CARELESS JUSTICE

Also by Arthur Haberman

The Making of the Modern Age
Impressionism and Post-Impressionism: Private Lives/Public
Worlds (co-author, Fran Cohen)
Civilizations: A Cultural Atlas
(senior editor and author)
The West and the World: Contacts, Conflicts, Connections
(co-author, Adrian Shubert)
1930: Europe in the Shadow of the Beast

Toronto Justice Series
Poetic Justice
Social Justice
Wild Justice

Anthologies
The Making of the Modern Age, Ideas in Western Civilization
On The Edge: Literature and Imagination
(co-editor, Fran Cohen)
The West and the World, Selected Readings
(co-editor, Adrian Shubert)

To Helen and John
To celebrate our long friendships,
Arthur

CARELESS JUSTICE

ARTHUR HABERMAN

VIADUCT
PRESS

Library and Archives Canada Cataloguing in Publication

CIP data on file with the National Library and Archives

ISBN e-book edition 978-1-55483-481-5
ISBN trade paperback edition 978-1-55483-482-2

To Jan

"If one really wishes to know how justice is administered in a country, one does not question the policemen, the lawyers, the judges, or the protected members of the middle class. One goes to the unprotected...and listens to their testimony."
— James Baldwin

Part One

I

The result made it the trial of the year in Canada. Emerson Echoiman was found liable of defrauding two people who placed their money in his trust through his hedge fund.

The judgment in favour of the plaintiffs, Sam Markson and Susan Refarrel, exceeded two million dollars.

Echoiman was a public figure, an international businessman with an out-sized ego and a habit of using his very large vocabulary to prove his superior intelligence to himself and others. He didn't take the stand in his own defence, something he now believed was bad advice given to him by his lawyers. Though an appeal was filed immediately and he was again advised to remain silent in the ongoing case, he couldn't resist making a statement on the steps of the courthouse after the verdict was delivered.

"This is outrageous and malevolent," he said. "It is a verdict that a more sophisticated legal system would not have delivered. I am again reminded that this country is nothing but a backwater. The appeal will certainly be upheld. It reflects badly on the justice system."

Ten years ago Echoiman had renounced his Canadian citizenship in order to accept a knighthood from the United Kingdom. One of the reporters asked, "Sir Emerson, do you think this would have happened in England?"

"Absolutely not. British justice would never have reached this verdict. Even in America entrepreneurs are permitted to ply their trade. Only here are the regulations so restrictive of free enterprise and opposed to the normal workings of capitalism. No wonder wealthy people have a difficult time in this confining environment."

His lead lawyer, Olivia Maylor of the firm of Sachs LLP, managed to get him away before he did further damage to his public persona.

There was a second part to the narrative related by the media. The lawyers for Markson and Refarrel were a small firm, Clark LLP, composed of five people in their late thirties who had challenged both Echoiman and the large and powerful Bay Street firm of Sachs LLP representing him.

Celia Rogdanovivi was the lead lawyer for Clark. The media decided even before the trial that it was something like David taking on Goliath. And David won. Rogdanovivi was careful in her victory. "The justice system proved itself," she said. "My clients were duped. Now the law has restored the funds that disappeared into the pocket of someone found liable for fraud."

As a columnist for *The National Post* put it:

…There are often times when the court of law and the court of public opinion don't coincide. That happened recently in Toronto when Karim Bogasha, accused of regularly sexually harassing a number of women, was found not guilty in the courts. We all felt that something then was wrong with the system because even he admitted to acts which were ugly.

Today, the law and the public agreed. Emerson Echoiman thought he was invulnerable, that he could get away with fraud because he was smarter and bigger than all of us. The law said "no" and the public agrees. He decided to put himself above all of us, and many are delighted that he just had a hard fall. Good for Ms. Rogdanovivi and the little firm of Clark LLP.

Celia received many emails, texts and calls congratulating her. Three were especially meaningful.

Her school friend Detective Constable Nadiri Rahimi, with whom she worked on a murder case over a year ago, emailed her to say how thrilled she was that the new small firm did such a fine job.

Detective Inspector Daniel Miller, the head of Homicide in Toronto, who had a special place in Celia's heart because of how sensitively he handled a very delicate matter that could have gotten her and her partners in very serious trouble, called to say how happy he was that the firm and Celia had done the just thing inside the system. "I'm enormously pleased, both with the outcome—you know that I've had dealings with Echoiman as a cop—and with the way it was done. This more than justifies everything we discussed a year ago. Good for you and your partners."

Joshua Black, one of the wealthiest people in the country, whose offices were near those of Clark LLP, dropped by several days after the verdict. Black had given some business to Clark as a way of encouraging the firm's new mandate. Clark's five lawyers devoted ten per cent of their time pro bono to legal aid for people who could not afford legal fees and another ten per cent, also pro bono, to what they called 'interesting cases,' like the Echoiman trial, where they felt that justice needed a bit of help against the wealth and forces of power that rich people could and did muster.

Black was the opposite of Echoiman. He was low-key, modest, and a believer in sharing his wealth and in public service. He and Celia had gotten to know one another and she regarded both him and Miller as mentors.

Black had a coffee with Celia. "You did very well," he said. "I knew I was being smart in hiring you for a bit of my business. Let me know how I can help in any other way."

"You've been great, Mr. Black," said Celia. "Really

supportive. I do have a question. If you remember, about a month before the trial, *The Star* had a story on its front page about the case filed against Echoiman. It was really sympathetic to my clients and to us. In fact, it began the tale of the little guys against the big blowhard and the little firm taking on the power of Sachs. I've asked a lot of people who knew about the case at that time if they planted it, and everyone says 'no'. You're nearly the last person on the list. So I'm asking, "Did you get in touch with *The Star*?"

Black smiled. "Technically, no. Actually, yes. I had my administrative assistant get in touch with someone there, indicating that they might find it an interesting story. They did. So, I'm responsible, though I think I merely pushed up the interest a bit because once the trial began, I think the same narrative would have been written."

"The mystery ends. For a moment, Sachs thought we did it. Happily, they took our word. Why?"

"I did it because I thought that Echoiman deserved the publicity. He could have turned it around by then admitting he was operating on the margin of legality — now we know it was beyond the margin — but he doesn't know how to apologize. He's one of those people who even when they know they're wrong, insist that they are right. Now he attacks Canadian law because he can't take responsibility for his actions. Anyway, I hope it didn't do any harm. I thought it might help."

"No harm at all, Mr. Black. If anything, it helped to convince my clients to keep going. This is confidential. Echoiman's lawyers offered a very handsome settlement. Ms. Refarrel and Mr. Markson turned it down because they wanted more than money. They wanted what happened. To see Echoiman found liable in a court of law. And they thought that even if he was not found guilty, the public would reject his innocence."

"Good for them. I've looked at the case carefully. I don't think the appeal will get anywhere. The judge handled the case with great sensitivity to all the legal niceties. Where does your ten per cent go from here?"

"Probably the Altonis. We're still looking into their activities to see what kind of case we can make. We may be what Susan Refarrel, a retired English teacher, called 'quixotic.' Still, we want to have at least a chance to tilt whatever windmill we decide to investigate. I'm going to relax a bit now, get back to normal lawyer's work, and see in a few weeks whether it's worth pursuing."

"You've earned the down time, Celia. Tell me. Are you still practicing the cello each day? When I told you I majored in music, you said you were taking it up again."

"I am. After ten years not doing it because I worked for Wilson, Campbell on Bay Street and had to clock insane hours. Every day. I cheat sometimes and don't give it the promised hour, but I'm getting back to it. I remember telling you that Danny Miller told me that it was important to have some beauty in my life. He was right. He's a far better violinist than I am a cello player, but it gives me pleasure."

"Sounds good. I have a request. As a member of the board, I have tickets to the Saturday night concert of the symphony at Roy Thompson Hall. My daughter was going to join me, but her husband's father is ill and they need to go out of town to visit him. Would you join me? It's an all-Tchaikovsky program, including his fifth symphony, full of Russian despair and hope at the same time. I think you'd enjoy it. I like attending with people who know something about music."

Celia smiled, both with her mouth and her eyes. "I'd be delighted. What a nice offer. Thanks."

"Excellent. Give me your address and phone number and I'll arrange to have my driver pick you up. I have to be at the hall early on a board matter. We can meet in the lobby."

"Sounds good. Now, Mr. Black, Louise told me she wanted to see you about a small matter related to Green Real Estate. If you have time."

"Tell me where she is and I'll stop in on my way out. See you on Saturday."

II

Anna Crowe now worked full-time for Tom Pendleton, the owner of an art gallery in Yorkville and the minority owner of the Stenbrook Gallery in the Distillery District.

Only several months ago Toronto's art community was shaken by the murder of Anna's former employer, Chantal Stenbrook. Her gallery specialized in Quebec artists and the murder, investigated and solved by Danny Miller, was committed by the husband of the owner of a competing gallery, thinking he was helping his partner.

Then, Anna worked part-time for Stenbrook and also part-time for a design shop in the District. Now, Pendleton, a close friend of Stenbrook, collaborated with Stenbrook's heir and sister to continue her work. Anna, fluent in French as a result of a B.A. in French literature from York, and with an M.A. in design from OCAD, was given the full-time job of managing the day-to-day work of the Stenbrook Gallery. As part of her new job, her first full-time work since graduation, Anna occasionally worked in the Yorkville gallery when Pendleton was away.

Anna had turned thirty in the last year and she used the marker to change her life, as she put it, to prepare herself for the long haul of adulthood.

She had been engaged in two matters which she had kept private, in addition to working part-time and designing jewelry which, though sold in the design shop, didn't come close to making enough income to survive, much less live decently.

She was not beautiful, though several men and some women told her she was attractive. She had black hair and an oval face. Her eyes were green, her nose a touch tiny for her face, her lips full, her body curvy. Her face was a lively one, and people liked talking to her because she showed that she was attentive to what they were saying.

Five years ago Anna decided to become an escort. She got a friend to help her make a web-site and she rented an apartment near the lakeshore for her work. As June August, what she thought of as her *nom de travail*, she hosted a number of men, most of whom she thought of as decent people who were either lonely or needy, or both. A few of the men, those who were vulgar, or who wanted to be violent, or who treated her as an object, she only saw once. Soon, she had a clientele which was regular and comfortable. In one instance, that of an accountant who was a partner in one of the major firms in the city, she became a travelling partner and they had spent ten very pleasant days together in the south of France for each of the last three summers.

The other private matter was both simple and dangerous. Anna was recruited by a group of three men who blackmailed mid-level members of hedge funds and other financial firms. June August was the lure, and the encounter was then filmed and recorded. All of the men blackmailed—there were five of them over the course of nearly two years—had families. All earned a lot of money in salary, bonuses and investments. The group asked for what they thought was a small amount of money—usually eighty thousand dollars—to destroy the evidence and then to disappear. As a result, Anna managed to put away her share, which was one hundred thousand dollars.

Anna ended both her escort business and her involvement with the blackmailers when she turned thirty and entered full-time employment. She used the money from the scheme to purchase a small loft on King Street West. It was time, she thought, for a serious, stable life.

The Pendleton Gallery in Yorkville was one of the major art dealers in the city. Last month it began showing a group of master drawings and paintings that Tom Pendleton was selling on consignment from an estate. The forty-one images included some by Dutch masters, including Lucas van Leyden, Jean Baptiste de Wael, and Rembrandt, and some Impressionist and Post-Impressionist artists, including Sisley, Renoir, van Gogh and Cezanne. The drawings ranged from $1500 for a small de Wael to $100,000 for the van Gogh. The most expensive painting was a small Renoir, whose price was not listed.

For a week when Pendleton was travelling, Anna was asked to work in Yorkville. It could be boring, for she was there basically to welcome browsers and potential buyers, and she had little to do other than to make some interesting conversation with a few of the visitors and to look after some paperwork.

On the Tuesday at about two in the afternoon an elderly woman accompanied by a middle-aged man entered the gallery. They said hello in the European fashion and Anna responded in turn. Then they started to look at the images. "We were drawn in by the Cezanne and Rembrandt drawings in the window," said the man. "Do you mind if we browse?"

"Not at all. That's part of why they're here. Take your time. Let me know if you have any questions."

They wandered about and when they came to the second wall, the woman stopped in front of the van Gogh. She looked carefully and then said, "*Gott im Himmel*. Michael, come and see."

The man hastened over to look. He turned to the woman. "Mother, do you think it's the same one?"

"It could be. I would bet on it."

The two went to the desk at the rear and saw Anna.

"May I ask a question, young lady?" said the woman.

"Of course."

"Tell me how you got hold of the van Gogh."

"Forgive me, Madame, I don't know. The owner of the gallery is out-of-town. I usually work at our second gallery in the Distillery District and I didn't have anything to do with this show. Can I inquire why you're asking?"

The man replied, "My mother and I think it may have once been in our family."

At that moment two women entered the gallery. Anna thought she recognized one of them and she called out, "I'll be with you shortly."

Anna turned to the pair in front of her. "How fascinating. Did someone in your family sell it some time ago?"

"No," said the man. "By the way I'm Michael Gelernter and this is my mother, Minnie Gelernter."

"I'm Anna Crowe. Now tell me how the drawing left your family."

"As far as we know," said Michael Gelernter, "it didn't leave our family. It was taken. By the Nazis in 1939. They also took our aunt and uncle and sent them to Treblinka."

Anna gasped. "Do you mean you didn't sell it? I don't know the rules or the law well. Could it possibly actually belong to your family now?"

"Possibly," said Minnie Gelernter. "I have some photos that my parents—my father was the brother of the owner of the drawing—took with him when he left

Germany a few days afterwards. Some were taken in my aunt and uncle's apartment and show some of the works that they collected on the wall. Do you mind if we walk around and look to see if there are any others we recognize?"

"Of course not. Please take your time. May I get you some water or a cup of tea?"

"Water would be good."

The Gelernters walked about and thought they recognized two others, a Boudin painting and a Cezanne drawing.

While they did so, Anna greeted the two middle-aged women. "We're just browsing, if you don't mind," said the fair-haired one. "To be frank, I doubt that we could afford to buy. But some are very beautiful."

"Take your time," answered Anna. She turned to the second woman. "I think we've met. In another gallery in the Distillery District. Aren't you the detective working with Inspector Miller?"

"Of course," answered the woman. I'm Nadiri Rahimi. And you're Anna....."

"Anna Crowe. We met when my former boss, Chantal Stenbrook, was murdered."

"And you were very helpful. Are you working here now?"

"In both places. Tom Pendleton bought an interest in the Stenbrook Gallery to help keep it open."

Nadiri turned to the other woman and introduced her. "This is my friend Debra Castle. Debra, this is

Anna Crowe. She really helped us in the Stenbrook murder."

Anna said, "Hang around, please. Something really interesting is happening and I need to see to the two others in the gallery. Wander around at your pleasure."

Anna went to the Gelernters and asked, "Find anything else?"

"No," said Minnie. "Forgive me, I need to sit. This is something of a shock."

"Of course." Anna and Michael Gelernter accompanied her to a chair and they sat on a couch opposite.

"Ms. Crowe, will you be here tomorrow?" asked Michael.

"Yes."

"We'd like to return with some of the photos. That would let us know if they are really the ones that were in the family or if we're imagining it."

"Please do. Can you come in the morning? I'll definitely be here between ten and twelve."

"We'll do so. This is most strange and amazing."

"It has to be. Mrs. Gelernter, do you want me to call a cab?"

"No. That's kind. If I could sit here for ten minutes, I'll be fine."

"Stay as long as you like."

After the Gelernters left, Anna asked Nadiri and Debra to sit. She made some tea for the three of them, and told them what just happened.

"Can that be so?" asked Debra. "Don't you have

something called provenance which gives you the history of the work and its ownership? Rare books have that."

"We do," answered Anna. "I don't know where Tom got the works. I usually work with Quebec artists in the other gallery. But there are a lot of stories about how Nazis and others stole works of art in Hitlerian Germany and in the war. And then they turn up many years later in the hands of people who claim not to know anything about the history. It's a terrible story, not only of theft but of greed."

"I'm a librarian, Anna," said Debra. "And I know that this sometimes also happens with rare books and manuscripts. What are you going to do?"

"I don't know. I'll wait until tomorrow. If they're still certain that they were the paintings in their family then Tom will have to deal with it. I've never encountered anything like this."

"Could I ask?" said Debra. "I'm trained at research. This is fascinating. If you need some help in finding out, I'd be pleased to work with you. Not as a job. Just something that's interesting, even exciting."

"I can vouch for her skills," said Nadiri.

"I'll let Tom know. You may have a deal, Debra. The Gelernters are returning tomorrow with some photos taken in 1939 which will be revealing. Do you want to come and take a look?"

"I don't go to work until twelve," Debra replied.

"They're coming between ten and twelve. I think

they'll be here early."

"Yes, I'll be here," Debra replied. This is fascinating."

The three women lingered over their tea and became better acquainted. When Nadiri and Debra left, Anna said, "Come visit me soon at the Stenbrook. We have some really fine Quebec cityscapes and landscapes on view."

"Thanks," said Debra. "We'll do that. We're exploring the city. I've never been there."

III

Danny Miller was a little worried. He felt that the Homicide Squad was stretched almost as far as possible.

The murder rate was more or less what it usually was. But there were two sergeants ill, another on family leave, and two constables seconded to other matters. On top of it all, Danny's associate, Sergeant Ron Murphy, who ran the day-to-day operations of the squad, was on vacation. They were stretched.

This morning he got a call from 53 Division. There was a murder in a building on the southwest side of Rosedale. He needed coverage and he couldn't take it himself.

He summoned his partner, Nadiri. "We have a new homicide," he told her. "All I know is that it's in an apartment building near Rosedale Valley Road, on the ravine. We're short. So I'd like you to look into it, with Taegan as your partner. Technically, I'm the lead detective. But, in actuality, it's yours. You need to brief me regularly, at least once a day."

"Thanks, sir. I'm on my way."

Nadiri had been in charge of cases before, but none of this magnitude. She managed to immediately get hold of Taegan Brown, another constable who had regularly worked with Miller, and they drove the short distance to the site.

The building had a strange configuration. It was located on the Rosedale ravine and had nine stories. However, five of those stories went down the ravine, where there was an entrance. Hence, the top four stories, which were in Rosedale proper, met the zoning requirements of the neighbourhood that no building be more than four stories high. There was a second entrance, at the top, into the sixth floor.

Nadiri parked in the ravine and entered, showing her badge to the constable guarding the entrance. "It's on the fourth floor," he said, "outside apartment 412."

The body was that of a man of about fifty, slumped in close to a fetal position on the carpet in the hallway, with a knife in his back. The man had worn glasses, which were on the floor next to him. He had silver hair and a short grey beard. Also on the floor were a magazine and two unopened pieces of mail.

Nadiri and Taegen looked around. In addition to the constable guarding the site, there was a man standing there.

"Who are you?" asked Nadiri. The man was about an inch taller than her five feet seven inches. He too was in his fifties. He had a florid face and a paunch above the belt of his plain brown pants.

"I'm Bill Rourke. I'm the manager of the building."

"OK," replied Nadiri. "First, I want you to help this constable put up yellow tape and I want no one else near the site except the forensics people who are on their way. Now tell me who this is."

"He's Richard Hall, Dr. Richard Hall, as he likes to be called." He pointed to the door, which was in a corner of the building. "That's his apartment."

At that moment, Emily Chow and her forensics team arrived.

Chow was characteristically brief. "Where's Inspector Miller?" she asked, knowing that Nadiri was his partner and having worked with both on other cases.

"I'm in charge at the moment," answered Nadiri. She turned to Taegen and introduced him. "This is Constable Taegen Brown." Chow nodded by way of greeting.

"What do we know?" Chow asked.

"Very little. We just got here. The body is identified as Dr. Richard Hall. The apartment here is...was... his."

"Good. Now we'll get to work. I'll look after the body. I'd like the team to have a look in the apartment before you go in."

"Sounds good," replied Nadiri. "Let me know when we can do our own search."

Nadiri took Rourke aside in order to question him quietly.

"What happened?" she asked.

"The body was found by one of his neighbors down the hall. Susan Lopate in 409. She said she looked at it and then immediately called down to the desk. I came up and then called 911."

"Did you touch anything?"

"No."

"Did Ms. Lopate touch anything?"

"I don't know. You'll have to ask her."

"Tell us about Dr. Hall," said Taegen.

"It's a story, officers. He's a psychologist. As far as I know he has a private practice. You can google him. In this building he's one of those people who stir things up. He doesn't like how it's managed or how the board does its business. This has been going on for at least the seven years I've been here. He continually writes letters to the board telling them they're not doing a good job, criticizing this and that. At meetings of the shareholders he usually has a prepared speech attacking board decisions. Sometimes he tells the board that they're incompetent, sometimes he says they don't respect anyone else. Not happy language."

"Does he have enemies in the building?"

Rourke did some thinking. "Enemies isn't the right word. Frankly, he's a pain in the ass and he takes up a lot of time better spent on other matters. He has a few followers. Most people put up with it, though it requires patience. Most people would just like him to go away. One of the board members describes him as a guy who isn't happy unless he's unhappy. He said he wished Hall would find someplace else to deal with his anger."

"That may be insightful," said Taegen. "We'll see."

They waited in the middle of the corridor for another five minutes before Emily Chow came along.

"Nadiri, Taegen. It's very simple. He was attacked sometime between an hour and three hours ago, between say one and three. The knife did it. He was killed from behind, probably walking to his apartment with his mail."

"What about the knife?" asked Nadiri.

"It looks like an ordinary kitchen knife that you could buy anywhere, from Canadian Tire to any kitchenware store. I'll look at things more carefully in the morgue. If there's anything more to say I'll be in touch."

"Thanks, Dr. Chow. Can we get into the apartment?"

"In about fifteen minutes. There's not much that's obvious, and the team is taking whatever prints they can find."

When they entered the apartment, Nadiri and Taegen found a very pleasant two-bedroom suite with a balcony looking over the ravine.

The furniture was mixed, though comfortable, and the second bedroom was used as a study. The books were mainly in the area of psychology, some texts, and a number dealing with obtaining happiness in a hard world. There were several works on Canadian history, and some on the history and community of Rosedale. The few works of fiction were English classics—

Dickens, Thackeray, Shakespeare and others.

Nadiri surveyed the walls to look at what art was displayed. She was now very interested because in the last several months, after they starting dating, she was being taught about art history and criticism by Debra. All the images were landscapes, most dark, none original. 'Boring', she thought.

Taegen had gone into the kitchen and now reported that he didn't think any knives were missing.

"Let's reserve going through his study and his office," suggested Taegen, "until we question some of the people here."

"Good idea," said Nadiri. "Let's seal the apartment and we'll return."

Nadiri and Taegen went to the sixth-floor entrance where Rourke's office and the concierge desk were located. Two other men and one woman were gathered in Rourke's office, all probably retired, thought Nadiri.

They all stood when the two detectives entered and introduced themselves. One of the men said he was the current president of the Board of Directors of the building, which he called Newcastle Apartments. He was, he said, Kenneth Ames, a retired judge. The woman, the Treasurer, was Pratiba Shanla. The other male was the Secretary, Alan McMemeny.

There wasn't enough space in Rourke's office and, in any case, Nadiri wanted a private conversation, not one at the entrance to the building or in the lounge area. "Is there a space we can go to talk?" she asked.

"Oh, yes," replied Ames. "We have a board room on the fifth floor." Rourke produced a key and the six of them left to go to the committee space.

As they navigated the corridors, Nadiri remarked to the group, "It feels as if there's a lot of corridor space. And because of the unusual configuration of the building it seems like a maze."

"It is a maze," said Shanla. "Visitors sometimes have a difficult time finding their way. Even newcomers sometimes get lost looking for things. We have a pool, a gym and a library. Lots of lockers. No floor is quite the same."

"It must give you some feeling of security," said Taegen.

"That's true, detective," said Ames. "But it's also a bit scary at times. I read a lot of mystery novels and I sometimes imagine that there's a body or a threat around one of the corners, especially at night."

"Well, it happened, Judge," said Nadiri. "The body appeared."

They settled themselves in the committee room. Rourke went to a fridge and produced six small bottles of water.

Ames spoke. "Tell us what happened. All we know is that Bill told us that Richard Hall was found dead outside his apartment. Before you start, I should note that nothing remotely like this has ever happened here. It's an old building, built in the mid-1960's. That's why it's a co-op. There was no condominium law in Toronto until 1967. As far as I know, and I've been here seventeen years, we've not even had a theft in all this time."

"That helps," said Nadiri. "We don't know a lot yet. Hall was certainly murdered. Detective Brown and I did a cursory survey of the body and the apartment and didn't find anything pointing to the killer or the motive. It's very early days, people. We got here a little over an hour ago."

"Tell us about Dr. Richard Hall," said Taegen.

The three officers of the co-op looked at one another to see who would start. Silently they agreed on Pratiba Shanla.

"He was a contentious person, officers," she said. "Bill told us he briefed you on that. Most people here are retired and most are very civil. There's a sense of community. For example, we have the usual governance apparatus—committees like Grounds and Budget—but there's also a Caring Committee which helps residents who might be ill or incapacitated. And there are groups that play bridge regularly or watch films. There is even a group that regularly meets to play chamber music. They give a concert once a year. And we have an annual art show of works produced by residents. We like to think we're a community, not just a bunch of apartments.

"Dr. Hall was the exception. There are several others. He was determined to interfere with virtually every major matter. For example, when we tabled the budget once a year, we knew we could expect a long letter from Dr. Hall indicating where we erred or where we were spending too much money. Sometimes he would distribute the letter to others. Recently we permitted a group of residents who were supporting refugees to have a gathering in the lounge to celebrate the arrival of a family. Dr. Hall complained that they were noisy."

McMemeny leaped in. "It wasn't only that he complained, officers. He was rude. He would write notes to other residents stating that the board—he did this for fifteen years, so it didn't matter which board—was incompetent. He said we treated our staff badly, which outrages me, among others. At one of our open meetings he said that Ken had contempt for all the other shareholders. It was impossible to have a normal conversation with him."

"We get it," said Nadiri. "Thanks. We may want to talk about this again and, Mr. Rourke, I'd like to see some of his recent correspondence, going back about three years."

"It occurs to me," said Taegen, "that Hall seems, in the building, to be someone who makes everything political and confrontational. You—he looked at Shanly—told me this was really outside the normal code of behaviour. Did he have any allies?"

"A few," said Ames. "We could supply you names if you like. Not enough to change the tone of the community, but enough to take up a lot of time and to be a constant annoyance."

"He also had a couple of friends from the staff," said Rourke. "He continually claimed they were being treated badly and a few were drawn to him. Most found him just loud, but a few saw him as someone sympathetic."

"I'll want their names, Mr. Rourke," said Nadiri. "Now, before we leave, can you think of anyone who might have done this?"

"I did give it some thought sitting in Bill's office," said Ames. "The answer is no. There's no one who comes to mind. But you and I know, officer, that sometimes killers are the most unlikely people."

The others shook their heads, agreeing with Ames.

"We'll get on with our work," concluded Nadiri. "We'll probably want to talk again and you'll certainly find us around the building in the next several days. Mr. Rourke, no one is to enter apartment 412. No one."

"I hear you," replied Rourke.

Nadiri and Taegen left the building, got into their car and went to the homicide office to report and to get on with the case.

"Any thoughts?" asked Nadiri.

"He sounds like a terrible person. I'd like to investigate his professional life before saying anything. I'll bet a lot of people won't mourn him for long."

"We'll see, Taegen. Sometimes, that kind of personality gets some people who love him and others who really dislike him. Not much in between. Let's find a few who liked him before we go further in our thinking."

When they got to the office, Nadiri said "Give me ten minutes and then we'll report to Inspector Miller."

When they met with Danny, they reviewed what they had found. Then Nadiri added, "I googled him on a site called 'Rate your Psychologist'. I got some of the same things. Half the patients say he was unusual but he helped them. The others, all giving him a score of one out of five, say things like....she consulted her notes....he was determined to make a diagnosis that was totally wacky; he told them to see their GP and get pills; he was habitually late and didn't listen; he was more concerned with his car breaking down than he was in the patient, etcetera."

"We've experienced all this in other murders," said Danny. "What do you think?"

"I think, sir," said Nadiri, "that we have very little to go on at the moment."

"What about all the statements about his lack of courtesy?" asked Taegen.

"We have to be careful about that," said Danny. "If we take that as the way to go, we eliminate a lot. It could be one of his patients, you know. There's violence in the medical world, including the world of mental illness. And it just could be something personal that we don't know about."

"Well, sir," said Nadiri, "I think we go back and slog it out. We need to talk to lots of people."

"Have you talked to the neighbor who found him?" asked Danny.

"Not yet."

"Start there. Also, get a look at his office and his files. Dig into his behaviour."

"Will do, sir." Nadiri looked at Taegen. "Let's go. We have a lot of research to do."

IV

Debra Castle came the next day to the Pendleton Gallery at a few minutes after ten. She brought coffee and croissants for Anna and herself.

The two women exchanged histories over their breakfast. Anna told Debra about her growing up in Toronto, and Debra talked about some of her experience as a youth in Vancouver. Both were circumspect about pieces of their lives, Anna because she didn't want to reveal her having been an escort and having been engaged in a blackmailing scheme, and Debra because she was by her upbringing and her nature a very private person, especially about her never having known her father and being raised by a mother who was ill and an addict, and who died when she was eighteen.

At 10:30 the Gelernters arrived. Anna welcomed them and then introduced Debra, telling them about her background as a librarian and researcher.

"We brought the photos," said Michael. "We'll need to look again, but we're reasonably certain that the van Gogh, the Boudin and the Cezanne are the same as

those on the wall of our relatives' apartment in Berlin."
He opened a briefcase and took out a file.

They spread the photos on the coffee table. They were in the grey of the time, Debra noting that the grey was most appropriate to the events of the era.

"Yes," replied Minnie Gelernter, "I think that Spielberg was right to film *Schindler's List* in black and white. The times are not caught in color."

Anna produced a magnifying glass, and the four looked at the pictures. Then, Anna said, "Let's take the photos to the images."

The four went to the three images with the photos in hand. They spent a quiet time doing the comparisons.

Michael looked at Debra and Anna. "What do you think?"

"I'm no expert in that period," replied Anna. "But on first glance it seems that they are the same."

"I agree," said Debra. "Still, none of the four of us has the expertise to pronounce this with certainty. However, I think there's enough here to warrant further study. What do we do now?"

Anna looked at Minnie and Michael Gelernter. "I think we should discuss this with Thomas Pendleton, who owns this Gallery and who is showing these on consignment. He's on the west coast at the moment, doing some business there. He'll be back next week. With your permission, I'll email him with a summary of what we've found. Then I can set up a time for you to meet with him."

"That sounds fine," said Michael. "Have you had any experience like this before?"

"No," answered Anna. "But there are others who have had similar experiences and there will be a way of finding out what we need to know. I wish I could tell you more. This is a first for me."

Debra entered the conversation. "I did some work in graduate school with manuscripts that were donated to the rare book library at the Robarts. It's a very complicated business. The key is to find out the history of ownership, or at least the history of who claimed ownership. It's sometimes murky."

"First, we need to talk with Mr. Pendleton," said Michael. "Anna, could you set up a time for next week?"

"Of course. I know Mr. Pendleton will want to do the right thing. He's a very professional and responsible person."

"Good," said Minnie. "We look forward to meeting him."

Anna closed the Gallery on Hazelton and Yorkville at six in the evening and walked to the Bay Street Subway Station. She took the subway west to the Ossington station and then the bus south to King Street, near her loft. When she exited the bus and started walking the two blocks home, she heard a male voice call out behind her, "June August. Hey, June August, wait for me."

She had prepared herself carefully for this moment. Every day she remembered that in a city the size of

Toronto this kind of random encounter could occur, especially because she sometimes worked in the downtown area. She reminded herself not to stop, not to flinch, to simply walk on. She did flinch for a millisecond, and did walk on.

The voice caught up with her. "Hello," he said loudly, almost a shout. "You're June August."

"Excuse me" she said, "I don't now what you're talking about."

"Cut it out, honey. You're that escort. We fucked about three years ago. Then you wouldn't see me anymore."

Anna responded, "Should I call the police? I won't give you my name, but I'm not your June August. And don't talk like that to me."

"Bullshit. I know who you are. You wouldn't answer any of my calls or emails afterwards. You rejected me. Don't you know that I'm an important person? Women like to go to bed with me. I don't need your bullshit."

Anna took out her phone. The street had lot of people walking on it. She wondered if she should yell for help. Instead, she said "I don't know who you are. I'm dialling 911. If you touch me, I'll scream."

The man said, "Fuck you, June August. I know where you work. I followed you from Yorkville. I know you live near here. Remember this. You haven't heard the last of me." He turned and walked away.

Anna did remember the man, though she forgot his name. She made a mental note to look it up if it was still on her email or phone. He had connected with her through her escort service, all wit and charm over the phone and for the several minutes the two talked when he came to visit her at the apartment she had used on the waterfront. Then, in bed, he became rough, not just strong but with a need to slap and hit. She recalled that she managed to stop it and throw him out, hurling after him the envelope of money that he had left on the coffee table. She also remembered that he wouldn't go away and attempted to contact her several times. She ignored everything and eventually he did go away. Until now.

Anna circled around several streets before going home, checking as best she could that she was no longer being followed. Once she got to her loft, she sat still for some time in thought. She reached no clear conclusion about what, if anything, to do.

V

It was a Wednesday. Danny stayed in the office until six-thirty, eating a sandwich he had bought when he went out to lunch. Then he went to Bloor Street, to the Royal Conservatory of Music, to the weekly practice of the Bloor Street Chamber Group.

The group were a bunch of amateur musicians who gathered together weekly to practice and play music from the seventeenth and eighteenth centuries. About half of the thirty in the chamber orchestra were music teachers, several in the Conservatory, some from York University, the University of Toronto, and two from a secondary school, Rosedale Heights School for the Arts. The others were from various professions, including a person who owned and operated a small corner grocery store, an accountant, a psychiatrist who had a master's degree in music from Yale, a woman who owned a chic clothing store and a cop.

Danny and his older sister Ruth were encouraged in their music by their parents. Ruth played the piano well, and Danny was started on that instrument. He decided at age six he wanted an instrument of his own and made enough of a fuss to get to switch to the violin. From that moment, the violin was a central part of his life.

He played well enough to join the group eleven years ago, though not well enough to move him out of the back row of the violin section. He sometimes wondered if he was still in the group as a courtesy, though he was reassured by many that he belonged.

The group was led by the thirty-six-year-old Gabriella Agostini, who had been their first flautist and had moved into the conductor's chair four years ago. Since then their reputation grew in the classical music world of the city and Gabriella had very successful visiting conductor engagements in Victoria, Seattle and Winnipeg. She now had an agent and was getting inquiries about working with other symphony orchestras.

About three years ago, Gabriella and Danny became a couple. They both found that life was far richer shared with a kindred soul and Danny felt that he had finally found the love of his life. Each had their own home, not far from one another, and the arrangement became one which was celebrated by friends and family, most importantly by Danny's sister and by his son Avi.

This week they were practicing Telemann's Violin Concerto in G Major, with their first violinist, Grigori Lapuchenkov, as the soloist. It was a short piece, about fourteen minutes, and they worked through it to the point that they could do a full run-through at the end of the session.

"Terrific," said Gabriella when they were through. "I still want to work on some of the allegro section. But it's fine. Grigori, you were really splendid this evening." They all applauded in the manner of players, by using their instruments.

"OK, people," said Gabriella. "Summer is coming in a few months, and we have our annual concert in seven weeks. The Telemann makes it on the program."

A hand was raised in the viola section. "Are we still getting requests to do professional performances?" asked Sheila Ratten.

"Yes, but we agreed to remain as we are," answered Gabriella. "Again, as we agreed, we'll do two performances at the St. Jacobs Music festival at the beginning of July, as we have the last two years. Nothing else. I like it that we're asked. I like it better that we do this simply because we love doing it."

Everybody nodded. They had had this discussion a year ago and they were now fully determined to remain amateurs. They all knew that the group would fall apart if people were expected to give up their day jobs in order to try to make it as professionals.

"What about you?" asked Benny Grunbaum. "Are you here for the Fall?"

"I'm booked in Minneapolis for two weeks in October and then back in Victoria just before Christmas. I'm concerned about this, but I think it can work. As

I've said before, if not, we need to discuss it."

"No problem, Gabriella," said Benny. "We want you here." There was a loud chorus of assent, which pleased Gabriella immensely.

She looked for anyone else who might want to speak, found no one indicating so and ended the evening asking everyone to look at the Valentini they were doing so they could work on a few sections next week.

It was Danny's custom to take his car to the session, park it in a nearby lot and drive Gabriella the short distance home to her condo on the southeast edge of Rosedale. He waited on the side as two members spoke with Gabriella one-on-one about their interpretation of certain sections.

As they walked to the car, Danny said, "Well, you're still beloved, my girl. Everybody sees how we have gotten better since you took over."

Gabriella smiled. "It's just my girlish charm, Danny."

"That, too, which you have in abundance. Seriously, we are probably 50% better than we were three years ago. And people like the sound you produce. It's a lot clearer and defined than what we did with Andrei. Much more suited to the kind of music we play."

"You know, Danny, if I've learned anything since I've been guest conducting these last two years, it's the need to find the right sound for the piece we're doing. The Chopin I did with the Victoria Symphony started me on this. I began conducting it as if it was written by Bach and it was terrible. I really had to adjust."

"But you did."

"I've heard your colleagues on the Homicide Squad—and the Chief, for that matter—say that one of your strengths is that you're not wedded to a single method for solving murders, that you change your method to suit the crime. That actually helped. I had to change my sound to suit the piece, not warp the piece by fitting it into my sound."

Danny smiled. "Whoever thought that police procedure would help a conductor. Not bad."

They got into the car and Danny exited the lot and turned left onto Bloor Street to take Gabriella home.

"What's happening with you in the squad?" she asked. "We haven't talked about it in a while."

"We're stretched. Not because there are more killings. Because some people are sick and Ron is away. I can't wait for him to return so that I can take up an interesting case, if one arises. I'm getting antsy. I gave Nadiri a case of murder in a co-op on the other side of Rosedale from you. Technically I'm doing it, but it's really in her and Taegen's hands."

"She's smart. I'll bet she's ready."

"I think so too. She had a rough patch personally a year ago but that's changed. In fact she has a new partner, a woman her age who's a librarian. I haven't met her, though Taegen tells me she's very nice."

"That's very good. Nadiri has a lot to offer a relationship."

"What about you?" asked Danny as they turned left on Sherbourne.

Gabriella's day job was as a director of music at St. Michael's Choir School. "The same. We're sort of getting to the end of the year at St. Mike's. I'm thinking about Friday. You know I'm doing Shabbat dinner this week. An Italian Shabbat dinner."

"I remember. Do you want me to do anything?"

"Not at all. I'm always helping Ruth. This week I'll take over her kitchen and she'll help me."

They embraced as Gabriella exited the car. Danny waited for her to get inside the building. When she did, she turned around and they both waved. He drove the short distance to his home on the Danforth feeling a warm glow inside.

VI

Since his divorce several years ago, Danny spent Friday evenings at the home of his sister and brother-in-law, Ruth and Irwin Feldman, where they had a traditional dinner welcoming the Sabbath. His son, Avi, now fifteen, spent the whole of every other weekend with the Feldman family, and was regarded by the Feldman children, Deborah, 22, and Leo, 19, as a younger brother.

The Feldmans were what is now known as modern Orthodox Jews in their observance. They followed the dietary laws, honoured the Sabbath, and were important figures in their large synagogue congregation. Danny was less observant and less traditional, something of a skeptic in his relationship to the theology. However, he found comfort in tradition and ritual, though not in the prayers.

Hence, since the Feldmans didn't travel on the Sabbath, Gabriella took over Ruth's kitchen in order to prepare her Italian Sabbath meal. She had been wanting to do this for some time, as a way a thanking the Feldmans for their warm acceptance of her and of the relationship between a man raised as an Orthodox Jew and a woman of Italian Catholic background. By now, she was one of the family, with a special relationship with Deborah, who admired and respected her deeply.

When Danny entered the house at about six in the evening, he immediately knew something different was happening. In place of the familiar Friday night odors of home-made gefilte fish, chicken soup, and brisket, there was tomato and the south of Europe in the air.

He went into the kitchen, hugged his beloved older sister and kissed Gabriella and sat down. The custom, for years, was for Ruth to give him a nosh, usually chopped liver or gefilte fish or a cup of matzo ball soup. Tonight, Ruth placed a piece of fish in front of him, accompanied by home-made challah. He tasted it. "This is wonderful," he told Gabriella. "What am I eating?"

"You'll learn later."

Gabriella already had a reputation among the family as a wonderful cook. She regularly cooked kosher Italian meals for Danny, Avi, Deborah and Leo at Danny's place, for Danny kept kosher at home both by choice and because that meant that Avi and the family could eat at his table.

"Delicious," said Danny. "Any guests tonight?" he asked Ruth, for the Feldmans almost always invited guests to welcome the Sabbath.

"Yes," answered Ruth. "The *chazzan* and Lotte Marcus are coming and we asked Sidney and Pearl Adelstein."

"I'm glad to see Elie and Lotte again," said Gabriella. The cantor of the synagogue and Gabriella had developed a warm relationship, for he had trained at the Curtis Institute in addition to his cantorial background and he was very interested and knowledgeable about both sacred and classical music. "Who are the Adelsteins?"

"I don't know them either," added Danny.

"He's visiting this year at Osgoode Law School. He's at NYU. They rent a house nearby and they've joined our shul for the year. Nice people."

Danny finished his nosh and said, "I think I'll go upstairs to say hello to Irwin and leave you two to your creations."

"He's in his office," said Ruth. "He'll be glad to see you."

Danny and Irwin had, for some years, a very careful and cautious relationship. Irwin didn't like the fact that Danny's observance of the religious laws was far more casual than he had been taught as a child. As well, he found Danny's joining the ranks of the police a strange choice for someone who was clearly able to do law or another acceptable profession, and rightly chalked it up to Danny's determination to carve his own future rather than follow what was thought appropriate, what he sometimes termed Danny's rebellious spirit.

For his part, Danny found Irwin more rigid than he

would like and more formal than he needed to be. Still, both men loved Ruth more than either could articulate, and that bound them in a truce. However, over the years they learned that each had misjudged the other, and by now they had developed a warm and trusting friendship.

When Danny appeared at the door of his office, Irwin smiled and invited him in.

They exchanged small talk and then Danny asked, "How is the firm handling the loss in the Echoiman case?"

Irwin was for the time being the acting managing partner of Sachs LLP, the firm that represented Emerson Echoiman. There had been a crisis in the firm recently, one in which two major partners were involved in trying to unduly influence the handling of the case by the plaintiff's firm, the small Clark LLP. It also involved Joshua Black, who had been a major client and who withdrew all of his affairs from Sachs. Irwin was navigating all this, trying to get some stability for Sachs and to protect its professional reputation.

"You know I never wanted the firm to represent someone like Echoiman in the first place," he said. "But that happened and we had to follow through on our undertaking. Frankly, Danny, for your ears only, I think the judge made the correct decision. I spent a lot of time looking at the documents. I think we represented him well. But I think the evidence proved him liable. He'll lose the appeal he insists on making. I'll be happy when it's over. Then we can get him off our hands."

"I know Celia Rogdanovivi of Clark well," said Danny. "You know she helped me and Nadiri on the Harvey case. I think she did a fine job."

"No argument from me," said Irwin. "I give them credit. I wish I could hire the whole of Clark, but they've taken another road."

"Maybe that road is something other young attorneys will also take."

"Perhaps. Still, Danny, I don't think the time of the big firms is over."

"Well, you need to think about it. People like me and Gabriella can't afford you, if we needed representation. I'd be tempted by something like Celia and Clark."

"You make a point. Right now, I want to get Sachs to a place where I can leave the temporary managing role and be a full-time lawyer again."

At that moment, Avi appeared. He hugged his father who gave him a big kiss on the top of this head. "Uncle Irwin, Dad, Aunt Ruth told me to tell you that our guests have arrived."

"Then let's inaugurate Shabbat," said Irwin, and the three went downstairs.

After they greeted their guests, the group moved into the dining room. The eleven took their places and still standing they held hands and sang traditional songs welcoming the Sabbath. Ruth lit the Sabbath candles, quietly saying the blessing. Irwin then chanted the blessings for the wine and the bread and they sat, Ruth informing the guests that Gabriella had made an Italian Shabbat meal.

Gabriella came out of the kitchen with a large platter of fish. "It's called *Baccalà alla Vesuviana*," she said. "In an English cookbook it would be called something like Salt Cod with Tomatoes and Capers. I made it in small portions because it's an appetizer, an antipasto. A little different from gefilte fish. Remember Italy is a Mediterranean country and Italian Jewish cooking is closer to the Sephardi tradition than to the eastern European cooking that you're used to."

They each took a portion. "Oh my god," said Leo. "This is terrific. What's in it?"

"The cod, capers and special San Marzano tomatoes," replied Gabriella. "Also, onion, red pepper, mint and parsley."

"Stunning," said Irwin. He turned to the guests. "We're used to this from Gabriella. Every time she cooks for us something wonderful appears."

"It's terrific," said Pearl Adelstein. "Like the coast of Italy."

"Gabriella, you did it again," said Deborah. She continued, "Uncle Danny, do you know the firm of Clark LLP, the people who took on Echoiman?"

"I do," said Danny. "And I know the lead lawyer in the case, Celia Rogdanovivi, very well. Why do you ask?"

"Before we go further with this conversation," interrupted Ruth, "we should tell our guests about the famous case that finished recently."

Irwin summarized the case and talked about the small firm taking on his large Sachs LLP.

"Why aren't the lawyers in Clark working for some of the big firms?" asked Sidney Adelstein. "You'd think they would want a bigger career."

"That's part of my question, Professor Adelstein," said Deborah. "I researched the firm and they all did work for large firms and left to form a small one. They do a lot of pro bono work."

Adelstein turned to Irwin. "Is this a trend? Are many doing this?"

"Not many," replied Irwin. "Some. I understand they didn't like the work they were doing in the several large firms they joined. They gave up careers that easily would have led to partnerships."

"Are they surviving?" asked Adelstein.

Danny answered. "They're doing OK, Sidney. They make less money than they did on Bay Street, but they seem happy in what they're doing. If I may say it, I think they feel that they wanted to get back some of the idealism that originally drew them to the law."

"It's a gamble."

"They know that," said Danny. "They're in their late thirties. Five partners. Some have kids. They decided to do it and so far they're above water."

Avi interrupted. "Gabriella, can I have another portion?"

"Me, too," said Leo.

"Of course," said Gabriella. She smiled. "I know you guys. I made extra. I must tell all of you that I never had this with challah before."

It works perfectly, Gabriella," said Lotte. "You're as good a cook as you are a conductor."

"It's Ruth's challah, remember," said Gabriella. "I can't match it."

They finished the first course and Deborah, Avi, Ruth and Gabriella rose to help take in the dishes and serve.

They next brought out soup. "Chicken soup," said Gabriella, "called *Brodo di Pollo*."

"Some things are sacred for our tribe," said Ellie Marcus. "And chicken soup is in our soul."

"It's a little different from the usual," said Irwin.

"Not really," said Gabriella. "I used celery, carrots and onion in the stock, some basil and peppercorns. I think what you're tasting is the fennel. That would be different from Ashkenazi soup."

"Yummy," interposed Leo.

"So, Debbie," said Danny. "You haven't yet answered my question. Why are you asking about Clark?"

"I'm thinking of applying to work there in the summer. You know, first year law student looking for some experience in a firm."

"I thought," said Irwin, "that you had applied to Wilson, Campbell and they made you an offer."

"They did," said Deborah, "but I like what Clark is

doing. Their idealism, as Uncle Danny called it, seems good to me."

"But," said Sidney Adelstein, "if you do well at a large firm, that opens the door to a possible position after you graduate."

"I don't know that I want to work for a large firm," Debbie replied.

"What do you mean?" asked Irwin.

"Daddy, we've had this discussion before. No offense meant, but I don't want to be in a place that protects people who avoid taxes or who charge so much that ordinary people can't use them."

"I'll defend your father," said Sidney Adelstein. "The large firms provide a service and they contribute to our economic well-being as well as to a civilized society under law."

Gabriella entered the conversation, wanting to help Deborah. "They may do that, Sidney, but they also defend very nasty people who abuse women and others who use the law to enrich themselves. Forgive me, I have a lot of respect for your profession. Still, it isn't always as high-minded as it makes itself out to be. The Panama papers are not only full of people who avoid taxes, they cite law firms who help them to do so."

"Don't you think, Gabriella," answered Adelstein, "That everyone is entitled to good representation."

"Of course I do, Sidney, but Karim Bogasha, who is clearly someone who abused lots of women, has the money to hire the best lawyers, who charge about a thousand dollars an hour. You must admit that the rich have an advantage. If he was poor he'd have had a young lawyer doing legal aid work."

Danny decided to try to turn down the heat of the conversation. "Well, we're still in a world which is imperfect. Frankly, Debbie, I can see the attraction of Clark. If you're going to work in the summer to get a sense of what lawyers do in their daily lives, I think Clark will give you as much of that as any other firm. I know the partners and they're decent people."

Ruth looked around. "Time," she said, "to move on with our meal."

Avi, Deborah, Gabriella and Ruth again rose and moved into the kitchen with the empty soup dishes. "I need a few minutes, people," said Gabriella.

The conversation at the table turned to more ordinary topics including comparing New York and Toronto, both at the center of finance, culture, and power in their countries.

After ten minutes Gabriella and Ruth each came into the dining room with casserole dishes clearly based in a pasta recipe.

"What would an Italian meal be without pasta," said Lotte Marcus. "It smells terrific."

Gabriella started serving. As she did so, she said to those at the table, "This is a pasta casserole that has two names. It is usually called *Tagliolini colla Crocia*, which means Crusty Fettuccini. But it's also called *Ruota di Faraone*, Pharaoh's Wheel, by many Jews.

It's a dish that's traditional on Purim in Italy, though it's also served on Shabbat, especially on the Shabbat when the Torah reading is the escape of the Jews through the Red Sea. It's fettuccine which is boiled and then mixed with salami or beef sausage and raisins. Then I bake it to finish it off. Some use pickled tongue instead of salami, but I didn't want to take a chance that one of you might not like tongue. So it's salty and sweet at the same time."

They all waited until everyone was served and then dug in. "Oh, my god," said Pearl Adelstein, "this is sensational. I want the recipe. It'll be a big hit where we live in Brooklyn Heights. How did you know how to do this?"

"Credit my Nonna, my grandmother," said Gabriella. "She took me in hand as a young child and taught me all her secrets. She really raised me. She lives forever through my cooking. Our two cultures are very similar in regard to the family."

"Bless her," said the Cantor.

The conversation moved to the discussion of the two cities. The Adelsteins were happy New Yorkers, though they had praise for Toronto. "The social culture is wonderful. New York has variety, but you people celebrate it more," said Pearl. "They are both fine places to live."

When they finished the pasta—the two boys taking a second portion—Ruth prepared tea as Gabriella bought out dessert. It was two Apple-Apricot Crostadas, tarts which would easily feed the eleven at the table.

The group happily had the sweet and ended the meal by saying and singing the traditional grace together.

They lingered, not wanting the pleasant time to end, talking about their work, the Yankees vs. the Blue Jays, and giving the Adelsteins tips on what to further enjoy in the city.

After the guests left, Danny and Gabriella joined Avi, Deborah and Ruth in the kitchen to help with cleaning up.

Danny returned to the topic which Deborah raised earlier. "Now, Debbie, tell me what you're going to do about Clark."

"I just wanted your opinion about the firm and its members, Uncle Danny."

"You have it. They're good people. They want to use the law to make the society better. Like everyone else, they don't always succeed, but they're making a difference, as in the Echoiman case."

Deborah turned to Gabriella. "I was going to ask Uncle Danny to put in a good word for me at Clark. Do you think that's right?"

Gabriella smiled. "I'll give you what I've learned is a Jewish answer. Do you think it's right?"

"I didn't think about it until tonight's discussion. I think that's how the big firms work sometimes. But I'm not certain it's right. I should apply and rely on my own abilities. I don't want to use the family tie in the wrong way."

"Good for you," said Danny. "Not that I don't think

you would be wonderful, but I don't like to give you an advantage that another applicant can't have because I know the partners. It's not my style and, let me add, I don't think it's Celia Rogdanovivi's style. Apply on your own. See what happens."

"Will do," said Deborah. As Danny and Gabriella were leaving, she hugged them both. "I know you're always on my side, my lovely aunt and uncle."

"Always," said Gabriella.

VII

The first meeting between Tom Pendleton and Minnie and Michael Gelernter took place on the Tuesday of the next week. Anna Crowe and Pendleton had exchanged emails over the last several days, and Pendleton was anxious to clear up the matter. Anna, with Tom's consent, invited Debra Castle to attend.

The Gelernters had brought their photographs and, after serving tea and cookies, Pendleton took his time looking at them.

"What do you know?" he asked.

Minnie answered. "We know, Mr. Pendleton, that our relatives in Berlin were collectors. On a modest scale. They were not people like Courtauld or Barnes who ended up with museums. They had some money, loved art, and on occasion purchased something for their home. Then, as we know, the world tumbled out of centre. The Nazis passed their anti-Semitic laws, Jews were in danger, and they began opening their camps.

"I was told that my relatives didn't want to leave,

like many. They believed that they, too, were German, and didn't want to be driven out by the hatred around them. Finally, in 1939, they were arrested on whatever charges were made up. They were sent to prison, then to a camp. They lost all their possessions. My father got away, made it to London, married and then came to Canada."

"Have you ever tried to get restitution?" asked Pendleton.

"Yes and no. The German government in the post-war period gave money to a fund which my parents shared with many others. Otherwise, all was lost. My parents started again from nothing."

"What a sorry tale," said Debra.

"We're not unique," replied Michael. "In fact, what happened to our family is ordinary. Our best estimate is that forty relatives disappeared in the Holocaust."

"What's the legal situation?" asked Anna. "If you prove these paintings belonged to your family, are they then yours?"

"It's very, very complicated, as far as I understand," said Pendleton. "The courts decide. But there has to be proof and there has to be some evidence that they were stolen. Also, what happened to the works since that time, maybe passing through many hands, is taken into consideration."

"What do you think we should do, Mr. Pendleton?" asked Minnie.

"Please call me Tom. I know what I'm going to do.

I'm going to take down the van Gogh, the Cezanne, and the Boudin and store them. They will no longer be part of the sale. Then, I'd like to inform the current owners. This group of paintings is being shown on consignment. They are currently owned...." He smiled.... "or thought to be owned, by a couple. I also feel I need to inform the current owners about this."

"What next?" asked Michael.

"That's up to you, Mr. Gelernter. If I were you, I'd get a lawyer with some experience in these matters to begin with."

"What needs to be uncovered?" said Michael

"My guess...I've never encountered this professionally before...is that you first need to trace ownership. Who owned them after 1939? What is the provenance?"

"How do you do that?"

"Two ways," said Debra. "You can work backwards or forwards. My guess, having done this with rare books, is that it will be easier to work backwards. I would suspect things get murkier the further back you go."

"Who owns them now?" asked Minnie

"Do you mind if I reserve my answer to that," said Tom. "I'd like their permission to reveal their ownership. I think that would make life easier for everyone."

"We will get to know, Tom," said Michael. "But if you think this is the best way, we'll go along."

After this exchange, the five continued to sit and talk. The Gerlenters talked about the family's history, Tom discussed what he knew about provenance and ownership, and Debra told some anecdotes about her research experiences. The whole matter was, as Anna said in summing up the meeting, "a puzzle both scholarly and moral."

VIII

Nadiri seemed to be getting nowhere in the investigation into the murder of Dr. Richard Hall.

She and Taegen first spoke with the neighbor who found him, Susan Lopate. She was in her eighties, short and a bit bent, though clearly spry and sharp.

In answer to their first question, she said, "I touched nothing, Officers. I saw the body, I saw the knife and I called the desk. When Bill came up I retreated to my apartment."

"Was he a good neighbor?"

"Frankly, no. He was sometimes rude and would pass by me as if I didn't exist. Sometimes he greeted me kindly. He was totally unpredictable and I found that disturbing. So I avoided him as much as I could. When I saw him, I tensed up. I was polite, no more."

"Did you ever have a conversation?"

"Never. He often walked with his head down and ignored me. I'm told by others that they received the same treatment, so after a time it stopped annoying me. This is a friendly place. He's one of the few who lacked manners."

Interviews with others on the floor yielded much the same information. People were shocked that a murder took place in what most called 'Newcastle'. Richard Hall wasn't mourned.

Nadiri and Taegen then went to Hall's office and looked through the files. This was the second time Nadiri was involved in the murder of an analyst. The first, William Gentrey, was prominent in the city and in the profession. His files were organized, his notes on patients clear and respectful.

Hall's files were a jumble of papers, put together neither alphabetically nor by when the patient began to see Hall. The notes in the file were sometimes sparse. When not sparse, they were sometimes not on topic, Hall reminding himself to make a call, to shop for food, to commenting on current events or slights he thought he had suffered from Newcastle and professional colleagues. When on topic they were unsystematic, often using terms like 'bullshit', 'boring', or 'why do I have to suffer this?'.

After a careful examination, Nadiri and Taegen singled out five patients who had a history of violence and who should be interviewed.

Going back to the building, Bill Rourke, at Nadiri's request, had put together a file of Hall's memos and letters to the Board, or to specific board members, or to Rourke as manager over the last five years. Hall was an equal opportunity insulter. He accused the Board of ineptness and, in a recent matter concerning New-castle and their employees, of incompetence and of contempt for the residents, who were shareholders in the co-op. When Rourke sent Hall a form letter indicating that he was over a month in arrears for the regular monthly fees, Hall replied nastily and threatened to get his lawyer to sue. Recently, Hall drafted a three-page letter which he distributed to all the units, all 225 of them, asking for support to call a special meeting of the shareholders to throw out the current Board. Kenneth Ames was called the worst president Newcastle ever had, something not unique since Hall had called earlier presidents the same thing.

"What happened to the last three-page letter?" asked Taegen of Rourke.

"Nothing," he replied. "He couldn't get enough support. This is a case of the little boy crying wolf. He's used up whatever goodwill he might have had."

"Who are his friends?" asked Nadiri.

"In the building there are two shareholders who often supported him, Amy Dickson in 824 and Donald Remuch in 532. He also had some friends among the staff, especially two of the staff who supported the union in recent matters, Belinda Kramer and Bezallel Jones."

"Was the union issue contentious?," asked Taegen. "I note that he spent most of the three pages talking about it and staff."

"It was," said Rourke. "I could tell you about it, but

I think you should hear about it from the executive group, Judge Ames, Ms. Shanla and Mr. McNemeny. They know more than I do about what occurred."

In meeting with the three officers soon after, Nadiri and Taegen heard an interesting tale about labour relations.

Newcastle came to be, about eight years ago, one of the few unionized buildings in the city. The staff—including cleaners and those on the desk—unionized as a result of believing they were being treated unfairly.

"And, Officers," said Pratiba Shanla, "they were correct. The Board at that time tried to pay them far below scale and to offer no benefits. So we became employers. Most other big condos and co-ops hire a firm to take care of these matters, and it's the firm that is the employer and the firm gets a fee based on a contract negotiated with the building."

What occurred, Nadiri and Taegen were told, is that the union, called Together, turned out to be mainly a hotel union and it found the work required to look after the five full-time and eight part-time employees servicing Newcastle to be far more expensive than any union dues it received. "So over the years Together came to ignore Newcastle," said Ames, "to the point of missing negotiating deadlines."

"We reached an impasse about six months ago," said McNemeny. "The contract was over, they didn't answer any requests for negotiation. We presented an offer which they ignored. Then they halted the negotiations we were having with an arbitrator. We were faced with a possible strike. We could have locked them out, but that was not in anyone's interest."

So, they said, the Board found a service provider who did this for other buildings and firms, and the provider agreed to hire the employees that were at Newcastle and to provide continuity of service.

"Most of the employees were content," said Ames, "for they felt let down by the union. So all the employees with the exception of two signed a formal application to the Ontario Labour Relations Board requesting that the union's representation be terminated. Moreover, we made certain they got decent raises, their benefits were enhanced because they were now with a larger group, and the part-timers could even get more work from the firm we hired because they had other buildings."

"Sounds sensible," said Nadiri. "What was the problem?"

"Two employees turned down the offer to continue while working for the new service provider. They claimed we were union busting and they were loyal to the union movement."

"They were let go?" said Taegen.

"No, Officer," said McNemeny. "They turned down an offer which was better than what they had. In one case the person had been with the building for a long time which meant there was a decent severance settlement coming to her, which she received."

"So they stood up for a principle?"

"So they said," Ames responded. "Though sadly Together did nothing to help them."

"Any flack from the shareholders?"

"Yes," said Shanla. "It required a few meetings to sort it out. But there were people who were convinced that all this was part of some conspiracy. A few, like Richard Hall, accused us of hurting our employees. You read about that in the correspondence. A few others were upset because they claimed it would cost more money and fees would rise."

"Does it cost more money?" asked Taegen.

"Marginally, Officer Brown," said Shanla. "I'm the Treasurer, as you know. Giving people a raise costs more money. Giving the police a raise costs more money. But we are also saving money because we are no longer employers and don't do payroll. Moreover, we had some very healthy lawyer fees in the past as a result of having a union which we no longer will have to pay. So, a bit more is the answer, but not a serious number."

"Thanks for your candour," said Nadiri. "We'll take it from here. We now have some more people to interview."

Later that day the two young detectives had their daily meeting with Danny about the case.

"What do you think, sir?" said Nadiri. "We're getting nowhere on this one."

"You can't let it defeat you that easily," said Danny.

"You know that. We've been in this place before when working together. You keep plugging away."

"We know that, sir," said Taegen. "I just wanted a eureka moment."

"Not for this one, guys," responded Danny. "What do you think you do now?"

"We interview the five patients," said Nadiri. "That's called plugging away."

"Anything else?" said Danny.

Nadiri and Taegen looked at one another, each hoping the other would have the correct answer. It was as if they were back in a classroom as Danny's students.

"What do you mean?" Nadiri finally said.

"I'll give you a hint. Who else do you interview?"

"I got it," Taegen answered. "We interview the two people who supported him in the building and two employees who continued to support the union and were his friends."

"Right on, Taegen," said Danny. "Plugging away means being totally comprehensive. So, guys, you have nine interviews to do. Come back here when you're finished. If you get something, we'll go with that. If you get nothing we'll decide how to proceed from here. We're nowhere near being totally puzzled."

"You know, sir," said Nadiri. "You're known in the force for your insights. No one really gets how determined you are."

Danny smiled. "My mother said I had two flaws. I was impatient and I could be stubborn. I'd like to think

I've learned some patience over the years in this job. But I remain tenacious. Don't let it go."

"Yes, sir. C'mon Taegen, let's get back to work and be stubborn."

IX

The five partners at Clark LLP held their weekly office meeting at their regular time on Wednesday morning. Informally, Louise Xavier, who had excellent organizational skills and was appropriately obsessive, became the equivalent of managing partner, though none of them wanted that title, and chaired the session. She was joined by Celia Rogdanovivi, Arnold Aronovitch, Robert Jensen, and Ken Trussman.

"The financials look decent," said Louise. "We are even putting some money in the bank for a rainy day. Getting the big contract with Green Realty from Joshua Black made a difference."

"Good stuff," said Ken. "How is Black as a client?"

"As nice as could be," answered Rob who, along with Louise, had some background in acting for real estate developers and handled the account. "Actually, he's very smart also. I can see how he made his money."

"Very smart as in clever?" asked Arnold. "Another rich guy who beats the system?"

"No. He's our kind of guy," answered Robert. "He

just thinks two steps ahead of most people and works through complexities with ease."

"I agree," said Louise. "He's the opposite of the kind of rich guy like Echoiman and others."

"Sounds very good," said Ken.

Celia kept quiet and smiled to herself. She and Joshua Black were developing a friendship and she regarded him highly. This was good to hear from her colleagues.

Louise took over. "As long as we're on the subject, let me say two things. First, the publicity we received out of the Echoiman case, not that we asked for it, has done some good. We're getting inquiries. Soon, I think we'll have to turn down some business we would ordinarily have accepted a year ago."

"Do you remember Irene Walsh from Sachs, who wanted to join us?" asked Celia.

"Sure," said Arnie. "A really good lawyer. We decided not to expand, to keep ourselves small. We don't want to start growing into what we left."

"Right," said Celia. "When I met with her to tell her, I suggested that she find a few others like herself and us and start her own small firm. Let me say that I got this from Joshua Black who said that ten firms of five lawyers who wanted to practice in a decent way could do a lot more good than one firm of fifty. Again, good advice. So she recently founded a firm with three others. It's called Kent LLP. She told me they thought it an in-joke that two firms like ours would be called

Clark and Kent.

"Boo," agonized Ken.

"I like it," said Arnie.

"Anyway, we could direct some of the business we can't handle to them. I told her we would help with advice. They're working hard. This assist could help them to get off the ground. And we would not insist on referral fees as some firms do."

"Sounds good," said Louise. "Are people OK with this?"

They all nodded.

"Second bit of business," continued Louise. "Now that we have dealt with Echoiman, we need to decide who's next. We still have to fulfill our pledge to put ten percent of our time into 'interesting cases'."

"Well, there's Michael Lubente and his so-called loan companies," said Rob.

"And there are a lot of people avoiding taxes by sending their money out of the country," said Ken. "The Panama Papers are only one source for finding this out."

"And," said Celia. "There are the Altonis with two pieces of ugliness, as we know. I did a little research one evening and found out on LandlordWatch.com that of the 100 buildings in Toronto with the most violations they own eleven of them. James Altoni is called the Violations King by people interested in this kind of stuff."

"Don't they have another business, besides being

slum landlords?" asked Louise.

"Yep," replied Celia.

"I remember," said Arnie. "They own a mortgage company which seems to specialize in giving mortgages on homes in Toronto which are very risky for the lender. The kind of thing where the borrower can't get a loan elsewhere."

"You got it, Arnie," said Celia. "Then, if the borrower defaults, which happens often, they foreclose as soon as legally possible and take over the property. Usually, they tear down what's there, build something new and make a big profit."

"What do you think?" said Louise to the group.

"Altoni," said Arnie.

Louise looked around the table. "Altoni," said Ken. "I agree," said Rob. "Me, too," said Celia.

"OK, it's Altoni. Who takes the lead?"

"Celia, if she wants it," said Ken. "You already did some research."

"It's someone else's turn," said Celia.

"I'm happy putting a lot of time into legal aid," said Arnie. "It suits me and I get a lot of satisfaction from it."

"Me, too," said Louise.

"I'll help, Celia," said Robert. "But you should lead."

"Done. Go for it, girl," exclaimed Louise.

They started to rise, impatient to get on with their work, but Louise said, "One more thing, guys. It won't take long."

"We got a call from a law student who wants to work for us this summer and I interviewed her. We haven't discussed if we want to do this."

"We don't have a lot of space," said Rob. "We're tight."

"We are. But all of us are scheduled for holidays in June, July and August, so there will always be a desk available."

"What would he do?" asked Celia.

"She. Not he. She'd do whatever we wanted her to do. Mainly research I expect," said Louise.

"Do you like her?" Arnie asked Louise.

"I do. She's a first-year student, very high grades for her B.A. and at Osgoode. She researched us and said she'd work for minimum wage, or for nothing, because we might not have the funds to hire her. She reminds me a lot of me when I was her age. A young idealist. I like the fact that she found us and persuaded me to interview her. When I told her she could make a lot more money working for a Bay Street firm, she said she knew that but she wanted to learn here."

"Sounds good," said Ken. "But I'd be unhappy if we didn't pay her something reasonable."

"We can do that, Ken," replied Louise. "I agree. We'll pay her half of what she would earn on Bay Street, which is about what we take home. Do we think this is a good idea? Does anyone else want to interview her?"

"I'm for it," said Celia. "But only one student. We

can't take more."

The others nodded.

"Are you sure you don't want to see her first?"

"We're fine with your decision, Louise," said Arnie.

"OK She starts June 1."

"What's her name?" asked Rob of Louise.

"Deborah Feldman. That's it. Let's go do some work."

X

Nadiri and Taegen managed to get hold of the five patients and the two former employees of Newcastle over the next few days.

Three of the patients were eliminated on the strength of solid alibis for the time of the killing. The other two were interesting.

The first, Allan Saltmann, had a history of violent episodes. He was in his mid-twenties and recently had been convicted of assault in a case involving a feud over a parking spot with another driver. He paid a fine, was placed on probation and was told to get medical help.

The interview took place at the station. Saltmann was told that he was not being charged. Rather, as a patient they needed to get some information.

"What did you think of Dr. Hall?" asked Nadiri.

"He was a little crazy himself," said Saltmann. "I liked that. I've been with other shrinks and they're all so nice and sweet and then they tell you you're crazy and give you some pills. This guy was unpredictable.

Sometimes he'd ask me to talk about stuff—like how I felt about school or even which baseball team I rooted for. Sometimes he'd talk about himself."

"Do you think he helped you control your tendency to be violent?" asked Taegen.

"Nah. We never talked about it. He told me to get some pills from my doctor and a prescription for more, but I never did it. I don't like taking pills. He was late a lot, as if that gave him some power over me because I had to wait."

"Have you done anything violent since the parking incident?" asked Nadiri.

"Nothing. The judge made it clear I would get jail time if it happened again. I did one thing. My Uncle Louis said that I should join a gym and take up boxing, because that might get some of the energy out of my system. So I did it. He gave me the money to pay the gym. It's been cool."

The interview went on in this manner until Nadiri and Taegen gave up any hope that Saltmann was a serious suspect. They ended it and thanked him after another fifteen minutes.

Taegen turned to Nadiri after Saltmann left. "Unlikely," he said. "He has no alibi, but I don't get any rage against Hall. Actually, his uncle helped him far more than Hall did, but his anger isn't directed at the shrink."

"I agree," replied Nadiri. "Let's be careful. We're looking hard for something to grab onto. Let's not let that guide our questions."

"Good point. The boss would agree."

The next interview was with Amanda Lescot, a thirty-year-old woman who was an addict with a history of break and enters, as well as threatening some people in order to get money to feed her habit.

"Do you work?" asked Nadiri.

"I get jobs here and there, mainly waitressing in bars. I also take some visitors, if you know what I mean."

"What caused you to see Dr. Hall?"

"I served some time two years ago. I'm still on probation and my officer said I should do it."

"What did you think about the sessions with Dr. Hall" asked Taegen.

"They were bullshit. Sometimes he asked about what he called 'dramas'....

"Do you mean traumas?"

"Yeah, that's it. He told me once that something that happened in my childhood was my problem. More bullshit. Then once he said that I should go to school to get my high school diploma and then go to university. Sure, I have all the money in the world to live like a rich person. Garbage."

"Why didn't you stop?"

"I didn't want my probation officer to get angry. I have to keep her on my side. At least Hall didn't do the thing most people do to me. He wasn't superior. At times he just mumbled. Sometimes he complained about his condo or about his car. He wasn't a happy guy. I don't know much about what he does, but he was as nuts as the rest of us."

Taegen and Nadiri also brought this encounter to an end quickly, realizing that nothing was to be gained by pursuing it further.

"So," said Taegen. "Let's move on to the two former employees at Newcastle."

Bezallel Jones was somewhat difficult to find. He had moved from the address they had from Bill Rourke and he had changed his cell number. It took a few hours, but they located him in an apartment near the corner of Eglinton and Oakwood.

They knocked on his door at two in the afternoon.

"Go away," they heard. "I'm still in bed."

"It's the police Mr. Jones," said Taegen, using his best street accent, the locution he grew up with.

"Oh, shit. What now."

"We just need to talk, brother. Open the door."

Jones took a few minutes and then appeared. He opened the door but didn't invite the two cops into the apartment.

"You got a warrant?"

"We don't need no warrant. This isn't a search. We just need to talk."

"I don't want to talk," replied Jones and he tried to close the door.

Taegen easily prevented the door from closing and said, "Look, man, we just want to talk. We talk here or we talk in the station. You choose."

"What are you gonna do? Arrest me?"

"Yeah. This is about a murder. The murder of Dr. Richard Hall. So if you keep this up, we'll arrest you and take you down to the station and let you stew for a few hours."

Jones opened the door. "Come in, officers of the law." He bowed. "At your service, ma'am and sir. Forgive the look of the place. I wasn't expecting such important guests."

They sat in a dishevelled living room. However, both Nadiri and Taegen noticed that it was clean. 'Messy but clean' thought Nadiri. 'Lived in.'

They explained why they were there.

"I heard about the murder," said Jones. "I'm sorry about it. A lot of people found Dr. Hall a pain, but he was straight with me. He tried to explain why the bosses wanted the union out."

"What about you? Why didn't you continue at the co-op?"

"I was part-time, only ten hours a week. There was no future in it. I'm working nights now at a restaurant, helping with the cooking, full-time. They pay better and I get some meals. I just decided it wasn't worth working at the co-op now."

"Did you support the union?"

"Look, the union meant a lot to some of the full-time people, especially Belinda, but it made no difference to me. Dr. Hall explained how the bosses wanted to save money on our backs by getting rid of the union, so, yeah, I voted on the side of keeping the union. I'd do it again. I'm in a union now at the restaurant and the wages and benefits are decent." He looked at Taegen. "You know, brother, you get nothing on your own. We got to stick together."

"I agree, brother. I'm in a union myself. And my partner and I stick together."

"Good. That's what we need to do. Our lives matter, man."

"Did you have any problems working at the co-op?"

"Yeah. Sometimes with the guy in the office, the Irish guy with the belly. He got upset if I was late. He got very upset if I missed a shift and only told him an hour before. But sometimes I got better work and I had to take it."

"What about Dr. Hall?"

"A weirdo. A good guy. He cared for the little people."

"OK, Mr Jones, that's it," said Taegen. "A lot easier than going down to the station, don't you think?"

"Look, brother. I can see you're OK. But I've been harassed now and then by your people, so I'm a little standoffish."

"No sweat," said Taegen.

"We thank you for your help," added Nadiri.

As they left and were walking down the stairs, they heard from above, "Stick together, brother and sister. Stick together."

Belinda Kramer had a job in another apartment building as a cleaner, working days. They had called her at home and arranged to see her at her apartment in Parkdale at seven that evening.

Kramer was in her fifties, white hair somewhat astray, a lined face indicating a life lived with some hardship. Her apartment was small and impersonal, as if she was living there temporarily.

Kramer seemed distraught. She wandered around the living room for a while, seemingly aimlessly. The two detectives were patient and let her get to the point where she offered coffee or tea. "Actually, water would be good for me," said Nadiri. "I'm fine, ma'am," answered Taegen.

"We're investigating the murder of Dr. Richard Hall," said Nadiri. "We know you knew him well and we thought you could help us."

Kramer again stood up and walked about. Her eyes blinked while talking. "How could I help you? You know I don't work for Newcastle anymore."

"We do know that," said Taegen. "Where are you working now?"

"I was out of work for a month after the new people took over. Finally, I found a job cleaning at a supermarket. I was not happy about it because it paid a lot less, but that's what I could find. Now I'm working for a building around Yonge and Eglinton."

Nadiri took over the interview, both she and Taegen thinking that Kramer would be more comfortable with a woman interrogator. "How long did you work at Newcastle?"

Kramer again stood up. This time she went to straighten out some newspapers on the coffee table. Her face continued to be in motion, as if she couldn't control its movement. Finally, "Eighteen years."

"Were you happy there?"

"It was good at the beginning. Then the Board tried to cheat us, so I helped to start the union. I can't say I was always happy, but it was exciting and I thought I was doing something worthwhile."

"Did you know Dr. Hall at that time?"

"We met in the corridor, while I was cleaning. During the time the union was being started, he was very encouraging. He invited me into his apartment and we would talk. He was helpful and he was clear that the Board was abusing us. After a while we got into the habit of having a weekly cup of tea. On Wednesday in the late afternoon, after my shift. I thought of him a friend."

"Did anything happen in the eight years that the union was there?"

"A lot." She paused for a time. "A lot. I applied for a job at the desk, which paid more, and got it. Then, the Board went after me. They kept a file of everything that went on and tried to prove that I was not fulfilling my responsibilities to the security of the building. They demoted me about five years ago. I grieved and we won. They went after me again and demoted me again.

I grieved and we lost. So I went back to being a full-time cleaner."

"Was Dr. Hall involved in all of this?"

"Yeah. He tried to help. He got a few people in the building to support me and he advised me along the way. But we lost."

"Did he advise you recently?"

Kramer's posture changed and her face seemed to scrunch up in a menacing way. There were tears.

"He advised me to support the union. He told me and Bezallel that the Board could never get rid of the union. I went to the union and they weren't any help. It's as if they didn't care except for the dues we paid. Dr. Hall still said he was absolutely certain that if we supported the union all would be fine. He told me to turn down the offer of a job with the new guys. 'They'll only exploit you,' he said. 'They're on the side of the Board.' So I turned down the offer and got my severance."

"Do you regret that?"

"Now I do. I didn't realize what was happening. I thought Dr. Hall was thinking about me and the others. But I realized later that he only wanted to make the Board look bad so he could look good."

"Did you talk with him about that?"

"Yeah. We continued to meet weekly for tea. I told him that I was a lot worse off because I followed his advice. He got very angry and screamed at me, telling me that I was stupid and didn't understand what was best for me."

"What did you say?"

While telling this story, Kramer became even more animated and upset. "I told him that he didn't suffer because of his advice. Only Bezallel and I suffered. Everybody else kept their good jobs. A year ago he said he didn't want to see me anymore. That I was ungrateful for all he had done for me and I was no longer his friend. He told me never to knock on his door again."

Kramer again rose and paced around the small room. She was crying openly.

When she got settled Nadiri asked, "How did you respond to Dr. Hall when he told you he was no longer your friend?"

"I told him that I wished he was dead. All he did was hurt people."

"Did you do anything to Dr. Hall?"

"Not then. I felt alone. I had nobody in my corner. I relied on him. I thought he was a person who cared for me."

"You said not then. Did you do anything recently?"

More pacing. A very long silence.

"I want to hurt him. I want to do something that would show what he did to me."

"Did you hurt him?"

"All I wanted to do was to hurt him."

"When was this?"

"Five days ago, maybe six days. All I wanted to do

was to hurt him."

"What did you do?" asked Taegen

"You know. I took a knife and stabbed him when he was returning from getting his mail. I didn't mean to kill him. I'm not sorry he's dead. He was not really kind at all. He was lousy. He hurt people."

"How did you get into the building?"

"When I returned the keys, I kept one. The entrance to a door in the garage."

"How did you leave the building?"

"That's easy. There are lots of ways out on every side where no one sees you."

Nadiri spoke formally. "Belinda Kramer, we are arresting you for the murder of Richard Hall. We will be taking you into custody. You have the right to retain and instruct a lawyer without delay. You have the right to contact any lawyer you may wish. You also have the right to free legal advice from a legal aid lawyer. And you have the right to remain silent. Do you understand?"

Kramer looked down at what she was wearing. "Can I change my clothes?" she asked.

"Yes," said Nadiri. "But I will have to go with you."

Taegen called for a police car while Kramer changed. They went downstairs, put Kramer in the police vehicle and followed it to the station lock-up.

"We got lucky," said Nadiri to Taegen as they drove to the station. "If she hadn't confessed, we might still be nowhere."

"Well, the Inspector was right. We needed to plug away."

Danny was in his office. Nadiri and Taegen asked to see him immediately, to report.

Danny listened to what happened and remarked. "It seems too simple. I've never solved one this way."

"She confessed, sir. This isn't like some others where we confront the criminal with the evidence and they fold. It's as if she just had nothing else. Her life isn't a happy one and she felt betrayed. So she confessed."

"No argument about that, Nadiri. We'll need to interview her again. Does she have a lawyer?"

"She said she didn't know of any," said Taegen.

"Did she make any other calls?" asked Danny.

"One. To a friend," answered Taegen. "She said she didn't have any family except a sister in Australia who she hasn't seen in fifteen years."

"Not good enough," replied Danny. "Let's get to legal aid. I'm not sure why I'm saying this, but let's make certain we find someone good to represent her. This is unusual enough to be sure we do the right thing."

"Should I call Celia's firm, Sir?"

"Not a bad idea. If they can't handle it there's another firm like them that has started recently. Celia will know."

"Do you have some problems, sir, with what we have done?" asked Taegen.

"No, Taegen. Not at all. You both did well. My problem is that I don't feel entirely comfortable about what happened. Not with how it happened. I just want to take the usual pains to be right."

Kramer stuck to her confession when Danny took part in the next interrogation with Irene Walsh as her lawyer. It seemed open and shut.

XI

Tom Pendleton arranged a second meeting with Michael and Minnie Gelernter the next week. He had asked Debra Castle to continue to do some research and she was present. Anna Crowe was looking after the gallery in the Distillery District.

The Gelernters brought along their lawyer, Helen Oakhurst from the large firm of Babcock, Melton LLP whose specialty was copyright law and associated matters.

"First," said Tom when they were seated and he had provided refreshments, "I can tell you who the owners of the paintings are at this time."

"That's good," said Oakhurst. "At least we can start from somewhere."

"They are James and Jeanette Altoni. You may have heard of them. They are among the most important collectors of rare books in the country. They tell me that they bought a lot at an auction at Sotheby's in order to get some books they valued. The lot included the paintings which are hanging here and are on sale.

And, of course, the three by Boudin, Cezanne and van Gogh, which I took down."

"I know of the Altonis," said Debra. "They've donated some books to the Fisher Rare Book room at the Robarts Library. They have a reputation as sophisticated collectors."

"Could I ask, with respect," said Oakhurst, "What is Debra's role here?"

"She's assisting me," replied Tom. "Debra is a head librarian at a branch in Toronto and is trained as a researcher."

"How have the Altonis responded to your telling them about the three images?" asked Michael.

"They were moderately annoyed, because they regarded it as an unwanted complication. However, they agreed the images should not be offered for sale until matters are cleared up."

"Do they know," asked Oakhurst, "that it might take years to get this clear?"

"We didn't discuss it," replied Tom.

"Years?" asked Michael. "We can prove ownership in 1939 and we can prove that the Nazis took them."

"Can I say something?" said Debra. Everyone nodded.

"I did a lot of work this past week in this area. There are over one hundred thousand works of art that the Nazis confiscated which are still outstanding. Each piece, or pieces taken together, has its own history and legality. I agree it should be simple, but it's not."

"I don't know what you mean," said Minnie.

"Let me give you a few examples. Recently it was learned that more than ten thousand works of art which were looted were given in 1949 by the Americans to West German and Austrian authorities for restitution. As it turned out, many of them were claimed by people who owned...Debra raised her hands and put quotation marks around the word 'owned'...them after they were looted. In short Nazi families claimed them. One example is that Hitler's private secretary, Henriette von Schirach, claimed over 300 paintings. The Bavarian authorities arranged what they called 'return sales'. That is, a lot of the works were sold for small sums of money to Nazi families, including the family of Goering and some others tried at Nuremburg."

"My god," exclaimed Minnie.

"There are more stories like this, Mrs. Gelernter. Several years ago, finally, after having to go to the United States Supreme Court, the famous Klimt painting 'Woman in Gold' was returned to the family that commissioned it originally. The Austrian state fought it to the end.

"My point," continued Debra, "is that each piece has its own history. More than that, each piece has its own legality. And I don't have to tell you that legal action takes both time and money."

"Debra is correct," said Oakhurst. "I'm certain both of us could cite many other instances of injustice. The question is to get the courts—sometimes it is courts in other countries—to say it belongs to you."

"But it does belong to us," said Michael.

"Mr. Gelernter," said Debra, "if I had the power, I'd turn them over to you now. But works of art, like rare books, are commodities. They have value. They have prestige. People will want them."

"What do we do now?" asked Minnie. "I'm not leaving this matter simply because it's difficult."

"We find out their history," said Oakhurst. "We get people like Debra to help us. Then we decide where to go to ask for restitution. Remember, a lot of people may have handled them in the last seventy years."

"I'd like to help in any way I can," said Tom. "This is new to me."

"I, too, would like to help," said Debra. "I know more about books, but the research skills are transferable, I'm sure. Let me say that I'll do this voluntarily. It's interesting and I'll learn a lot. And besides, as far as I can see, there's a big moral issue here. We can't let the Nazis win."

"Good for you, Debra," said Oakhurst. "We'll call on you if we think you can help."

Oakhurst turned to the Gelernters. "Let me warn you, there will be some agony. Do you want to go ahead?"

"Yes," said Minnie. "We need to keep reminding these people what they did."

They ended the meeting on that note and the Gelernters and Oakhurst left, thanking Tom and Debra.

"What happened to the Klimt?" asked Tom.

"It ended up in the Neue Gallery in New York, put there by the niece of the woman in the painting, Adele Bloch-Bauer. The family had commissioned the portrait and everyone agreed that the Nazis had stolen it. Even that didn't matter to a lot of people. The Austrian authorities put every obstacle in the way of the niece, including financial ones. It took years."

Later that day Debra went down to the Distillery District where she was meeting Nadiri. The two of them had been exploring the city together, wandering aimlessly sometimes like a pair of *flâneuses*, going to specific places on occasion. Debra had never been to the area. Nadiri had only been there during a murder investigation during which she had met Anna Crowe. Now, they had arranged to visit Anna at the Stenbrooke Art Gallery there and to walk about.

Nadiri arrived first at the gallery. Anna greeted her with a hug and brought out some coffee. As they were talking Nadiri's eyes roamed around the walls. "I like some of this stuff," she said. "Debra's been teaching me about art and I'm getting a feel for it. I even checked the walls of the man who was killed in my most recent case. Unbelievably boring."

"They're the works of three Quebec artists," said Anna. "I like the ones by Léa Pastore best. Do you want to get a closer look?"

They walked about. Pastore's works were not large, some of them very colourful and careful everyday scenes, from still lifes with pots in them on interesting backgrounds to fall scenes in brown and gold and winter ones in shades of white with sleds and people in colourful clothing.

"Wow," said Nadiri, "I wish I could do that."

"So do I," said Anna. "I can make jewelry but I'm not a very good painter."

"But you went to art school, so you're a lot better than me." Nadiri pointed to work about 50 x 35 centimetres, called 'Un bouquet de douceur', which was a still life with flowers in a blue jar slightly to the left of centre, and an apple and pear next to them on a table. "I'd love to have that on my wall at home."

"So buy it," said Anna.

"You're kidding. I've never bought a work of art in my life."

"Start now. It's beautiful. You picked well."

"It's probably a million dollars."

"Of course not. In fact, it's twenty-five hundred dollars. Less than a holiday. Go for it. You'll be saving money because it's already mounted on a board. It doesn't need framing, which can be costly."

Nadiri was excited. "I don't usually buy things this fast."

"You picked well. I met Léa when she brought her works here. She's not yet well known. When I saw her stuff, I thought they would be priced at double what's on the sheet."

"I don't trust myself."

"Who do you trust?"

"Debra. You."

"Well, I vote yes. Let's wait for Debra and see what she thinks."

Nadiri spent the next five minutes going back and forth between paintings. Then, Debra arrived.

"OK, Deb," said Nadiri. "I'm besotted with one of the three artists and might buy my first painting. Which one do you like?"

Debra took her time. Finally, she said "I like Lea Pastore and Frederic Telsalle. I don't like the stuff by Pierre Remarque. They look too much like paint by numbers. Not enough of a personality. I like Pastore best."

"Which one?" asked Nadiri as Anna hovered in the background, smiling.

"That's not fair, Nadiri. I like her style and her way of seeing the ordinary world. You may like one better and I may like another better."

"All right. Pick three."

Debra again took her time. "I've decided," she said after a full five minutes. "I like, not in order of choice but the three best for me, 'Les bois de lumière', 'Un bouquet de douceur', and 'Portrait en rouge'.

"Yes" shouted Nadiri. "Anna voted for it and you just voted for it. I'm buying 'Un bouquet de douceur'."

"Great choice. I love it. Can I ask what their asking for it?"

"Twenty-five hundred."

"A bargain. Buy it, girl."

Nadiri turned to Anna. "Do you take credit cards?"

"Of course. We also allow privileged customers to pay for a work over six months if that makes it easier for you."

"Done. I'm excited."

Anna wrapped the painting and gave it to Nadiri. "Are you going to walk around?" she asked. "The District really is an interesting place."

"That's the plan," answered Debra.

"Could I show you my jewelry? It's being displayed in a shop on Tank House Lane, where I used to work part-time. I can close the Gallery for fifteen minutes. Tom doesn't mind."

They walked on the old bricks in the nineteenth century setting of the large Distillery to the design shop. Both Nadiri and Debra admired Anna's work, which was clearly very sophisticated and, occasionally, very playful. Debra bought a necklace and put it on.

They hugged their goodbyes as Anna went to reopen the Gallery. Nadiri and Debra then walked around, taking in the shops, stopping to buy some chocolate that they couldn't resist, looking at the restaurants and enjoying the ambiance. Nadiri carried her painting with both hands, hugging it to her body.

At about 6:00pm Nadiri said, "Time for your cooking lesson, Deb."

When Debra started taking Nadiri to the AGO, McMichael and some local galleries, Nadiri realized that her friend was really knowledgeable and was introducing her to this new world. She told Debra that as a way of thanking her she wanted to teach her how to cook.

They had gone to restaurants together and Nadiri had cooked for Debra. Soon she realized that Debra knew virtually nothing about food or getting around a kitchen. Debra admitted it. "I live on pasta with ketchup, meatloaf and scrambled eggs mostly," she said. "How awful," replied Nadiri.

This was a result of Debra's unusual history. She was raised, if that can be said, by a mother who was ill and an addict. She never knew who her father was and there were no other relatives. Her mother tried but didn't have the resources or the strength to do much. So Debra was on her own very early. Then her mother died when Debra was eighteen. She was determined and she loved books, which she says saved her life. She managed via work and loans (and the kindness of a landlady, a beggar in Point Grey who lived on the street, three teachers and some strangers) to get through a B.A. in four years at UBC. She then got a partial scholarship to do graduate work in library science at the University of Toronto and, knowing no one in Toronto when she arrived, succeeded at that. Now, at forty, she was the head librarian of one the branches of the Toronto library system and had even published several articles in professional journals on the subject of determining the authenticity of rare books. Only two years ago did she celebrate paying off her student loans.

Nadiri thought Debra to be perhaps the most resourceful person she had ever met. "I wouldn't have made it if I had your history," she told Debra. "Without my sister and my family, I would have fallen apart." She also thought Debra to be very smart. But there were gaps. One of them was that no one had ever taught Debra anything to do with cooking. "We survived on KD, minced meat and ketchup," said Debra. "What's KD?" asked Nadiri. Debra laughed. "Kraft Dinner, of course."

So Nadiri took Debra in hand and they had a cooking evening every so often. She even had to buy kitchen tools for Debra that Nadiri took for granted: among them, two decent frying pans of different sizes, a pot in which to make a stew, a salad spinner (Debra rarely ate vegetables and fruits which astounded Nadiri), a spatula, tongs, and decent knives. She also, one evening, brought along a spice rack with ten spices, oregano and basil included, that Debra hardly knew existed.

Nadiri started from scratch, not getting as nearly complex and sophisticated as she usually was in the kitchen. 'This is like teaching someone who has read much more than me and is very worldly as if she was in cooking kindergarten,' she thought. Tonight, she was going to teach Debra how to make rice which was interesting and some spicy shrimps and scallops.

Nadiri directed, but Debra was expected to be active. "The way to learn how to cook is to cook," said Nadiri.

"I feel unbelievably awkward," replied Debra. "This is like learning a language at forty, instead of learning it at four."

"But you like to eat interesting food," said Nadiri

"Sure. As long as someone else makes it."

They laughed through it all and when they were done they enjoyed the duck fried rice and the shrimp and scallops with garlic, ginger, thyme and oregano.

"The result is worth the agony," exclaimed Debra. "I hope I get to feel comfortable one day."

"You will. It's like learning how to ride a bicycle. Once you do it, it comes easy."

"Guess what?"

"What?"

"I don't know how to ride a bicycle."

"Oh, my god."

"I do know, though, how to do desert."

"I don't believe you."

"Join me in the bedroom and I'll show you."

Nadiri giggled. "With pleasure. You do that very, very well."

XII

With the Richard Hall case finished, Danny gave Nadiri and Taegen some time off. Ron Murphy was returning in two days from his holiday which meant that Danny would take for himself the first difficult and/or interesting case that arose. He was anxious to get back into the street.

A week after Belinda Kramer was charged with murder, Danny picked up a message that he was requested to call Judge Kenneth Ames. Though Danny had never met him, the name was familiar. He answered the same afternoon.

"I need to meet with you, Inspector. Forgive me for using my status as a judge to ask you to do this. It's important. It has to do with the recent murder of Dr. Richard Hall. I'd like to meet with you and Detectives Rahimi and Brown as soon as possible."

Danny arranged for a meeting in his office the next day.

Before Ames came, Nadiri asked, "What do you think he wants, sir?"

"I've no idea. Perhaps he has some information which is pertinent to the case. I made a few calls and everyone I spoke with said that he was a careful man and a decent judge."

"That was my impression, too," said Taegen. "A responsible guy."

When Ames arrived, he was dressed in a suit and tie, not like the ordinary retired person. He was courteous and he praised Nadiri and Taegen for their work.

"Judge," said Danny. "I don't understand the purpose of this meeting. Certainly it has to do with the murder of Richard Hall."

"It does indeed, Inspector. I've thought hard about what I am doing. I'm here to tell you that Belinda Kramer did not murder Richard Hall."

Danny nodded.

"But she confessed," said Nadiri.

"And she continues to say so while being held for trial," added Taegen.

"So she does, officers. But she didn't do it."

"How do you know?" asked Nadiri

Ames took a deep breath. "Because, Officer Rahimi, I did it. I killed Richard Hall."

Danny put up his hand to ask for silence from his colleagues.

"Why, Judge Ames, are you telling us this now?" Danny said.

"Because I thought about it and I couldn't abide someone, Ms. Kramer in this instance, taking the responsibility for something I did."

Danny was silent, leaving time and room for Ames to continue.

"I had no difficulty with the idea that I could harm Dr. Hall and get away with it. I have no idea why Belinda Kramer confessed to the murder, but she did. We hardly know one another so it can't be about me. In my time I've seen a few false confessions. They happen with some regularity. But now I would have to live with the fact that Ms. Kramer would be punished for a criminal act that I did. I found that unacceptable, even unbearable, this last week. Hence, officers, I am confessing to a murder."

"You are aware, Judge Ames," said Danny, "that we will be arresting you in a minute or two."

"Of course. I would expect nothing less. I know the consequences of this confession. I don't like to think about my life from this moment forward, but I accept that it will be very different from what I imagined my last years would be. Still, my wife died two years ago and the only child we had died five years ago in an auto accident. Like many on this planet, I am alone. I suffer from depression and this might help explain what I did."

"Can you tell us what happened?" said Danny.

"It's simple, Inspector. Far more simple than I imagined it would be, even with my experience on the bench. Dr. Hall made my life unpredictable and mean in the last few years, since as president of the condominium I had to deal with his madness and rudeness nearly every day. I broke. I decided to kill him. I took a knife that I had purchased at Home Hardware, waited for him in the stairwell—I learned from the desk that he went for his mail at the same time most days—and struck him in the back. I returned to the stairwell, went upstairs, had my regular daily meeting with Bill Rourke and then went to my suite, number 723. Though it was early, I did pour some whiskey for myself. That's it. Done. As you know, I was never a suspect. I expected to get away with it easily. And I did. Then Ms. Kramer confessed and I had a moral dilemma which I decided to solve by coming here today."

Danny spoke. "Kenneth Ames, you are under arrest for the murder of Richard Hall. You may get counsel and you may use the phone to do so. You have the right to keep silent."

"Thank you, Inspector." He held out his hands. "Do you want to handcuff me now?"

Danny didn't answer. He just said, "Officers Rahimi and Brown will escort you to a holding cell, Mr. Ames. They will provide you with a phone to call an attorney and anyone else you think necessary."

Ames rose slowly. He suddenly looked weary and bent. Nadiri led him out of the office and Taegen followed at his rear.

Nadiri and Taegen returned to Danny's office after finishing the paperwork on Ames, wanting to talk about what had happened.

Danny asked them to hold off. "We need to sort out all this. I have to talk with the Crown Attorney and, I think, the Chief. And we do have to make arrangements to free Belinda Kramer. Give me a few hours. I wish Ron were here. He's so much better than I am at this sort of thing." He looked at his watch. "It's now a little before two. Meet me here at five and we'll work it through."

When they returned, Danny was finishing a donut that accompanied his coffee.

"All done, sir?" asked Taegen.

"Not quite. But well enough along that we can talk. Do any of you want to start?"

"Sir, I was stunned, but you weren't," said Nadiri. "I had been certain that it was Kramer who did the killing, but I remember you hesitated. How come? What did you see?"

"I didn't see enough to feel it was not Kramer. I thought it *might* not be her. Why? It came too easily. So I thought it was one of two things. Either she simply wanted to confess and not go through the whole hard process, or that she made a false confession."

"I've heard of that," said Taegen, "but I've never encountered it."

"Me neither."

"I have," said Danny. "Twice in the past. Once when I was even more of a rookie than either of you. The interrogation was something we wouldn't do now. A hot, windowless room. Relentless questioning and harassment from the cops doing the interrogation. Exhaustion. Coercion. So the guy confessed to stop it all. It's the sort of thing you hear about during wartime. Not as bad as the Bush-Cheney torture, but bad."

"What happened?" asked Nadiri.

"I don't want to go deeply into it now. Let's just say that eventually, against the odds, two junior cops got to the truth. But some nasty stuff was done to the guy who confessed in the meantime."

"And the second time?" asked Taegen.

"Very different. The confession was made to get attention. The technical term for this is 'voluntary false confession'. A little man wanted to be known as the clever killer of an important person. In fact, in that case, five years ago, we had three voluntary false confessions. People lined up to get this odd fame. To answer your next question, it was fairly obvious and we finally got the killer. Not through a confession.

"The psychology of this includes people who genuinely believe they are guilty of a crime, mainly done through those interrogation techniques we now deplore. They internalize the guilt after a time. I've never encountered this."

"What about Belinda Kramer? What do you think?"

"Let me ask. What do you think?"

Nadiri smiled. She was used to her boss turning questions back. "Well," she replied. "I hope you don't think we used inappropriate questioning techniques."

"Of course not. I ruled that out immediately. I'm

certain any film of what happened would show you both were professional in every way."

"Then, there is the attention-getting thing," said Taegen. "I don't sense that was the case. If anything, Kramer was wiped, exhausted, tired, not interested in publicity."

"I agree," said Nadiri. "That leaves the category of her believing that she actually did the crime."

"I don't think that works here," said Taegen. "It looks like we're out of reasons."

"No, Taegen," said Danny. "We're not out of reasons. We're out of categories. That is, those three are what the experts usually list. That doesn't mean that Kramer didn't have a reason for confessing. It just means it's not explained in the usual way. The experts need at least one more category. Let's abandon those three reasons, though we might use part of some of them, and ask simply: Why would Kramer make a false confession? I want to add that whatever we come up with would need to be checked by trained psychiatrists, so it does fall under the category of speculation, not fact. At least not yet."

"What do you think, sir," said Nadiri. "And please don't now ask what do we think. You're ahead of us."

"All right. Let me say this is tentative. Speculation. What I sometimes call cheap psychology.

"I think that Kramer felt betrayed by someone she thought was her champion, her best friend and supporter. She admired Hall and then he abandoned her.

Or at least she thought he abandoned her. She may have developed a psychological dependency here, given that she had no real family. Then she got stuck in a job which she felt was awful, all because, she felt, she listened to Hall. She's depressed, maybe clinically so, alone. She wants to act but she doesn't know how to do so. Maybe she even wants to harm Hall.

"You interrogate her and she has a wish fulfillment. Hall is dead. Killed. She can have a kind of revenge, what I would call in fancy philosophical language, metaphysical revenge. The wish becomes an act. The statement 'I killed him' helps her to deal with her problems. Does she think she really killed him? Not then, when she confessed. Would she eventually have thought she really killed him if Ames didn't confess? Maybe down the line. We'll never know."

"Poof," smiled Nadiri. "A new category. The wishful confession."

"Could be," said Danny. "If we were scholars we'd write it up as a case study.

"There you have it. That's what I think. Am I correct? We may never know. I do know that Kramer has been assigned a senior social worker and a team to help her get back into the world. That includes a psychiatrist. Since there would be doctor-patient confidentiality, we may never know."

"Is the case finished?" asked Taegen.

"I think so," said Danny. "Of course tomorrow someone else from the condo could march into this office and also confess, but I think it unlikely. Let's move on. Time to go home. We'll come back tomorrow to something new."

Part Two

XIII

I don't know where I am. It's a basement somewhere, dank and ugly. It's a space about ten feet by eight feet with a small toilet in the rear. A bedroll on the floor. No windows. I think I've been here two days. Maybe.

I remember leaving the gallery in the Distillery District and walking west to get to Parliament Street. Then I remember a man coming up to me and asking for directions to Front Street. Somebody came up from behind and put a cloth on my face.

I woke up in the back of a small truck, I don't know how much later. My hands and feet were tied. My clothes were all messed up. My blouse was unbuttoned. I still had my bra on. I looked up and there was a guy with a balaclava on his face holding a sawed-off broomstick.

I asked for water. He laughed.

I decided to try to get my head clear and find out where we were. Or where we were going. I couldn't see out, so I thought I'd count the number of times the truck slowed down or stopped.

Useless. We were definitely out of the city because the truck hardly stopped. How far out of the city, I didn't know.

When the truck stopped the driver came into the rear. He too had on a balaclava. He blindfolded me. I tried to make conversation, but no one answered anything I said.

They carried me blindfolded into a house, took me down some stairs and here I am, locked up.

They soon untied me. The guy who was the leader touched my breasts and my vagina, so hard that it hurt. "That's what you get, you bitch," he said. The first thing he said, I recognized the voice. It was the same man who stopped me on the street, calling me June August and revealing his anger. I know his name, at least the name he used, but I'm not going to let him know that I know the name.

They took my watch so I don't have any sense of time. They bring me some food every so often. Not the leader, the other guy who was watching me in the truck. He says nothing except that he bangs on the door and says "move back."

When he opens the door I try to see something, anything, but there is nothing there, just a wall and some stairs. I try to listen for something, anything, but there is only silence.

Yesterday, when he delivered what looked and tasted like Chef Boyardee gook from a can I asked him, "What's going to happen? What do you want?" He shrugged and then closed the door.

I've read about this kind of thing. How do you pass the time? How do you keep your sanity?

I tried to make up stories. I'm not good at that. My stories are like remembering the lyrics of songs. I get two sentences going and then nothing.

So I decided I'd design and draw. Whoever you are out there, I've designed a necklace that is so remarkable—all coloured glass like an abstract work of art. I'll sell it cheap. Just please come and order it. I'll give it to you free. I made some earrings from bauxite. I have a bracelet for you, all colours of the rainbow. Please. Come and get them.

I sleep. I don't know if I'm sleeping in the day or night. I think that my food is brought during the day, but who knows? I try to sleep all the time, but I can't.

What's going to happen? Will I ever get out of here? Will I see a sunset again, so beautiful? Nature does it better than we humans can ever do.

Who knows that I'm gone?
Who cares?
Do you miss me?
Is anyone looking for me?

XIV

There are several pedestrian bridges in the city of Toronto. One of them, the Glen Road Pedestrian Bridge, is near the middle of the city, linking Glen Road in the southwest corner of Rosedale with the Sherbourne Subway Station and the corner of Sherbourne and Bloor. It goes over the Rosedale ravine at that spot, which has Rosedale Valley Road, an artery known by some and used to get to the lakeshore quickly, at its centre.

The bridge in early June made for a fine walk, for the ravine was filled with many kinds of trees, all now lush and green. If you walked from Glen Road to Sherbourne you could turn left and see the tree canopy, and you could turn right and see both the canopy and the outlines of buildings in town. For many it was part of what could happen in this city—a pastoral walk on the edge of the main part of the city. If you knew your way, you could even use it to walk as far as Lake Ontario via the ravine.

On the southern side of the bridge, there was a kind of urban oxymoron. You could take steps to go up to

Bloor Street, or you could take a small tunnel to get to a subway entrance and the neighbourhood on that side. The tunnel was filled with graffiti, some of it rude, none of it claimed by aficionados of the genre as art. It was very badly lit and very dark at night. Many people, including the elderly and those with baby carriages, avoided it at night because it had a sinister feeling and a reputation as being a place where drugs and money were exchanged.

On a balmy Thursday night in early June, a bit before ten o'clock, which meant there were still some remnants of daylight, three teenage boys of seventeen crossed the bridge together to go to the subway. They were coming from a friend's house on Dale Avenue where they had gone after school at the nearby Rosedale Heights School for the Arts, had supper and jammed for several hours in rehearsal for an end-of-year performance at the school.

They crossed the bridge, entered the tunnel together and found there the body of a mature woman of about fifty. They dialled 911 and were told not to touch anything and not to leave the scene. A police cruiser arrived four minutes later and the two policemen cordoned off the area. A half hour after the boys called, Detective Inspector Daniel Miller arrived, soon followed by Detective Constable Nadiri Rahimi.

Danny huddled with the policemen and was reassured that nothing was disturbed. He was looking at the body when Nadiri arrived to join him.

The woman was lying on the ground mid-way in the tunnel, near one of the walls. She was well dressed and a handbag was lying by her side. One low-heeled shoe was on. The other had fallen off fifteen feet from the body, which meant that she may have been running away from someone. There were knife wounds in her back and, as far as Danny could tell without touching the body, at least one knife wound in front.

Danny turned to talk with the boys and saw Dr. Hugh O'Brien coming from the bridge side, probably after parking on Bloor and going down the stairs.

"Good evening, Danny," he said. "It looks like you have another body in Rosedale."

"Maybe, Hugh. Maybe she's from elsewhere. We'll know shortly. How are you?"

"Very well, Danny, though my children are trying hard to drive me crazy."

Danny smiled. "It goes with the turf, Hugh. How old are they?"

"Twenty-one and nineteen."

"Well, Avi is fifteen and hasn't yet gotten to that side of things. But my older sister has two kids of about the same age as yours. They are fine people, Hugh, but they do drive her nuts sometime. I think we should all remember that they think we drive them crazy."

"Both statements are true, my good man. Still, I love them more than life itself."

"Of course."

"Speaking of life, Danny, is there anything I should know before I do my examination. My forensics team will be here shortly."

"I know very little, Hugh. Her handbag is on the ground. I thought I'd let your people do their job before I went through it."

"I'll get to work, Danny. I'll let you know what I find and when you and Nadiri can go through the scene."

Danny turned to find the boys. They were waiting with a policeman at the top of the steps. Danny saw a bench nearby and asked the boys to sit there.

"I just need to talk with you guys because you found the body," he said. "We'll let you get home pretty soon. Have you called your parents?"

One of the boys lifted up his phone. "Yes, sir. They're on their way to pick us up."

"Tell me what you found in your own words."

The three boys told their story quickly. At its end, one of them said. "There's nothing much to say, Inspector. Do you know who she is?"

"Not yet, but we'll know shortly. You all did what a good citizen should do. Thanks. We may need to talk again, but that's it for now. Hang out here. I'll send an officer to keep you company until your parents arrive."

Danny and Nadiri waited on the bridge until O'Brien and his team were finished.

"It's pretty clear," said O'Brien. "She was killed by the two wound entries in the back. Then, the killer made certain with the third wound in the stomach. I'll know more about the knife when I do the autopsy."

"How long ago?"

"Not long at all. My guess is between an hour ago and two hours ago. Perhaps I can narrow it down when I look at the body, though I doubt it. It's all yours, Danny and Nadiri."

The two looked at the body still sprawled on the floor. The middle-aged woman was wearing a summer dress and had on a necklace and earrings. Her shoes were low heels, of good quality. Her face was pleasant, though she had some scratches on her left side as a result of falling. Her hair was dyed black, some grey at the roots.

When they opened her handbag, they found that she was Amelia Broadhurst, and that she lived nearby, in one of the two low-rise condominiums on the Glen Road side of the bridge. She had the usual contents in the handbag—a brush and comb, keys, a small make-up kit, a set of plastic cards ranging from a Visa card to one which indicated membership in the Art Gallery of Ontario. She also had one which gave her entrance to a private school, The Castle Frank Academy, located not far away. She wore a wedding band.

When they finished in the tunnel, Danny and Nadiri walked across the bridge to her address on Glen Road. They found an answerphone system which had a listing for Broadhurst and Lin and punched in the number.

A man answered. They identified themselves, entered

the building and made their way to apartment 403 on the top floor.

"Something is wrong," said the man waiting for them at the open door.

"We need to come in, Mr. Lin," said Danny.

Lin tightened his lips, brought them inside to the living room and sat. "Something happened to Amelia," he said, his intonation making it a question.

"Yes, Mr. Lin," said Danny. "I'm the bearer of very bad news. Amelia Broadhurst was attacked in the tunnel near the pedestrian bridge. She died of her wounds a short time ago."

Lin had tears rolling down his face. He simply hunched over in his chair and absorbed the news. After a time he looked up. "You're certain she's dead?"

"Yes. She was examined by an excellent forensic pathologist."

Nadiri asked, "Is there someone we could call to keep you company, Mr. Lin?"

"My brother lives not far away. Amelia's sister is in the Junction along with two nieces. I need to inform them."

"Of course," said Nadiri. "Can you give us some information now or would you rather speak tomorrow? This is a homicide and our job now is to find the killer or killers."

"I must first call the immediate family. Then, I think I can talk. Talking is better than sitting doing nothing."

They learned that Broadhurst and Norman Lin had

been married for twelve years. "We met when both of us were in our late thirties." He mused. "A first and only marriage for both of us. Life was wonderful with her. I hadn't known it could be so rich."

Lin said that he was a city planner and he worked for that office at City Hall. Broadhurst was indeed a teacher at The Castle Frank Academy. "Drama and History," he said. "They'll tell you. She was a remarkable teacher."

"Mr. Lin, do you have any idea why this would happen?"

"No, Inspector. We lead...led...quiet lives. We loved walking, going to the theatre, some travel, talking about our work, reading to one another, cooking. Everything. I know of no enemies. It must have been a random killing. Maybe a robbery? I worried about that tunnel when one comes out of the exit at the station. Bad planning and lighting."

"Where was your wife?"

"She was at the weekly meeting of Voices, a female choir that meets in the west end, at Runnymede United Church. Several friends are also in the choir."

Norman Lin's brother appeared. The two simply hugged one another for a time.

Danny felt that Lin had done as much as he could on this terrible night. "Mr. Lin, I think we should talk again in a day or two. We will need someone in the family to formally identify the body at the morgue. We can do this tomorrow."

His brother offered to do the difficult task. "I'll do it," said Lin. "I need to see her."

"Either Officer Rahimi or I will be there, sir. Can we send a car to pick you up at, say, eleven o'clock in the morning?"

"Sure. Now I have too much time."

"What do you think, sir?" asked Nadiri as they walked to their car.

"Frankly, Nadiri, I don't know what to think. At this moment we have the death of an ordinary good citizen married to another good citizen. There's no handle. Yet. Let's get some sleep and follow up with the school and family and friends in the morning."

XV

That same day, Celia Rogdanovivi began to assemble a case against the Altonis. She had done some research and was ready to try to find an avenue of interest that she felt would work in court. The new young student hired by Clark LLP, Deborah Feldman, was assigned to join her.

"You'll work on this case, Deborah," said Celia, "for half your time. The other half will be spent assisting whoever needs help with what we might call normal lawyer's work. We all think that you should get a general feel for what lawyers do everyday while you're here this summer."

"Sounds good, ma'am. You tell me where to go."

"First, I find the ma'am, while proper, annoying when we're alone together, or even when we're with the other partners. Call me Celia. Save the ma'am for more formal moments or meetings."

Deborah nodded.

"Now, let's look at the file and see what we might pursue."

They read for a while. Deborah then said, "You know, the mortgage scam is something a lot of people relate to. Perhaps we could get some of those whose homes were foreclosed to take action."

"I thought the same thing for a while. There is a big 'but'. The 'but' is that nothing illegal was done. They loaned people money who wanted loans. Those people were risks and couldn't get loans through normal channels. Then some of those who took out what are really sub-prime loans in the famous American terminology couldn't meet their payments. So eventually they got a foreclosure notice and the Altoni's company took over the property. They usually wanted the land. They tore down what was there, redeveloped and made huge profits."

"That," said Deborah, "is a scenario that a lot of people will find scummy."

"It is scummy. The 'but' is that it isn't illegal. It's deplorable and immoral. Still, it's legal. In a democracy you are allowed to make a bad deal. For example, suppose the firm contracts to provide certain services at a fixed fee to person A. It turns out that it takes a lot more time than was expected and the firm suggests to person A that it should be paid more. Person A says: 'We made a contract. I expect you to live up to the contract.' That's it. There is no legal remedy that the firm can turn to."

"You mean it's like you make a trade between the Yankees and Blue Jays. You trade pitchers. The guy who went to the Blue Jays is terrific. The guy who went to the Yankees is either a bum or he gets injured the first time he throws a ball for them. The Yankees can't say, "Excuse me, we want another pitcher."

"You got it. Not unless the Blue Jays hid an injury. But both pitchers would have undergone health checks. You make a bad deal, you live with it. It's legal. In fact, the Blue Jays General Manager will be praised. Look what happened with Donaldson, an MVP."

"If we took the Altonis to court for the loans, they'll lose in the eyes of the public."

"Not good enough, Deborah. We want something like Echoiman, to have at least a good chance to win in court. We want them to be crooks in the civic world, which they are.

"No," continued Celia. "I think we need to go the route of the building violations. There are several buildings owned by the Altonis in which the tenants claim there are mice and vermin all the time, where there are leaks in apartments that are not fixed, where the floor is badly damaged or coming apart, where the top floors have regular leaks from the roof, where the halls are filthy. Negligence. Big-time negligence."

"Sure. But aren't the tenants supposed to take their complaints to either what are called the Investigation and Enforcement Unit or the Landlord and Tenant Board. Those are supposed to provide remedies."

"Two things. We can argue that the Landlord's repeated failure to repair roof and plumbing leaks and to control the presence of pests on the premises is a breach of the Landlord's covenant to the Tenant in the lease for what is called "quiet enjoyment," meaning that the Tenant is entitled to use the premises for the purpose for which it was intended in the lease, namely to live there as his home. Hence, damages should be paid and the court should order remedies.

"We can also only take on a case in which the tenants went to one of the two remedial bodies and won but nothing was done. We can then argue that going back to those bodies is useless. We need the courts."

"That sounds good, Celia," said Deborah. "I have a question. Why haven't the tenants done this?"

"Simple answer. Because they have no money to hire lawyers and they work so hard they have no time to deal with it. That's why we're here. We'll do it for them pro bono. The Altonis depend on this. They can hire firms like Hardings or Sachs or Wilson, Campbell to defend them. They pay an hour more than the people in their buildings who work hard earn in a week. Sorry, I'm getting preachy. It really bothers me."

"That's what attracted me to Clark, Celia. No need to apologize. It's an appalling system that totally favours the 1% or 10%. My uncle, who is a really smart man and works for the city has said he couldn't afford to hire those firms if he needed a lawyer, though I think in his heart he wouldn't want to. So if the upper middle-class can't get the best representation, imagine what happens to the poor." Deborah laughed, "Whoops, now it's my turn. I'm getting preachy too."

"Enough high-minded words," said Celia. "They don't win cases. Your job is to check out the five worst buildings, places which are dreadful and where many violations are on record. Also, where some tenants have tried to take action. Find which two would provide the best cases."

"And then?" asked Deborah.

"Then we need to persuade several people to join in an action. We take the Altonis to court and expose how they make their money in order to buy their precious rare book collection and play at being philanthropists."

"I remember," said Deborah, "my American history professor, in telling about the Rockefellers and Fords and Fricks, say, 'the first generations are robber barons, the second are captains of industry and the third are philanthropists.'"

"With the Altonis, the Echoimans and others, Deborah, they are robbers. They want to leap to being thought of as philanthropists. Let's get going and expose who they really are. This will take time. Remember, half-time for me and half-time for regular work."

XVI

James Altoni had asked Tom Pendleton to arrange a
meeting with the Gelernters. Tom invited Debra to be
present in case there were questions related to provenance. The meeting was also on that same day.

Debra had done some investigation on behalf of the
Gelernters and learned that the lot bought by the Altonis
at Sotheby's had been owned by a British resident, one
David Harrow, who had inherited the books and art
from an uncle, Sir Martin Harrow. She had tried to go
further back, but was not yet successful.

The Gelernters arrived first, along with their lawyer
Helen Oakhurst.

"Do you know what this meeting is about?" asked
Michael Gelernter.

"No idea," said Tom. "Perhaps it's about trying to
clear up the matter. We'll have to wait and see. Have
you people gotten anywhere?"

"Debra has helped," said Oakhurst. "We're working
on the other end with an associate firm in Germany.
They have experience in this sort of thing. We know

that the paintings were taken and that they were stored, along with many other pieces of art, jewelry and rare items, in a warehouse near Berlin. We'll keep going from there."

"Any guesses?" asked Debra.

"All conjecture so far," said Oakhurst. "They're going on the assumption that the allies, probably the Americans, found the warehouse. So now we're working with an American firm as well."

James Altoni arrived. He was introduced to the group.

"I'm terribly sorry about what happened to your relatives," he said to Minnie and Michael Gelernter. "I had some important books stolen about a year ago and I understand how awful that can be."

"You're correct, Mr. Altoni," said Minnie. "However, what happened to my aunt and uncle was far more horrific than the loss of three paintings or some rare books."

"Of course."

"As you know, Mr. Altoni," said Oakhurst, "Mr. Pendleton has taken down those images. We are currently trying to find out what happened to them over the last many decades."

"That would be good," said Altoni. "Perhaps I can shorten the process."

"What do you mean," said Oakhurst. "Do you have knowledge of their provenance?"

"Not at all. Beyond what you can get—have already

gotten, as I understand it—from Sotheby's."

"So how can you help?"

"Mrs. Gelernter, Mr. Gelernter, I am prepared to offer the Boudin, Cezanne and van Gogh for sale to you at a reduced rate. You can purchase them for a twenty-five per cent discount."

"What do you mean?" asked Michael. "We aren't even certain that you own those works."

"Think about it, Mr. Gelernter. Those works have great sentimental value to your family, especially to Mrs. Gelernter. It will take you years and a lot of money to ascertain who is the owner. This way you can have the paintings on your wall tomorrow. No one will ever question it. They can now be in your family forever."

"But, Mr. Altoni," said Minnie, "we believe that they belong to us. You are telling us to buy paintings that we own. Is this fair?"

"I'm doing you a favour, Mrs. Gelernter. You'll have to spend a lot of money to prove that you are the owners and that might not succeed. It will take a lot of time. You want the paintings. You can have them now at a cost which will probably be less than you pay your lawyers over the years."

"And now you want us to be part of the fraud, Mr. Altoni," said Minnie. "This is no better than what happened in 1939."

"You're wrong, Mrs. Gelernter," said Altoni. "As far as the law is concerned I now own the paintings. I bought them from the Harrows, a highly respectable

British family. I'm offering them to you at a reasonable amount, given their market value."

"And you will profit from all this, will you not?" said Michael.

"I will get money for goods that I own," answered Altoni.

"A *shanda*," said Minnie, "A *charpeh*."

"What does that mean?" asked Altoni.

"My mother is saying that what you are doing is a disgrace, a shame."

Tom and Debra tried not to smile.

"What do you mean? I'm making a business offer."

"If this is the kind of business you do," said Minnie, "I'll have nothing to do with you." She was angry. "You want to profit from other people's misfortune. Is that how you make money?"

"You don't understand," said Altoni.

"We do understand, Mr. Altoni," said Michael. "We refuse your offer. We prefer not to do business with you."

Altoni turned to Tom. "Put up the three paintings again, Tom. They're for sale."

"I can't do that. There are now questions of provenance and ownership."

"I own them."

"No, Mr. Altoni," said Oakhurst. "You possess them. The question of ownership is not settled."

Altoni, without any more words, turned and walked out.

"You may have made an enemy," said Oakhurst.

Michael responded. "He was our enemy before this exchange, Helen."

"Let's sit down and see how we can all help this process,' said Tom. "I'll make tea."

They had a good discussion, agreeing to proceed as they have been doing. Tom and Debra would continue working backwards. Oakhurst would work forwards with her German and American colleagues.

When they finished, Tom asked Debra to stay.

"Is there anything else I can do?" asked Debra.

"No. You've been great. There's something else I want to talk about. Have you seen Anna lately?"

"No. Nadiri and I went to the Distillery Gallery about a week ago. In fact, Nadiri bought one of the Pastores. Anna looked fine."

"She had a few days off. Then, three days ago she didn't come to work. That itself was unique. She is very, very reliable. She didn't call and when I called her at home and on her cell no one answered. I haven't heard from her at all. Yesterday, after I closed up I went down to her condo on King West. No one answered the bell. I got the superintendant and she said that she had not seen her in the last few days. I'm concerned."

"I know her, not well, but this is not like the woman I know. Does she have family?"

"She doesn't talk much about her history. I gather her parents are dead and she has never mentioned any siblings."

"What about her friends. Nadiri and I know her, but we only know her for a few months. I'm happy to regard her as a friend, but I don't know any others. Does she hang out with any group of people?"

"I don't know. I want your advice. What do you think I should do?"

"We, Tom. What should *we* do? I have an idea."

"Yes?"

"I'll call Nadiri. You know her. She's a cop, a detective. She'll know what to do."

"Yes. Do so. Right away. I have a bad feeling about this."

XVII

There are three hundred and forty-two nicks in the concrete blocks that make up the walls. There are eighty-one bumps on the concrete floor. There are forty-eight tiles in the bathroom. I think that in my condo there are seventeen things on the wall—posters, an Indian rug, two plates.

I don't know what to do. The man who is the leader, the guy who followed me, came down a while ago. He still wore a balaclava. He didn't say a word. He motioned me to sit on the one chair in the room. Then he hit me in the face. First with his right hand, then with his left hand. I was bleeding from my nose. He stepped back to take a look, seemed to smile under the balaclava, and left.

Maybe I should try to run. They may have made a mistake. There are no knives in the room, just a spoon and a fork. A fork can be a weapon.

I sometimes wonder why this is happening to me. If I was religious I'd probably put it down to my June

August life. God is punishing me and I now need to ask forgiveness. I'm not there. This is the work of a controlling vile man who thinks I need to be punished for hurting his ego. He's playing God. Maybe because God doesn't exist. Or if he exists—he has to be male—he doesn't care.

Who might look for me? I have friends but we don't see one another every day. Maybe Tom will do it. Maybe the condo people when they don't get my monthly cheque. Maybe Susan in the design centre.

I'm beginning to get some structure. I try to organize around meals. What I take as breakfast means that I will spend the next few hours designing in my head.

After lunch I try to remember stories, books that I've read and like. Who thought that the required university courses that I took because they were required would be so useful? I really liked Camus' The Plague. *I review it in my head, thinking that Camus was right. The plague is always near us, popping up when we don't expect it. It has interesting characters and a good plot. I carry on conversations with the doctor—I forget his name—and with some of the others. Earlier today I dreamed up a book called* Underground Woman. *The heroic figure is Liza, the prostitute.*

Supper stops all that and I look for things to do in my head. So far, that's not happening and I think I'm going crazy.

I worry about trying to get structure. Does this mean that I'm getting used to this? Am I giving in?

I'm dirty. There's a tiny bar of soap in the bathroom and I wash. One little towel, more like a kitchen towel for dishes. I'm still in the clothes I was wearing when they took me. My blouse is missing some buttons. I tried putting it on backwards, but it didn't fit. I close it as best I can.

I think I need to act. Maybe tomorrow—when is tomorrow?—at lunch.

XVIII

Debra called Nadiri on her cell phone. It was three in the afternoon and Nadiri was at her desk. "This may be an emergency. I'm with Tom Pendleton and we need your advice. Anna Crowe is missing."

She handed the phone to Tom and he and Nadiri had a quick conversation. After finding out the facts, Nadiri said, "You must file a missing persons report. Why not come down to our station. It's not far away. Once you file it we take action. There's a protocol, and it means that we can interview people and search her apartment, talk to neighbors, etc."

"Do I see you?"

"No. We're Homicide. Our office is in the precinct station, but you need to talk to the person at the desk. You can tell them that you spoke with me and I recommended that you file. That will get things underway. Keep me informed."

Nadiri sat for a minute and then crossed the floor and knocked on Danny's door.

When she entered, she said, "I just got some bad

news. It's kind of personal."

"Tell me."

"Do you remember Anna Crowe? From the Stenbrooke Gallery."

"Of course. A nice woman. Very helpful."

"Well, Debra and I have gotten to know her. It's a story I'll tell you another time. I just got a call from Thomas Pendleton. She works for him now. She's missing for a few days. He's coming down here to file a missing person's report on my recommendation."

"I'm very sorry. Do you have any idea why she might be missing?"

"None whatever. Debra and I have gotten to know her, and like her, but we haven't had a lot of personal exchanges. I know she lives alone in a condo loft she recently bought on King Street West. She doesn't have a partner. I don't know anything about family."

"Is there anything special we can do that won't be done by the people in the precinct?"

"That's what I was thinking about." She looked down, turning a bit away from Danny. "Maybe I could do the investigation."

Danny took some time, holding up his palm to indicate he wanted to think. Then, he said, "There are at least two good reasons why that shouldn't happen."

Nadiri nodded. "I know. One is that we're on a homicide case. The other is that I have a personal interest that might interfere with my professional judgment."

Danny smiled. "As usual, you're an A student."

"I still want to do it."

"Tell me how I deal with the two reasons you should-n't do it. What would you do if you were sitting in my chair and your partner made this request?"

"I'd give the same answer as you did."

"So?"

"So, sir, I'll tell you how I'll deal with your reasons. First, you can easily get another partner on the Broad-hurst case. It's early days. Second, Anna Crowe is not related to me or anything like that. We put that aside. We have an interest because she was helpful in an im-portant case. Then, if I'm assigned to the case, I work under a sergeant downstairs, so I'm not the principal officer."

"Not bad, Nadiri. I need to give it more thought. Let me ask. How important is this to you? Is it as important as if Debra was involved or your sister?"

"No. I wouldn't ask if it was one of them. Then, I wouldn't be able to function properly. Here, I sense something really bad. I can give it the interest and energy it needs."

"I still have to think about it."

"Thanks, sir. That's what I'm asking you to do."

She went downstairs to meet Tom when he came to the station. Debra accompanied him. She took Tom to the desk to fill out the forms.

While this was happening, she asked Debra, "What do you think?"

"I'm really worried. Tom said that Anna was very

reliable, which is what I would have thought. He talked to her super who said he saw her regularly, but hasn't seen her in several days. Something bad is going on."

"This will put an investigation in motion. I'll make certain it happens as quickly as it can."

"Can you be involved?"

"My question to my boss a few minutes ago. Technically, I can't be. I'm Homicide. I tried to convince him."

"What do you think?"

"Inspector Miller knows when rules need to be bent to get to the bottom of things. You know what I think of him. Any other boss would have thrown me out of his office. He said he'd think about it."

"I'd like to help," said Debra.

"Let's not put that on his table. We'll see what we can do."

XIX

Danny had seen Norman Lin that morning when he came to identify the body. Lin's brother accompanied him, which made things easier. They again conversed quietly. Lin said he did a lot of thinking, but he didn't know of anything that might be relevant.

Then, Danny and Nadiri went to The Castle Frank Academy, to meet at noon with the principal, Catherine Dunn. Dunn was in her late fifties, of medium height. She seemed very strong in her bearing. Her face had a determined look. On her door there was her name and the title, "Founder and Principal." There was another person in the room, introduced as Janine Tellpore, the Chair of the Board of Governors of the school.

"We are all very distraught, Inspector. Amelia was respected, beloved by many students."

"Tell me about her."

"I have a longish story to tell, Officers. As you will see, that's why Janine is here as well."

"We have whatever time you need."

"Good. Let me begin. Amelia was a great teacher.

Not good. Great. She taught History and Drama to the students from Grade 5 through 8 at various times. Every one of her students who auditioned for the drama programs for the Arts schools in Toronto beginning in Grade 9—the two main ones are Rosedale, very near, and the Etobicoke School for the Arts—was accepted. Her classes integrated the two disciplines. She taught History using dramatic techniques and role-playing. People came from outside to watch her work. There is no question she influenced the pedagogy in her areas in the province.

"Students adored her. Many of our girls saw her as a role model—open, caring and concerned. Warm. She is literally irreplaceable."

"What about her principal and her colleagues?" asked Danny.

"Not a problem there. A good team player. Someone who could listen as well as contribute. Pleasant. She had been offered more of an administrative job and she turned it down, saying she was happy with what she was doing. This school is beginning to be talked about alongside the big four girls' independent schools in this city, Havergal, where I came from, among them. She helped that to happen over the last eleven years she had been here."

"Dr. Dunn, am I guessing wrong, or is there an Achilles heel in all this?"

"Good for you, Inspector. There is something dark. How did you guess?"

"There's a reason Ms. Tellpore is here."

"I'll continue the story. Recently, in this past academic year, there have been some thefts in the school. Some gift certificates to Indigo, which were distributed to the staff at Christmas, were missing. They had been placed in the teachers' mailboxes in the office. Some were gone.

"As well, two students reported that cash had been taken from their wallets. Their knapsacks were lying around, as happens here and elsewhere, and when they opened their wallets money was missing."

"Did you report all this to the police?"

"No, Inspector," intervened Tellpore. "We decided to keep it in house. We hoped that we would find out what happened and then try to help whoever had done it. Moreover, Inspector, I'm a lawyer. The police would not have paid a lot of attention to missing gift cards in the sum of fifty dollars from a school which charges fees like ours. Frankly, I agree. They have better things to do."

"What did you find?"

"Several of the cards were used at three different Indigo stores. We managed to get the videos which were working at the cash registers. Amelia Broadhurst cashed them in."

"What about the cash from students?"

"We never solved it," said Dunn. "It stopped once we made it public. About five months ago. Nothing has happened since then."

"Have you ever had any problems like this before?"

"None. We're a small school. We started with twenty students fifteen years ago. We now teach nine grades, Senior Kindergarten through Grade 8. We have 258 students. If we grow any more we'll have to deal with finding new space. We're really a community, not just a school. People here look after one another. The big kids do look after the smaller ones."

"What happened?"

Tellford again stepped in. "We met with Amelia. That is the two of us and the two other officers of the school met with her. I also know her outside the school. Our husbands golf together and about once a year the two will join us and some others for dinner at the club. We presented the evidence. We told her we were not interested in harming anyone or even going public. If she needed counselling or some other support we would help find it."

"Sounds right," said Danny. "What was her response?"

"Amelia told us," said Telford, "that she was not the thief. She said that she had been given the cards by another member of our staff as a way of thanking her for some help that she gave to that person. She only realized they might have been the stolen cards after she had cashed them in, when we informed the community that this had happened after the Christmas holidays."

"Did you think this was plausible?" asked Nadiri.

"I didn't think it likely, Officer. But I didn't have the evidence to contradict her."

"So did she identify the person who took it, the third party?" asked Danny.

"This is when it gets strange. She said that she had spoken to that person—I would note she was careful not even to indicate the gender of the person—and had given her word that she would not inform on the person. She was helping the person, she said, and she was doing it as a friend. She felt bound by her promise."

"What then occurred?"

"We ended the meeting," said Dunn, "and decided to let it sit for a bit. I was asked to speak with her and to suggest she reconsider. I did so, hoping that would be the case.

"It didn't happen. Janine and I met again with her a few weeks later. We asked her to ask her friend to release her from her promise. She said no.

"At a third meeting soon thereafter, we told her that, in the absence of a third party who admitted to the theft or in absence of her identifying the third party, we had to assume there was no third party. This upset her greatly. Whether it upset her because she thought we didn't believe her or because her elaborate explanation was failing, I don't know. We again said that we would not go to the police. However, we told her we had conferred with our attorney and we would be taking steps to end her association with the school."

"And what did she do?"

"Several things. She told some parents that we were harassing her. Remember, she was beloved. With good cause. She had a lot of credibility among the parents. Then she got herself a lawyer and we were confronted with the possibility of damages and matters of that sort."

"She got tough."

"There's even more, Inspector. After this we tried one more meeting. We weren't certain she would accept our request to attend, but she came. We again asked that she inquire about being released from her promise. She said she wouldn't do that. It was a matter of honour, she said. However, for whatever reason she then volunteered some information. I'm quoting, Officers, because I wrote it down after she said it. She said, 'It really doesn't matter, anyway, because that person will not be at the school next year.' For that reason, she said, we should just let it go."

"Did she know that she was narrowing it down considerably?" asked Danny.

"I think, Inspector, she didn't think hard about what she was saying. She was improvising, I think, in order to tamp everything down."

"How many people will not be at the school next year?"

"There are three student-teachers who are placed with us from the Faculty of Education. There is one graduate student doing a doctorate at OISE, the Ontario Institute for Studies in Education, who is using our students and our data as part of her study. There are three teachers—at least as of now. One is retiring, the Dance teacher is moving to the west coast, and a third is moving to Bishop Strachan School."

"Seven."

"Yes, now it's seven. Not the whole staff. All this was compounded by Amelia telling a parent about this meeting and what was said, and the parent telling everyone she saw. So the staff knew what was said."

"Any response?"

"Anger. Some tears. In order to deal with all this we called a staff meeting which was attended by Janine representing the board."

"What happened?"

"It was civil, Inspector," said Tellpore, "but very tense. Some defended Amelia, saying we were harassing her. I was quiet but I insisted that there was no third person until there was actually a third person. The meeting turned when one of the student-teachers spoke. She got up, tears rolling down her cheeks and said that she felt betrayed. Now, as one of the seven people who were leaving, people were behaving differently to her, as if she were possibly a thief. And there were no grounds for any of this. She talked about the importance of her good name and how it was being dragged in mud for no reason other than someone saying that the thief was one of seven people. Maybe, she said, it was none of the seven people. Then she said, all of us have an idea of the identity of the likely thief.

She was emotionally distraught, she said, because of what was happening in this school, and her doctor had prescribed some pills. I know all six other people, she said, and they are the kind of people who would confess if they did it. If they are not confessing, then none of them did it. I don't want to carry this with me, she said, for the rest of my career."

"Wow," said Nadiri. "Powerful. Hire her."

"In fact, we shall probably do so in the future," said Dunn.

"Anything else?" asked Danny.

"That's what you called the Achilles heel. That's the story."

"What happened?"

"Nothing, Inspector. That meeting occurred five days ago. She was killed. Would she have resigned? I don't know. Would we have taken action to dismiss her? Yes. But all this is, as Janine would say, moot."

"Do you have any thoughts, Inspector?" asked Tellpore.

"Not yet. What you've told me is very important. It doesn't mean that I'll regard those seven people as the main suspects. There's much else to be learned before we narrow things down."

The room had been tense, for the drama of the tale affected the four of them. They sat and talked about the school and its history for a time. Then Danny and Nadiri left and returned to the office, where shortly thereafter Nadiri received the call from Tom Pendleton.

XX

An hour after Nadiri's request to be assigned to the Anna Crowe case, Danny called her into his office.

"You are temporarily assigned downstairs," he said. "You'll work under Sergeant Sara Bellucci on the Crowe case. You'll do this for a week at most. They're short and can use some help."

"Thanks, sir. I really mean it. I appreciate this. It's important to me."

Danny looked up and made a gesture of acknowledgment with his hands. "Now get going. Let me know what's doing."

Serafina Bellucci, Sara to most of her family and friends, though not to her parents, was known as a tough woman. Short, perhaps five feet two inches, the minimum requirement for females in the Toronto police force, and round in shape, she was a no-nonsense person, direct and forceful. As well, she had a record of solving crimes and working well with the local community.

Nadiri went downstairs and knocked on Bellucci's

door.

"Come in."

"I'm reporting in, ma'am, and ready to go."

"Constable, I understand you have some interest in the Crowe missing person case."

"I do, ma'am."

"I want no bullshit here. You behave professionally, which I hear you usually do. If you go off-track, I'll send you upstairs in a second. Do you get it?"

"Yes, ma'am."

"Good. Now tell me what you know about Anna Crowe."

Nadiri related her knowledge of Anna's life and said, "I know of no obvious reason that would make her missing. She seemed stable and happy. She had a good job and she had recently bought a condo."

"No partner?"

"Not that I or my partner know of. I would doubt it."

Bellucci looked at her watch. "It's a little after five. Let's get started in the morning. We'll go to her apartment and look around."

"I'd like to get started now, ma'am. I'm happy to do it without worrying about overtime. I think time matters. I'd rather not wait another half a day."

"I expected that, Constable. You have a reputation for pushing hard."

"I won't do it on my own, ma'am. Only with your permission. I did it once on my own a few years ago, when I was new upstairs. Inspector Miller nearly threw me off the squad."

"And rightly so. You should be glad you didn't do that to me. You'd be on the worst beat in Etobicoke in a minute."

Nadiri smiled. "So I hear, ma'am."

"You make sense. Take a partner. I know Connor Smyth sometimes works with Inspector Miller."

"He's good. We'll be a good team."

"Report to me regularly. Often. You understand?"

"Yes, ma'am."

Armed with the necessary papers, Nadiri and Connor arrived at Anna's King Street loft a little after six. They contacted the superintendent, who let them into the apartment.

It was a very pleasant small one-bedroom loft, well lit, giving the impression of being larger than it actually was. The first thing Nadiri did was to look and see if it was lived in, if there were any indications that Anna decided on her own, for whatever reason, to disappear.

"This is the place of someone who was coming home to it," said Nadiri. It was neat, but not so neat that it was pristine. There were a book and a magazine on the couch. One of the throw pillows still had the impression of Anna's back. The rugs in the living room were not quite straight. In the kitchen there were dishes in the rack in the sink, spices and salt and pepper shakers were randomly on the counter, a frying pan, unwashed, was on the stove. The bedroom had clothes on a chair.

The bed was somewhere between being unmade and made.

Connor asked, "Where do we start?"

"You take the living room. I'll start in the bedroom."

The made their way through drawers and closets and papers, but there was nothing indicating that Anna's life was strange or that she was in danger.

Nadiri then picked up a Mac Book Air computer and gave it to Connor. "See what you can do with this." she said. "I'll go into the kitchen."

The only things that Nadiri found in the kitchen that might be useful were telephone numbers on the fridge, stuck there with magnets from the AGO. There was a list which included the numbers of the super, a plumber, a handyman and other domestic necessities. And there were four small yellow slips scattered around. One was the home number of Tom Pendleton; a second was someone named Doris; the third was named Fay; and the fourth was named Charlie. Nadiri copied the names and numbers in order to follow up.

When Nadiri went back into the living room, Conner was still working on the computer. "Any luck?" she asked.

"No. I can't get into her email. I tried several obvious passwords, but nothing. I did get to the history and there's nothing strange. She did some work at home and there's a lot of art stuff from Quebec. And the usual stuff: CBC, some games, some YouTube music videos, etcetera."

"We'll take the computer. Some of our people will be able to crack it."

"What about the neighbors?" asked Connor.

"Of course. That's dumb of me. Come on. We'll knock on doors."

There were fifteen units in the condo. They found people home in nine of them. All knew Anna, some very casually, others people who conversed on occasion in the hall or the elevator. No one indicated that they perceived anything unusual in the last few weeks.

XXI

I made a big mistake. I chickened out at lunch and didn't try to run. I don't know why. I just feared doing it.

Then, after supper, I was lying on the mattress trying to figure out how to make the time go by. The door opened and the leader came in, face covered. He was naked.

"Get up," he said. "Take off your clothes."

I rose slowly and said, as if I didn't know, "What do you want?"

He came to me, pulled me to him and tore at my clothes. He beat me. He punched me in the face and the stomach. Then he raped me, screaming curses, telling me that I was a bitch, that I was a slut, and that I should never have thrown him out.

I went limp, hoping that would stop him, but he only became angrier and more brutal. At some point I passed out.

I regained consciousness. No idea how much time had passed. I was on the floor, naked, bloody. But I wasn't bleeding anymore. I was just very sore all over.

I didn't know what to do. I wanted to scream, but I thought that might make them angry and they would hurt me again. I knew no other person would hear me. I crawled over to the bedroll, covered myself and tried to sleep. I needed a head clearer than the one he left me with.

Now I had to make some fast decisions. This was no longer a horrific game, it was life or death. Now, definitely.

Sometime after I woke up, with aches in several places and with a big bump near my right eye, breakfast was brought by the second guy, the assistant as I thought of him.

I cowered in fear when he deposited the food, for two reasons. First, I was genuinely afraid; second, I wanted him to think I was broken, that I had no fight left in me. I felt like an animal trapped by cruel hunters.

I made a plan and I made a resolve. It had to happen at lunch.

XXII

The next morning at eight-thirty Nadiri and Connor reported to Sergeant Bellucci.

"What do you think?" she asked, after they told what they had found the evening before.

"I don't think she planned to disappear," said Nadiri. "Her apartment was lived in, clean but not especially clean, comfortable and a little messy. She expected to return to it when she left the Pendleton Gallery. Maybe she did return to it."

"The computer didn't reveal anything strange," added Connor. "I'm taking it to the lab after we finish and we'll soon get into her e-mail and any protected files. That's our best hope."

"I'm going to call the three people whose names and numbers were on the fridge," added Nadiri. "That might help."

"Do you think she might have been abducted?" asked Bellucci.

"No evidence of it, ma'am," answered Nadiri. "If it's a kidnapping, there's no sign of anyone asking for ransom."

"Foul play?" said Bellucci.

"Should we call the hospitals?"

"I think so," Bellucci replied. "There's too much mystery around this. There's stuff we don't yet know. I want you to dig hard. Something will come to light."

Afterwards, Nadiri called the three people. Doris was Doris Lescott. She and Anna had gone to OCAD together and remained friends. Lescott had two young children, no longer worked, and lived in Mississauga. "We meet about once a month," she said. "Anna sounded really happy the last time we talked, about three weeks ago. She felt her life was moving in the right direction. I don't know of anything strange or odd. This isn't like her. She's straight and orderly."

Fay was Fay Crowe. "We're cousins," she explained. "Her father and my father were brothers. She grew up in Cobourg and I grew up here in Toronto. When she went to school here we connected. She would come over to my parents' house for dinner once a month or so. Her parents died and I only have my mother left, and she's ill. We call one another every so often. We meet for coffee or lunch maybe five times a year. Neither of us have much other family. In fact, I have some family on my mother's side and Anna has no one left but me. We're not close, though we like each other. She's an artsy type and I'm a nurse so we have different interests. Still, its family."

However, Fay had nothing to say which threw any

light on what was happening.

No one answered the phone number which was 'Charlie'. From the prompt asking her to leave a message, Nadiri learned that he was Charlie Holt. She left an urgent reply, asking Holt to get in touch as soon as possible. Then, she got to the task of calling the hospitals.

XXIII

I got myself ready to try to escape. Better try to be alive than accept what seemed to be coming. I dressed as best I could. My blouse was by now better called a rag, but I got it to cover some of me. My pants were torn, but they were wearable. I noticed that even in these few days I had lost some weight. I got the thin blanket ready to take with me. If I got out who knows where I would be. Who even knows what day it would be? Would it be dark or light?

The assistant came down with what I called lunch. I had moved the bedroll closer to the door and was on it crouching like an animal, knees and hands holding me up. I had the fork in my right hand.

"Move back" he yelled as usual. He came in with the food on a tray. As he bent to put it on the floor I leapt up and pushed the fork into him. I aimed for his balls. Bingo!

He screamed and fell to the floor, holding his groin, clearly in pain. I jabbed the fork into him again, into his side, hoping to hit a kidney. Then I took the one wooden chair in the room and, while he was on the floor, I smashed it into his head. An arm came off the chair and I picked it up and beat him on his head again until he was unconscious. I'm ashamed to tell you that I didn't feel ashamed that I was hurting someone who was, at least after I first hit him with the chair, defenceless. I'll have to deal with that one of these days.

I grabbed the blanket and went up the stairs. I opened a door and it led into a small kitchen with just room enough to fit a table and a few chairs. But it had a window. A window. Light. The world. I heard in the background, very faintly, the sound of cars going by.

I went to the front door, opened it and stepped into the porch. Oh my god, what a surprise. I thought we were in the country, silent, far away from everything and everybody. I was prepared to just walk and walk and walk, hiding when I had to. Trying to find help.

I realized I had been kept in a small house. But it was on a road that had cars travelling on it. To the left there seemed to be country. To the right it looked like a small set of shops, houses, a gas station and some small manufacturing plants leading somewhere. I took that road, the blanket thrown around me. I looked up. The sun was high, in the middle of the sky. It was about noon.

I walked a short distance. Then there were a few buildings leading off the road with a sign, "Stratford Perth Museum". I turned right to walk to the entrance, which was in what seemed to be a very large old house.

There were some cars parked outside.

I opened the door and saw a woman behind a counter. She gave me a strange look. "I need help," I said. "I've been kidnapped and raped. Please call 911. I need help."

She immediately came out from behind the counter and told me to sit. She called out, "Christine, I need help. This is an emergency."

An older woman, my age, Christine, came and I told her the same thing. I had rehearsed it so many times that at that moment they were the only sentences in my head. "Call 911," Christine told the younger woman. "Tell them to send at least two policemen. Tell them one of them must be a woman."

Christine—I learned later she was Christine Donovan, the curator of the museum—took me upstairs to an office. She closed the door and helped me to sit down. She sat next to me and held my hand. She asked me if I wanted some water. I asked if she had water in the room. "No, I'll get it from the kitchen across the hall." "No," I said, "don't leave me alone."

I then asked her if the door to the room had a lock. She said no. I asked her to take a chair and place it under the doorknob so that no one could get in. She told me not to be afraid now. I asked her again the same thing. She got up, took a wooden chair not unlike the one I used to beat the assistant and placed it under the knob.

After a short time someone tried to turn the knob

*and get into the room. I cowered and moved back.
"Tell us who you are," yelled Christine. "We're the
police," said a male voice. Then, the young woman's
voice, "Christine, it's Hayley. I'm here with two police
officers."*

*"Stand back," yelled Christine. She left me and went
to the door and moved the chair. She opened the door
and let me see her look out. "OK, come in."*

*Two uniformed police officers, one male and one fe-
male, came into the room, Hayley following.*

*The female officer spoke. "Ma'am, we're going to
take you to the hospital. First, can you tell us who hurt
you?"*

*"They're in a small house not far from here. Two
men. The leader isn't there. The guy who helped him
may still be in the basement. Maybe even unconscious.
I escaped using a fork as my weapon and I beat him
with a chair like that one."*

*"Can you show us the house if we take you there in
our car?"*

"I think so. Maybe."

*The second officer called for back-up. "I need it
now," he said. "We have a woman who needs medical
assistance but we might be able to get one of her cap-
tors."*

*"We'll be moving out to the hospital in a few minutes,
ma'am," said the female cop. "Can you tell us your
name and where you're from?"*

"Anna Crowe. Toronto. Downtown Toronto. I live

on King Street West."

"The other cop had a device in his hand. He punched in something. Then he asked me, "C,R,O,W?"

"No. C,R,O,W,E"

He did something on the device.

"You've been reported missing. By someone named Thomas Pendleton. I'm going to inform the Toronto police. The person in charge is Officer Nadiri Rahimi."

I started to cry. For the first time since they took me. I cried and I couldn't stop crying. Christine held me and I cried into her shoulder for what seemed like a very long time. I tried to stop but I couldn't.

Finally, they signalled another police car had arrived. "We need to go," said the female cop.

I asked, not believing this was happening, "Where are we going?"

"To the Stratford General Hospital, ma'am. You need medical help."

"Can I go to the bathroom first?"

"Of course."

Christine helped me to rise and took my hand. "I'll take you, Anna."

I entered the museum washroom and peed. Then I looked in the mirror. In my head, the person in the mirror wasn't the person looking in the mirror.

The mirror showed a woman who had a black right eye and blue bruises on her face. She was asymmetrical. Her hair was a mess, tangled, dirty, all over the place. She had a vile looking blanket around her shoulders *and wore a rag which didn't really hide her bra. She stooped.*

I ran some water and tried to wash my face. I put some water on my hair and used a hand as a brush. I opened my mouth to see if I still had all my teeth. I wanted to look like Anna Crowe. Not possible. 'Not possible yet', I said to myself.

I straightened my body and left the bathroom. Christine smiled as she saw me. "Better, already," said this stranger who was turning into my guardian angel.

I tried to smile, though it hurt a bit. I asked her, "Could you come with me to the hospital?"

"Sure," she said, without a moment's hesitation. I hugged her.

On the way to the hospital, we identified the house. It was really very near the museum. I didn't walk far.

The second car went to the house to see what they could find. We turned around and they took me to the hospital.

XXIV

Nadiri received a phone call from the Stratford police as soon as they got Anna medical assistance.

"How is she?"

"Beaten up. She got away on her own and she showed a lot of spunk. She's being looked at now by a medical team at our hospital. A social worker is on the way."

"Will you let me know what's happening? She'll need support when she gets back to Toronto. I happen to know her and I can help with the arrangements."

"Will do." They exchanged names and numbers and addresses.

Nadiri reported to Sergeant Bellucci.

"I'm very glad," said Bellucci, showing a soft side Nadiri didn't know existed. "What a horrible experience. OK, Officer, you're off the case. Now you can be her friend."

"Can I stay on it officially for a short while, until Anna comes back to Toronto? The Stratford police are going to keep me informed and I can help to get her the support she'll need when she returns."

Bellucci did some thinking. "Yes, but nothing else. The case is closed. She's no longer missing."

"Thanks. Ma'am, what happens about the guy or guys who took her? What happens about the fact that she was sexually assaulted?"

"We'll open a new file. We'll work in tandem with Stratford. Let's see what they find. You told me that she showed them the house where she was kept—imprisoned is a better word—and that one guy might still be there. We'll learn about that and move along."

Bellucci looked up and gave Nadiri one of her tough looks. "And don't ask me about being on that case. We'll deal with it when it arises."

Nadiri smiled. "You took the words out of my mouth, ma'am. How did you know I would ask that?"

"I think I've figured you out, Nadiri. Besides, it's exactly what I would have asked if I was standing where you are and you were sitting where I am."

"Ma'am, you got me."

Anna underwent a long and complete medical examination. She was told there were no permanent problems and that her wounds would heal. The medical team insisted that she stay overnight in the hospital in order to keep an eye on things. Anna didn't mind at all. She welcomed a real bed, some decent food and a lot of TLC.

Nadiri called Tom Pendleton, Doris Lescott and Fay Crowe, all of whom were relieved. Then she called

Debra at the library.

"Do you know anything about her condition?" asked Debra.

"Not yet. I'll be in touch again with the Stratford police in an hour or so. I'll let you know."

"How's she going to get back to Toronto?"

"I haven't thought about that. By train or bus, I guess."

"No good, Nadiri. She shouldn't be alone. If you let me borrow your car, I'll go and get her."

"Good idea. Let's see. Depending on the timing, maybe we can do it together."

"That would be very good. I haven't driven a car in years."

When the police entered the house where Anna was held, they found a man in his early twenties in the basement. He was on the floor, looking dazed, still holding his groin.

"I'm bleeding," he said. "I had an accident and I hurt myself."

"Sure," said Officer Jill Partman, "and I'm your fairy godmother and I'll wave my wand and fix it. Who are you?"

"Billy Sadowsky."

"William Sadowsky, you are under arrest, charged with the kidnapping of Anna Crowe. You may call a lawyer. Anything you say may be used against you."

"I need help. I'm bleeding."

"I'll get you help," said Officer Joseph Elias, "but

first we're going to book you."

Partman called the station and asked that a doctor be available when they came in with Sadowsky. Then, she stayed with Sadowsky while Elias looked around the house.

When he returned Elias said, "There are envelopes addressed to Barry Depford." He looked at Sadowsky. "Who's he?"

"I need a doctor."

"Who's he?" repeated Elias. He leaned against the wall, casually, as if he had all the time in the world.

"He's my boss. I need a doctor."

"Does he live in Toronto?"

"Yeah. He works and lives there. This is a kind of country place. I need a doctor. Please."

They took Sadowsky into their car for the short ride to the station.

After he was booked Sadowsky was examined by the doctor brought into the station.

"You have bumps on your head and bruises to your face," Dr. McNaughton told Sadowsky. "They'll heal. You have a wound in your right side near your kidney. That'll heal."

"What about my balls? I don't know if I can pee."

"There's damage. I've never seen a wound quite like that. What was used?"

"A fork. The bitch used a fork."

"Very creative," said McNaughton. He turned to the police officers. "He'll need to see a specialist right way. I can't make a judgment here about his groin."

"We'll arrange it," said the sergeant in charge, Ken Wozniak, who then turned to Elias and asked him to step outside so that they could be private. "Where did they take the woman?" he asked.

"The General."

"Arrange to take Mr. Sadowsky to St. Michael's. We'll finish questioning him after he gets medical treatment."

Wozniak then went back to Sadowsky. "Remember this, Mr. Sadowsky. You're getting treated well and kindly. And then remember what you did to Ms. Crowe."

"Fuck you," said Sadowsky.

"I wouldn't have expected any other reply," said Elias, who escorted the handcuffed man to the car and then to the hospital.

The wheels started turning quickly. When Anna was asked she said she thought that the main figure in the kidnapping, the man who raped her, was named James Ford.

"How did you know him?" she was asked.

"I can't talk about that now." No one pressed her.

Wozniak called Nadiri and gave her the names. "I'll get more information when we have it," he added. "Right now, we have to look after Ms. Crowe and the guy we found, William Sadowsky, needs immediate medical attention."

"Thanks. By the way, we don't think that Ms. Crowe

should travel back to Toronto alone. A friend of hers has offered to drive and pick her up."

"Good. I'm told they're recommending she stay overnight in the hospital. I'll keep in touch."

There were a number of James Fords in Toronto, though only two Barry Depfords.

One lived on Nevada Avenue, a residential street near Steeles and Bayview. The second lived in a condo on Lower Jarvis Street Street, near the Toronto Ferry Terminal. Nadiri started with the latter.

She called the phone number listed, but got no answer. Then she googled the name and got something.

A Barry Depford was on Linked-in. He was listed as a property developer. There was a company called Depford Holdings, Limited, with an office in Scarborough.

Nadiri called the number. The phone was answered by a woman. "Is Mr. Barry Depford in, please?" asked Nadiri.

"Who's calling?"

"I'm Detective Constable Nadiri Rahimi of the Toronto police. It's important that I speak with Mr. Depford."

"How do I know you're not impersonating a police officer?"

"I'll give you the number of the police station. You can call and ask for me."

"I'll do that."

When she got Nadiri again, the woman said, "Sorry,

Officer, we've had people calling impersonating all kinds of officials. I'm Agnes Westcott, Mr. Depford's assistant."

"That's fine. I understand. Now can I speak with Mr. Depford."

"I'm afraid he's away. Can I help you."

"Do you have a contact for him?"

"He has a cell phone and I can give you the number. He told me yesterday he was leaving for a holiday. I don't know where he went."

"I'll take the number. Do you know someone named William Sadowsky?"

"Yes. Billy. He works for Mr. Depford."

Nadiri's heart quickened. 'We're getting there' she said to herself. "What does he do?"

"Anything and everything. He's a handyman, he does errands, he gets coffee, and he sometimes drives Mr. Depford."

"Do you know if Mr. Depford has a place in or near Stratford?"

"He has a house. This firm was started by his father. He bought it a long time ago as a vacation place."

"Thanks. You've been helpful."

Nadiri immediately went to report to Sergeant Bellucci.

"Fast. Good," said Bellucci. "I'll take it from here, constable. We'll find him. Either soon or not soon. But you can't hide forever."

Nadiri used her face and hands to gesture a question.

"No, constable," said Bellucci. "It won't work. A lawyer could use your friendship to compromise the case. Don't worry. We'll get him."

Nadiri tightened her lips. Bellucci added, "Check in with me every so often. I'll give you updates. Now go back upstairs and help your partner."

"Thanks, ma'am. I appreciate your understanding."

"Remember, constable, we women have to stick together. Especially in these kind of circumstances."

Nadiri went upstairs and looked in on Danny, who was on the phone. He waved to her to come in.

After he was finished talking, he said, "How is it going?"

"Good, sir." Nadiri briefed him on all the matters concerning Anna Crowe and said, "I wish I could have stayed on the case."

"This time you're pushing it too far, Nadiri," said Danny. "Bellucci was right. You're personal interest could actually get in the way. Trust your colleagues. They'll get Depford. The point is that Anna Crowe is safe and in a while she'll be sound. It could have ended very badly. A question. Did Sergeant Bellucci talk about asking Stratford to examine the house?"

"No. Why do you ask?"

"What if Anna wasn't the first?"

"Really? You think so?"

"Just a maybe. I think it needs consideration. Now, I'm glad to have you back. We have a case."

"Tell me about it."

"In a half an hour. Now I think I'm going to go downstairs and see Sara. Come back then."

Danny went down and poked his head into Bellucci's office. "Ah," she said smiling, "it's the star detective. To what do I owe the honor?"

Danny laughed. "All I have to do if I get a big head, Sara, is have a chat with you."

"It's good for you, Danny."

"It is. Keep it up. Now, thanks for letting Nadiri do the job."

"She's good. A bit too pushy, but good."

"Look who's talking about pushy. I'm here because of a thought I had when Nadiri briefed me about the Crowe case."

"Let's have it."

"Is Anna Crowe the first woman that Depford kidnapped? Could there be others? What about searching the house and grounds for bodies?"

"I knew you were smart, Danny. How about coming down and working with us plebes?"

"Do you think it's a possibility?"

"Yes."

"So?"

"So, my clever detective, I've already called Stratford and talked to their chief about it. I also have one of my people looking at outstanding missing person's reports. It's in hand."

Danny came close to blushing. "Sorry, Sara. I should

have assumed you would get to it as fast as possible."

"It's fine, Danny. I don't want to brag, but not all our colleagues are as clever as we are. Let's have lunch sometime."

"I'm buying," said Danny. "I feel embarrassed for having come about this."

"It's good for you, Danny. A harmless reminder of fallibility never hurts. But keep doing it anyway. I appreciate the interest. Now let's make a date. You're taking me to a very good restaurant."

XXV

Danny brought Nadiri up-to-date in the Amelia Broad-hurst case.

"It's quite a story, sir. All of a sudden she becomes a thief. It seems unusual."

"It does. There may be more to it. We'll see. In the meanwhile I have the names and addresses of the seven people who are leaving the school this year. I'm not at all certain that this is the path that will solve the murder, but we have to go there. Rather than always be together, let's split the work for a bit. Could you look into the seven people from the school to start. I think we'll probably have to talk with others from the Castle Frank Academy. But we'll start here. What I'll do is talk with Norman Lin again and some others and begin to piece together matters from her life outside the school."

"Sir, could I get about four hours off tomorrow morning. I'll work into the evening on the seven people. Debra arranged to pick up Anna in Stratford and take her home. She called in some favours to manage to get the day off. She told Anna she'd be at the hospital at

11:00. I'd like to go with her. Not only for Anna. Debra never drives and it might be wise for me to do it rather than she. "

"Sure. Let me know when you're back in the office."

"Do you think the killing of Amelia Broadhurst may have been random?" asked Nadiri. "Could she have been in the wrong place at the wrong time?"

"Doubtful. There was no robbery. Her purse and possessions, including her money, were intact. I'm not ruling it out, but it's not at the top of the list."

Danny met again with Norman Lin later that day.

"I thought long and hard about who might have done it," said Lin. "I don't know. Amelia was respected, she was really liked by lots of people. Ask at the school. Ask anyone."

"Is there anything strange that might have happened recently?"

"Nothing I know of, Inspector. We lead regular lives. We do our jobs. Both of us like our work and she took pride in her teaching. We have friends. We see family on occasion. We use the city. Go to the theatre a lot. That was one of her loves."

"What about any events or things that happened in the past?"

"Nothing."

"Did Amelia have any unusual habits or any incidents in the past that might signal something?"

"Not that I know of. A few times she referred to something that happened when she was nineteen. A kind of mystery. But when I asked her to tell me about it, she said she would someday. It was, she said, something she wasn't very proud of. A little mystery. But how could something that happened when she was nineteen cause her to be murdered at fifty."

"Unlikely, Mr. Lin," said Danny.

They talked for a further ten minutes, more a chat than a conversation between an Inspector and the husband of someone who was murdered. As he was leaving, Danny said, "I'm terribly sorry for what happened, Mr. Lin. I'll probably talk to other family members. I'll be in touch. Have you made final arrangements?"

"Yes, there'll be a cremation. Private. We're not religious. We'll have a memorial service and a reception afterwards next Tuesday. Do you want to be informed?"

"I do, sir."

"Just look in the *Globe* or *Star* in a day or two. There'll be a notice."

Nadiri stayed at the station into the evening, calling the seven women leaving the Castle Frank Academy at the end of the month in order to set up interview times and places. Two indicated that they thought the interview unnecessary because they had alibis for the evening of the murder. Nadiri told them that she didn't want to do this over the phone. "If so," she said, "we won't need much time. I still want to get your perspective on what happened." She managed to speak with five of the seven and she would be able to get going quickly the next day when she returned from Stratford.

XXVI

Right away, as soon as I was transferred to my hospital room after being examined, I took a shower. It was wonderful. I stood under the water for a long time. I washed my hair. I soaped my body. Strange. It was one of the most sensuous experiences of my life.

A social worker came to talk with me. She asked a lot of questions about the rape and my feelings. She seemed disappointed that I wasn't crying a lot or emotionally hopeless. She said I should get counselling. I told her that I'll look into it in Toronto.

The police came a little after that and asked me to tell the full story. I told them everything that occurred from the moment that the assistant asked me for directions in the Distillery district.

"You said you knew his name," asked Officer Shirley Ranke, the main questioner.

"I thought I knew the name of the main guy. The one who raped me. Do you know the name of the assistant?"

"The guy who worked for him is William Sadowsky."

"Did I do any damage?"

She smiled. "Yes, you did. There's serious damage to his testicles. He'll need an operation. He's in St. Michael's Hospital."

"I'm not sorry. I should be. But I'm not."

"I get it. Now, how did you know the person who raped you? By the way, his name is Barry Depford."

"Then I got it wrong. I thought it may be someone else."

She raised an eyebrow. Still, she didn't follow it up.

"Do you have him?"

"No. We're looking for him and Toronto is looking for him. It's really a matter of time. No one can hide for any length of time."

"What's going to happen to me?"

"We got in touch with the cop in Toronto, Officer Rahimi. She said she'd call you this evening. They're arranging for someone to pick you up to take you back to Toronto."

"I won't be alone? No bus? No train?"

"No. You won't be alone."

A few hours later—hours I spent just lying in bed or going to the bathroom a few times to see if I started to look like Anna in the mirror—Nadiri called.

"Bless you, Nadiri," I said. "And Tom. When they told me that Tom had filed a missing person report and you were on the case I was overwhelmed. I just cried for the first time since this occurred."

"Don't worry, girl. You're not alone."

I started crying again, on the phone. I felt a little stupid, but I knew Nadiri would get it. She just held on and let me cry.

Then she told me that she and Debra would be coming at eleven tomorrow to pick me up.

"I don't know what to say. How can I thank you?"

"Don't say anything. See you tomorrow."

The next morning, Christine and Hayley came to see me at about nine o'clock.

I tried to thank them but they shook me off. Hayley had a shopping bag. She put it on a chair and she pulled out some clothes. "We're about the same size," she said. "I thought you could use these."

She had brought sweatpants, a matching sweatshirt, a summer dress and a pair of socks.

"I can't take this, Hayley.'

"Please. It's all I could do."

"I'll use the sweats. Friends are picking me up in their car, so I don't have to really dress." Then I walked over to the locker where the nurse put what remained of my clothes. I took out the rag that was the blouse and the torn pants and put them in the garbage.

"Good riddance," said Christine. "A good ritual."

"Don't you have a museum to open?"

"It doesn't open until ten," said Christine. "Now, Anna. Tell us a little about yourself."

I talked about my design, my jewelry, and my working in the Gallery. They asked about where I lived and worked and I told them about the neighbourhoods.

They told me more about themselves.

Hayley left to open the museum. Christine said that, if I liked, she could stay until Nadiri and Debra came.

"Why are you doing this?" I asked.

"Because we women should take care of one another," she answered. "Besides, you seem like a really nice person."

"How can I repay you?"

"You can't, Anna. There are things you do in life for which there's no bookkeeping. I wouldn't want any repayment. I'm doing this as much for me as for you."

"You're amazing. I still am asking. What can I do?"

"Nothing for me or Hayley. Pass it on. Do some good for a sister in need. That's all."

"You're teaching me something."

"Well, I was taught it by a great woman teacher. I'm just following in her example."

"Tell me about her."

We had a wonderful conversation for an hour. She told me about her teacher and about her passion for local history. We talked about what food we liked, what art was our favourite, and even about a few hopeless men in our lives. I felt normal. This woman had many gifts to give.

"Could we not let this connection end now?" I asked. "Do you come to Toronto? Can I come to Stratford?"

"I do come to Toronto. My parents are gone, but I have an aunt and cousins there. We keep it up both ways."

"Promise you'll let me know next time you come."

"I will."

Debra and Nadiri came into the room a little after eleven. We hugged for a long time and then I introduced them to Christine, "my guardian angel," as I called her.

"I'm a librarian," said Debra. "Not much different than a museum director."

The three women chatted and then it was time to check out of the hospital. I didn't know how to say goodbye to Christine. I was wordless when I hugged her for the final time in this episode of my life. I know she understood.

Nadiri drove. Debra sat in the back with me. I related the story, at least the parts that they didn't know. I asked Nadiri, "What about Depford?"

"Oh, we'll get him. A very good sergeant is on the case. She'll not let up."

"How did you get to be on the missing person case? I thought you were homicide."

"I pushed a bit and my boss and the sergeant helped. It worked out fine. Remember, you freed yourself. You did it."

"What happens now?"

"We take you home. Life continues."

I got small in the back and put my arms around myself. Debra spoke, "I thought of something. Maybe, Anna, you'd be more comfortable staying with me for a while."

I shuddered. "I don't know if I can be alone yet."

"Then it's settled. You'll live with me for now."

"You're sure?"

Debra smiled. "I'm sure."

I took her hand. "I can't tell you how grateful I am." I told them about Christine and what she said when I tried to thank her.

"She seems a remarkable person," said Nadiri. "How good it was that you landed in her museum."

"You were due for some luck," said Debra.

"It was a very bad time. I'll never forget how good everyone has been to me. I'll pass it on, as Christine said. In some bizarre way, maybe I'll be a better person after this."

"So, Nadiri," said Debra, "drop us at Anna's place. We'll pack some stuff and then take a cab to my place." Debra looked at me. "Do you cook?"

"Not great. But I can make a few decent things. Some stir-frys, some fish, salads."

"Nadiri's been trying to teach me how to cook, but I'm not a very good pupil."

You can't cook?" I said. "How come?"

"A long story. I'll tell you mine and you'll tell me yours. Over time."

"I'm glad you said you're taking a taxi," said Nadiri. "I'm not sure I should leave the car in your hands. Besides, I need it for work."

"You can't drive either?" I said.

"And she can't ride a bike," said Nadiri.

"But you're one of the smartest and most capable women I know," I said to Debra.

"Thanks. But there are gaps. We all have an interesting history, Anna."

As I found out, she was right.

XXVII

The next morning Danny drove to the Junction, to a small house near Dundas Street West and Keele to meet with Amelia Broadhurst's sister, Joanne Alexander.

There was a family resemblance. Joanne was slightly smaller and her eyes were green rather than brown. But her straight nose, high cheekbones and thin mouth were similar to those of Amelia.

"I'm two years younger than Amelia," she told Danny. "I'm also a teacher, at an elementary school nearby. I'm home because this is my four over five year."

"What's that?"

"We can choose to take 80% of our salary for four years. Then, for the fifth year we're off at the same 80% of regular salary."

"That's smart. I hear that a lot of teachers experience burnout. It probably saves people for the profession. I wish we had that. Being a cop is also stressful."

"I'll bet it is. How can I help, Inspector?"

"You can tell me anything you've thought about regarding the murder of Amelia. It's not at all obvious. She seems to have led a useful and solid life."

"That's so. I've thought about it. We're not best friends, but we're close and we saw one another regularly. She was a gifted teacher."

"So I'm told by everyone who knew her. Any enemies? Anyone with whom she had bad blood?"

"Not that I can think of. She was creative, but not controversial. A good person. Very generous to her two nieces, who really loved her."

"Let me ask what might be an odd question. Is there anything in her past which I should know about?"

"What do you mean? Are you asking if she robbed a bank or something like that in the past?"

"I'll make it clearer. I've learned that she was bothered by something that happened when she was nineteen. Could it be useful to know about that?"

Joanne hesitated. "What could that have to do with a murder thirty years later?"

"Probably nothing, Ms. Alexander. But I need to know everything if I'm to get to a solution. Most of what I learn will be irrelevant. But sometimes an odd fact is a key to opening up a door."

"How public is this?"

"As far as I'm concerned, it's confidential unless it has to come out. I doubt that's the case."

"Do I have your word?"

"Yes, you have my word."

"All right. There's a story. Not many people know about it by now. Maybe only me and a few people who've disappeared from our lives. I don't even know if she told Norman, though they had a wonderful relationship."

"If you tell me I won't reveal that I know it to him either."

"Well, it may be one of those secrets that become deeper than it should be, simply because it's remained a secret for so long. If you know what I mean."

"That it's a secret," said Danny "becomes more important than the secret itself. Or, if it didn't remain a secret it might have disappeared by this time."

"Something like that. When Amelia was nineteen, in first year at Queen's, she was arrested in Kingston and accused of shoplifting. She took some socks and a blouse from a clothing store."

"What happened?"

"The police decided to just warn her, given that she had no record at all. Our mother took her to some counselling with a psychologist. She said that shoplifting isn't usually about being poor, which we weren't, or being a thief, which she didn't think was the case with Amelia.

"So what was it?"

"She said it was a sign of some need. In Amelia's case she suggested she was asking for help. It turned out that she was having a very hard time that year. Her roommates were not very nice, she felt she didn't fit in with her classmates, she felt isolated. And now she felt very ashamed for having shoplifted. Amelia was very straight, Inspector. She had trouble fibbing, and hated doing it, much less robbing."

"What occurred?"

"She left Queen's and enrolled the next year at York in their concurrent Arts-Education program. She was happy there. Did excellent work. Dean's list and all that. And that's the end of the story. As far as I know, and I know her, nothing like that ever happened again. She became a great teacher and contributed to lots of young peoples' lives."

"That's the big secret?"

"That's it. It seems absurd that she insisted on covering it up, because it was diagnosed correctly. It was a symptom of a young woman who was telling us that she was psychologically distraught. It had nothing to do with stealing in the end. I think she felt some people wouldn't understand. But I see this sometimes in young people today."

"Yes. You're correct, Ms. Alexander. It conforms to one of my favourite sayings. Things are rarely what they seem to be."

"Does this help you at all, Inspector?"

"Yes, I think it does. It gives me a perspective which is useful. Thanks for telling me."

"If it can help catch the murderer, I'm glad I told you."

"It might help. It certainly won't hurt."

Danny probed a bit further, though there was nothing useful to report. He then left to go back to the station.

His car was parked two blocks away on Dundas Street West. He decided to take the long way, to walk around a block or two in order to learn something about the Junction, now becoming one of the neighbourhoods of choice of Torontonians who couldn't afford the more expensive areas.

On Dundas itself there were some old stores selling cheap antiques, hardware and clothes. As well, there was a fish restaurant that had just been reviewed well in the *Globe and Mail*, a shop advertising home-made sausages of many varieties, a small Thai restaurant, a knitting shop, and what looked like a fairly new kitchen store selling, among other things, Le Creuset pots and pans. Dundas still had a dusty air about it, for it was one of the oldest neighbourhoods in the city, but, as Danny remarked to himself, dusty on the way up, not down.

The several residential streets he saw on his walk had the same mix. All old houses, some looking like they might fall apart at any moment, some redone and gentrified. Danny was very glad that so far the homes and stores were all low-rise. It had a human feel to it. He hoped that the city planners wouldn't permit high rise condos to spoil it.

When Danny returned to the office he and Nadiri met to exchange what they had found.

He first asked about Anna Crowe and told Nadiri

that he agreed that it was good that Anna would be staying with Debra for a while. "Debra must be very sensitive," he said, "if she took the initiative on this."

"That she is, sir. She surprises me all the time, in good ways."

"I'm happy for you. I'd like to get to know her."

"You will, sir. As she would say, it'll happen in its own time."

"Now, what have you found?"

"Not much. Really, I'm just getting to eliminate some people. I've spoken with two of the student-teachers. One has an alibi and the other one says she was alone at home because her parents were out. Her parents confirm it. I've also spoken with the teacher who's retiring and she has an alibi. I'm meeting later today or tomorrow with the others. What about you?"

"I got some interesting information from Amelia Broadhurst's sister, Joanne Alexander. She's also a teacher."

Danny told Nadiri the story of what occurred when Broadhurst was nineteen.

"Do you think this is meaningful? Do you think she was again signalling something?"

"I do," answered Danny. "We have to be careful not to make too much of it yet. Still, it appears that Broadhurst may have been under some distress. What it could be, I have no idea. I did some reading on shoplifting by people who are well-off and clearly it's what I called a referred signal. Of what, I can't be certain."

"What do you mean by a referred signal?"

"I'll give you an example which is physical, not psychological. Once, I had some pain in my left leg, running down the leg into my big toe. I went to my GP and he told me to take off my shirt. Of course, I reminded him that the pain was mainly running from my calf down. He laughed and said that the pain may be there but the cause of the pain was almost certainly coming from a nerve in my back. He called it referred pain. Luckily it went away with some anti-inflammatory pills and rest and never appeared again."

"So the psychological version is that she is stealing because she is in a kind of mental pain."

"Yes. But it could be something else as well. We'll put it in our heads for now as one piece of evidence that we'll keep in mind. Let's not go so far as to psychoanalyze someone we've never met. Maybe it's a key. Maybe not."

Danny stood up. "So," he said. "Let's keep going. You work the school and I'll see some of her friends."

XXVIII

Before going out to interview more people, Nadiri went downstairs to see Sara Bellucci.

Bellucci invited her into the office and said, "You've come at a significant moment, constable. I assume you're here to ask about the Depford case."

"I am, ma'am. I still have an interest."

"First tell me about your friend. Is she living alone?"

"No, ma'am. Another friend and I picked her up and took her back to Toronto. She's staying with that person for a while. I think she'll heal over time. She seems as good as she can be, given what happened. She talks about learning from the experience, which is good."

"Glad to hear it. This is informal, but it would be good if she stayed with the person—what's her name?"

"Debra Castle."

"It would be good if she stayed with Ms. Castle for a while."

"Why do you say that?"

"I just spoke with the chief of the Stratford police. He told me that they found the bodies of two women buried in the backyard of the house."

Nadiri gasped. "Oh, my god. That could have happened to Anna."

"I guess so, constable. She not only escaped. She saved her own life. But there's certainly more to it. They're doing forensic work on the bodies and we'll be comparing the results, when we get them, with unsolved missing person reports. I don't want to get ahead of the evidence, but it's highly probable there'll be matches."

"Of course, that makes Depford a killer, possibly a serial killer. What do we know about him?"

"He has an office, as you know. He calls himself a property developer. Actually, we discovered that he owns five apartment buildings in Scarborough. He inherited them from his father. He collects rent and manages them from that office. My guess is that they're not exactly prime buildings. He lives in a house in a good neighbourhood near the Bluffs. One he also inherited."

"So he's disappeared for now."

"For now is right, constable. We'll find him. Probably soon. He'll need money. He'll need lodging. My guess is that he's not all that resourceful."

"But it's moved from kidnapping and rape to suspected murder."

"Yep. There are a lot of resources being used on this."

"Can I call Debra Castle to let her know?"

"Yes. Does she live anywhere near Crowe's condo?"

"No. The other side of town."

"Tell her to stay away from the area where Crowe lives. Let's be careful for a while."

"I will, Ma'am. Thanks."

XXIX

The list of close friends of Amelia Broadhurst given to Danny by Norman Lin included four women. Danny set up appointments with two of them the next day, a Friday. He decided the case required him to work part of the weekend and the other two were scheduled for Saturday.

The Friday interviews didn't yield much. The first was with Aisha Hussmani, a friend for many years, the two women having met at university. She had become a lawyer, was married with two children, working now part-time.

"I'm staggered, Inspector," she said. "Amelia was among the kindest and nicest people I've ever known. We met regularly and on occasion we had dinner out with our husbands. As far as I know there is nothing out of the ordinary. She was a great teacher and a good friend. She was the kind of friend who always remembered my kids' birthdays and had a creative present ready for them."

"Is there anything in the past that might be worth

considering?"

"I've thought about it," said Hussmani. "Truly, I can't understand it. Even if you didn't love Amelia, which I did, you had to respect her. It makes no sense."

The second interview was with one of the teachers at the Castle Frank Academy, Maxine Wei. "I've known her since she came to the school," she reported. "Until this year she was the most uncontroversial person imaginable. She loved teaching and had no ambitions outside of the classroom. She was a really good colleague. I teach French and English and we sometimes teamed up. We ate lunch together with several others. I couldn't believe what was happening around the Indigo gift cards. I have no explanation at all for it. Frankly, if Amelia said someone else gave them to her, I'm inclined to believe it because I've never heard her dissemble in all the time I've known her."

The first Saturday interview turned out to be important. Danny went in the morning to the home of Nan Wright, further east on the Danforth from his own home. Wright was married, had one grown child, and the two, she explained, had been singing together in choirs for nearly twenty years.

"We were in a mixed choir together where we met, but about a dozen years ago we decided to move to Voices, partly because it was a women's choir and partly because of the director, who we really liked. Our families didn't socialize, though sometimes we went out to lunch or dinner together or with one or two other women. We would go to a movie together perhaps twice a year."

"Is there anything you can tell me that would help? You must have thought about this."

"Amelia was a fine person, very decent, really kind. There's one thing, Inspector."

"Tell me."

Danny could see that Wright was reluctant to do so. He let the quiet continue, giving her time to decide. She nodded, as if she had been talking to someone.

"Amelia didn't go to the choir this year. She told me that she had another commitment that she didn't feel she could discuss, and asked me not to refer to her leaving the choir if I happened to see Norman."

Danny sat up. "Do you mean to tell me that Amelia wasn't at Voices on the Thursday night of her murder?"

"She hadn't been at Voices all year, Inspector. Since September."

"This is important. Do you have any idea where she might have been those Thursday evenings?"

"We still met occasionally for lunch. Last month we went to Hot Docs to see a documentary on Edward Snowden. I did ask her once, but she said I needed to trust her and to please leave it alone."

"You must have had some ideas about what she did on Thursdays."

"I thought a lot about it. I wondered if she was ill and didn't want to tell Norman, and on Thursdays she had some sort of treatment. I asked her if she was well, and she replied she was perfectly healthy, citing a recent visit for her annual check-up with her GP. I wondered if she was being a Good Samaritan, helping somebody. You can see by these ideas how well I thought of her."

"Any other thoughts?"

She hesitated again. "Well, yes. I shouldn't say it, but it can't hurt now. I wondered whether she was having an affair." She smiled. "I do like 1940's movies, Inspector."

"Is there any evidence of an affair?"

"No. Not that I know of at all. It was just speculation. Amelia wasn't the type to have an affair. She was loyal and very straight. But still...."

They talked some more without getting further. But Danny was already putting together the surprise, the information provided by Amelia's sister and the theft of the book tokens. He cautioned himself to go slow with this, not to eliminate other possibilities.

The fourth friend on the list, Audrey Schmidt, with whom Broadhurst taught at a public elementary school before she moved to Castle Frank, had nothing new to offer.

XXX

Danny decided after finishing the Schmidt interview at 2:00 to have a normal weekend until Monday morning.

He went home and took a few hours of practice on his violin, getting ready for the annual concert in a few weeks of the Bloor Street Chamber Group, and thinking about the case. He felt he was getting somewhere. Now he had some threads, he thought. He'd need more information to figure out how to tie them together.

In the evening he picked up Gabriella and they went for dinner to their familiar and warm local restaurant, Elena's, where they had booked a table. Gabriella had a package with her, gift wrapped. When she gave it to Danny to carry, she said, "Notice how nicely it's wrapped. Your gifts look like they've been put together by a three year old. I think you do it purposely. It must be a man-thing that you haven't managed to conquer."

"Maybe. It goes back several years to one of Ruth's birthdays. Leo's gift and mine stood out for being hopelessly wrapped. So we now have a competition to see who can do it worse."

"Well, I'll tell him about this. You definitely win."

They walked companionably to the restaurant on the Danforth, holding hands. They had not been together as usual the previous night for Shabbat dinner at the Feldmans because Gabriella had an engagement with the St. Mike's choir which she directed.

The restaurant was one they went to regularly, a smallish place on the Danforth with no more than a dozen tables. It was a Mom and Pop place, with Elena in the kitchen and Constantine up front. Sometimes, when they were busy, like tonight, one or both of their children, a boy now 22, and a girl in medical school, 25, helped out.

When they entered Constantine and Gabriella kissed European style on both cheeks and Danny got a hug.

"Come," said Constantine, "I put you in a quiet corner. I'll bring an aperitif."

After they were seated, Gabriella asked, "Tell me more about the Anna Crowe story. You got as far as her escape last time we talked about it."

Danny related the whole tale, and ended by saying, "She's staying with Nadiri's partner, Debra Castle, for now. And Sara Bellucci is heading the search for the rapist, now thought to be a killer, in Toronto."

"What an ordeal. I don't know that I'd have had the courage to do what she did."

"Well, she may have maimed the guy for life in the process."

"The dream of every violated woman, Danny."

He laughed. "I can understand that. We still need to be careful. We don't know what's in Depford's head. So Debra's been asked to make certain she or Nadiri is with Anna virtually all the time."

"Have you met Debra?"

"Only once, really in passing. I know Nadiri's really happy and she tells me that Debra is as strong a person as she's ever known. She's a librarian. Nadiri mentioned that she's been on her own since she was a teenager. She has no family. Somehow, probably through sheer will and grit, she made a life for herself."

"Add intelligence to will and grit. She sounds interesting."

At that moment Constantine came to their table.

"What's on tonight?" asked Gabriella.

"We knew you were coming. So Elena made a roast lamb from the shoulder." He turned to Danny. "If you want meat tonight. We also have baked tuna. And there's the regular menu."

"We haven't looked at the regular menu in at least a year," said Gabriella. "Did you taste the roast?"

"Of course. Wonderful."

Gabriella looked at Danny. He then said, "Let's have the roast, with whatever salad Elena thinks is right beforehand. And you choose a bottle of wine for us."

"Perfect."

"I see Milos is helping out tonight," said Danny. "How was the convocation?"

"Wonderful. He got honours and he's on the Dean's list. It was a special day for us. This is why we came to Canada. So our children could get an education and live in a good country. His history professor, the one he loved most, greeted us at the reception—terrible food, by the way—and told us how proud he was of Milos. "He'll be a wonderful lawyer," he said.

"Don't slight yourselves," said Gabriella. "None of us, Constantine, myself included, could have gone anywhere without the guidance and support of our family."

"Thank you, Maestra," said Constantine. "It's not hard to tell that your parents also did a good job." He grinned. "And even the Inspector's. Now, I must look after another table."

"Salt of the earth, Danny. What a splendid couple."

"Did I tell you about Deborah?" asked Danny.

"No. Did she get the job?"

"Yes. She's working for Clark LLP this summer. Half-time with Celia."

"And she got the job on her own? No calls from her famous uncle?"

"Not a word. My guess is that Celia doesn't know she's our niece."

"How does Irwin feel about it?"

"I think he's secretly happy, admiring Deborah's idealism and spunk. He says that he thinks the Clark people should have stayed on Bay Street, but that's just for show."

Milos came with the wine and the salad. Then they

continued their conversation.

"Celia may find out about Deborah in two weeks, when we have our performance," said Gabriella.

"How is Celia coming?"

"I got a call from Joshua Black. Remember, when he came to dinner we invited him and his grandson. He asked if he could bring Celia along."

Danny raised his eyebrows. "Am I smelling a romance?"

"No, Inspector. As my favourite cop would say, don't jump too fast. Joshua said that Celia has gone back to the cello, that her firm is acting for one of his companies, and she has accompanied him to several concerts at the symphony because his daughter has been looking after her father-in-law. I think it's more of a mentoring relationship which is turning into a friendship. Nothing more."

"We may be in trouble at the concert. For the first time there are more requests for tickets than there are seats."

"I remember when the church was less than half full," said Danny. "It's all due to your allure."

"Flattery will get you somewhere, Danny, but it's not totally true. We have some better musicians now. Including at first violin, two violists and a cellist."

"Well, what are we going to do?"

"Nothing. The tickets are gone when they're gone. After all, it's free. Apart from the tickets all of us take for family and friends, we're just getting a lot of other requests."

They were, by now, into their main course. "Speaking of demand, what's going on with you?"

"I didn't want to tell you until it was settled. My agent, Leah Quinn at Goudys, is negotiating with Vancouver, Buffalo and Naples, Florida for the year after next. And maybe some others, she said."

"So this coming year it's Victoria a second time, Seattle and Minneapolis. And they're already organizing for the following year."

"The lead time is very long. You have to choose programs, you have to do marketing, and all that stuff. Leah said that if the reviews this year are good, then other things will open up."

"I'm pleased for you."

"I am too. I'm also scared. I had no idea this would mushroom. I'm not in the big leagues, but it looks like I'm moving up to the high minors."

Danny put his hand on hers. "You deserve it."

The roast arrived. "Heavenly," said Danny, after the first bite. "It's kind of Elena to do this for me."

"They're friends, Danny. They know how to be friends."

After they finished, they signalled to Milos. When he came over, they chatted abut the graduation ceremony.

"And next year at Osgoode," said Danny.

"Yes, sir. I'm looking forward to it."

"Can I give you one piece of advice?" Danny asked.

"Of course, Inspector."

"Don't ever forget why you are becoming a lawyer."

"What do you mean?"

"Let's just remember this," said Danny. "We'll have many more conversations as the next three years unfold."

Gabriella pulled out her package. She offered it to Milos. "This is for you. In celebration of your graduation."

"Oh my. I'm speechless. You're too kind."

"Not at all," answered Gabriella. "We adore your parents. And we love to see how proud they are of your accomplishments."

"It's their accomplishment too, ma'am. Without them, I'm lost."

"Smart boy," said Danny. "I'd be nowhere without my family."

"Me, too," said Gabriella. She raised her wine glass. "To family."

Milos swiped a glass from a nearby table and Danny poured him some wine. The three repeated the toast and they drank.

On Sunday morning, Danny woke early. He took some time to indulge himself in one of his favourite domestic moments. He looked at Gabriella sleeping, rubbed her back for a time, and thought about his good fortune. Then he went to do his Sunday routine.

He went to the Y at Bloor and Spadina with his

squash racket in hand in order to play his regular Sunday morning game. He was part of a group of a dozen or so men who showed up Sundays and played in rotation.

This morning he was paired with an old boyhood friend, Mike Ryan, now a lawyer and a prominent lay person in the Catholic community. They played hard, and Mike won the match by beating Danny 10-8 in the fifth game.

"You're playing better," said Danny afterwards, as they joined the others for a shvitz. "I finally got to the point of beating you twice in a row. But this time you lifted your game."

"I decided to get some coaching," said Mike. "I realized that time is becoming my enemy at forty-three. So I saw Solly and he helped me with my movement around the court."

"It looks like I should do the same thing," said Danny. "Time is the victor. Always."

After they dressed the group moved to the cafeteria for coffee, a bagel and some talk. Danny had promised them some time ago that he would notify them when the Bloor Street Chamber Group was doing its concert. He brought along two tickets for everyone and distributed them to those who could attend. When he got to Lenny Donnerstein He said, "Could we have a few words after we finish?" Lenny nodded and thanked him for the tickets.

When they were alone, Lenny asked, "What's up?"

"I need some professional advice," said Danny to one of the most distinguished psychiatrists in the city, the head of the psychiatric unit at Toronto General Hospital.

"For you or for the detective?" said Lenny.

"I could probably use it, Lenny, but I wouldn't ask you if it were for me. We're old friends. I need some clarification of an issue that's come up in a murder case."

"Go ahead."

"Why do people shoplift, Lenny? What's the motivation? I have a case—this is of course confidential— where the person murdered suddenly stole some minor things. There is something in her history, going back three decades, where this happened before."

"What happened before?"

Danny told Lenny about the incident of shoplifting by Amelia Broadhurst when she was a student and the diagnosis made at the time.

"Has anything occurred of this sort between then and the most recent incident?" Lenny asked.

"No. At least nothing that anyone knows about."

"Then it's highly likely that it was stress related again. She was sending a message."

"But when her principal and others offered to help, and to do it confidentially, she resisted."

"Danny, don't make the mistake of thinking that people in stress behave rationally. In fact, these days even political scientists and economists are changing their models because they made the wrong assumptions about motivation. She was asking for help but also she may have been ashamed to admit that she did so by doing some petty theft."

"Why else might people shoplift?"

"Lots of reasons. The most obvious one is to get the merchandise they're shoplifting."

"You mean sometimes a cigar is just a cigar."

"As our founder said. But his point was that it often is not just a cigar. When teenagers shoplift, it's often about consumer culture and its problems, but sometimes it's also a warning.

"Then, there are people who do it to get a kick. That is, it has some daring to it. Life is dull. This makes it exciting.

"And lots of other possibilities. This is one of the problems with trying to make psychology a kind of science. It's highly individual. If I had a dream last night in which an elephant was important and you had a dream in which an elephant was important, the two elephants will almost certainly point to different things. All related to our individual history and our psyche. Still, with your murdered woman, my best guess—I never met her after all—is that she was asking for help related to something very stressful in her life. That's as far as I can go."

"Thanks, Lenny. I may call on you again about this."

"Anytime, Danny. And Vicky and I are looking forward to the concert. I remember when you got your fine violin. What a moment of joy for a sixteen year old."

"It's been a friend, Lenny. I don't now how I'd get along without it."

Lenny smiled. "You and Sherlock Holmes, Mr. Detective. But let me say that you're a lot saner than him."

"Maybe. But the way Conan Doyle talks about him, I think he played better than me."

"See you next week, Danny."

Danny went home feeling that he still didn't have a good handle on the Broadhurst case, though he was getting somewhere. Gabriella was long gone, and he had the next few hours to himself. He decided to read in bed and wound up taking a half-hour nap.

At about five, Danny heard the front door open.

"Hi, Dad," called Avi, who was having dinner and sleeping over. Avi, now fifteen, would be away for the summer at Camp Shalom in New Brunswick, training as a counsellor. He was to leave in a little over two weeks, just after the school year ended. Danny and he had arranged this time together because they both knew that there would not be many more opportunities soon to do so.

They had no agenda. Both liked hanging out together and the relationship was so intimate that quiet time never was a bother.

They sat outside in the small backyard for a time, Danny with a glass of wine, Avi with a Diet Sprite.

"Abba," said Avi. Danny got the signal. Whenever Avi addressed him as Abba, the Hebrew for father, instead of as Dad, something important was following.

"Yes, son."

"I think I should tell you that I have a girlfriend."

Danny looked over at his beloved child, as always noting to himself those features which were from him, and said, "I won't ask if she's nice, because you wouldn't be with her if she weren't very nice. Tell me who she is."

"She's Molly Gerber. Sometimes she likes using her Hebrew first name, Malka. She's seen you at times when you pick me up, but you probably won't remember her. She's a year younger than me. Really nice. And really smart."

"Good. What are you going to do about the fact that you're going away to camp soon?"

Avi smiled. "That's the nice part. She's going too. For half the summer. July. So we'll see one another there. Mom's met her and likes her."

"Good. I'd like to meet her when that can happen."

"I thought, if you didn't mind, that she could come to the concert with me."

"Of course. I'd like that. So would Gabriella. Remind me later to give you an extra ticket."

"Also, you might meet her next Friday night. I spoke to Aunt Ruth and she invited Molly to Shabbat dinner. She lives about a kilometre away from Aunt Ruth and Uncle Irwin. An easy walk."

"That would be wonderful, Avi. I can see that you're happy. That's the important thing."

"You'll like her, Abba. She's got our values. She's shy but she gets angry when she sees injustice in the world."

"I'm certain I'll like her, Avi. I'm looking forward to meeting her."

And, only as he could, Avi changed the subject abruptly. "I'm thinking that next summer I'd like to go to Israel."

"I told you I support your decision on this. If it's important to you in terms of your spirit and your education, I'm for it. That doesn't mean I won't worry for your safety. I'm your father, that's natural. But these days the sometimes crazy world we live in isn't obviously safe anywhere. Not in Paris, not in Brussels, not in much of the US where guns are part of the culture. We have to live. And as Jews we have to live as if we were unafraid. You know what I think. I've told you many times. We have to pretend to live normally, knowing that we are pretending."

"Mom doesn't want me to go. Could you speak to her?"

It was a request Avi had never made before because Danny's former wife, Rachel, was at best coldly polite when the two of them found themselves in the same room. Often, she simply ignored him.

"I'll try, son. I'll give it a shot. That's a promise. I don't know how far I'll get, but I can try."

"Thanks, Abba."

"Now let's make supper."

The two of them had cooked together for many years, ever since Rachel and Danny separated. Danny purposely planned dishes that they could cook together when Avi was eating over. Tonight, he was going to make a beef stir-fry with lots of ingredients—peppers, garlic, onion, ginger, snow peas, satay sauce, salt and pepper—along with some rice. Watermelon for dessert.

They worked as a team, people who were familiar with one another. Once he knew what was to be made Avi got out the vegetables and garlic and ginger; Danny went to the fridge to slice the meat. As they chopped away Avi took out the wok and put in some oil. He took out a pot for the rice.

"When are your exams?" asked Danny.

"Starting tomorrow."

"So why aren't you upstairs, studying."

"It's math tomorrow, my best subject." Indeed Avi had done well in national competitions, even in one international one.

They ate, chatted some more, and then went into the living room. Avi put on the TV, for the Blue Jays were playing a rare Sunday evening game, an inter-league one, at the New York Mets. Danny read and Avi watched and they both had some commentary on how the Blue Jays might yet make the playoffs. Avi went to the fridge for some pareve ice cream in the fifth inning.

In the seventh inning Danny moved to the couch where Avi was watching. He sat next to his son, who put his head onto Danny's shoulder. There was little in life, if anything, that gave Danny more pleasure.

XXXI

At eight on Monday morning, Danny and Nadiri met for coffee. Danny related what he had learned about Amelia Broadhurst's past and his conversation with Lenny Donnerstein.

"Very interesting, sir. You probably got more than I did. I just got a strange feeling about something."

"What happened?"

"Nothing. The other student had an alibi, as did the Dance teacher who's moving to the west coast. The graduate student doesn't have a clear alibi, maybe half of one. That is, she was alone just long enough to maybe get from a restaurant where she ate with three friends to the bridge, but I don't sense that's so.

"It was the interview with the teacher moving to Havergal College, Nikki Papadoupolous, that seemed unusual. She's about forty, dark, interesting looking. She had been at the Castle Frank School for only three years, teaching math and some science to the same grades as Broadhurst. She told me that an opportunity came up at Havergal and that it was good for her career, so she was moving to the bigger, older school."

"None of this is strange, Nadiri."

"No. I'm not telling it right. I'll just go on, sir." Danny nodded. "She was totally out of it emotionally. I got the impression she was almost in mourning. I guess what I'm saying is that I thought her reaction to the death of her colleague, even if Broadhurst had become something of a friend, was out of proportion to the relationship."

"Maybe she's just one of those people who have their emotions close to the surface."

"Maybe. I just found it odd. We had to interrupt our conversation time and again because she couldn't get any control. I asked her when she met Broadhurst and she said it was when she came to the school. I asked her if they had a deep friendship. She said no, they were colleagues who liked one another. What I'm saying is that there was a disconnect between what was said and what was going on emotionally. That's all."

"What about an alibi?"

"None. Home alone. Home is near Bathurst and Bloor."

"What do you think we should do?"

"Not we. I think you should interview her. Maybe she'll be different with a male. Maybe I caught her at a bad time. I got an itch on this one, sir. I don't say that often."

"I've never heard you say it until now."

"Well, there it is." She smiled. "It's either I'm that

experienced enough now to sense when something is out of whack or that I'm out of whack. One or the other."

"I'll follow up. It can't hurt."

"Let me know."

That same afternoon Danny had a visit from Sara Bellucci.

He waved her into the office and offered coffee.

"I'm coffeed out, Danny. I have good news. We got him, as my favorite US president said about Osama bin Laden. He's in jail."

"Excellent news. I think Nadiri's in. Let me get her here."

When Nadiri entered Bellucci told the story of the capture.

"We figured he would surface somewhere or other. The Stratford police also set off a search, but I didn't think anything would come of it. Then, yesterday, we learned that he used an ATM in Scarborough to get a lot of cash.

"I presumed he had a hiding place and the cash was used to buy food and stuff. Then, one of my constables got a really smart idea. He said that Depford might be hiding out in one of his buildings—slums, really—in Scarborough. We did a search and we found him. It turns out that he gave Billy Sadowsky an apartment. Billy's in hospital and will soon be in jail. Depford used that apartment to try to hide.

"When we knocked he didn't answer. When we

broke in he was as scummy a guy as you would imagine. Bellucci lowered her voice two octaves. 'I'm just a sweet kind property developer'. We told him he was being arrested for murder and kidnapping and rape. 'Murder?' he said. When we told him we found the bodies of two women and they would shortly be identified, he folded."

"I'm really pleased," said Nadiri. "Can I call Anna Crowe and tell her he's in confinement?"

"Do it, Constable," said Bellucci. "Now she can walk the streets without fear. She's had a hard time. I've no doubt she'd be dead now if she didn't manage to escape. Depford's done. For many years. Maybe for the rest of his life."

Nadiri went to her office and called Debra's home number. No one answered. She then called Debra at the library and told her the news. Then she said, "I'm puzzled. I called your home and no one answered. Is Anna still staying with you?"

She heard Debra give a short laugh. "Yes, she's with me. She didn't want to be alone. So she's here in the library. I found some work for her to do. She's a lot better at it than most of my people. I'll get her. You tell her what happened."

Anna got on the phone and listened, her shoulders relaxing more with each one of Nadiri's sentences. When Nadiri finished the story, Anna said, "I feel a lot better. What can I do to thank you and Debra?"

"Just be yourself and live a good life," said Nadiri.

"That's one of the things I've learned going through all this. How about my taking you and Debra out to dinner tonight?"

"I'm game. Check with Debra."

XXXII

In the late afternoon, the appointment was for five-thirty, Danny went to see Nikki Papadoupolous at her apartment in what was once a large home on Manning Avenue between Bloor and Harbord. At first Papadoupolous suggested they meet at the school, but Danny didn't want to meet her in what could be a public place, nor did he want to have her colleagues think she was being singled out.

Papadoupolous greeted him outside and took him upstairs to a very pleasant irregular space which she had furnished with abstract paintings and antique furniture. As Nadiri noted, Papadoupolous had an interested face, one that seemed inquisitive. Her eyes were red and she carried tissues in one hand. She offered coffee and tea and had some cookies on a plate on the coffee table. Danny opted for coffee and looked around while Papadoupolous prepared it in the kitchen.

"You know, Inspector," she said when they were seated, "I spoke to another detective a day ago."

"I know, Ms. Papadoupolous," said Danny. "Constable Rahimi. She's my partner."

"Then why are we speaking today."

"Because I need to get some further information. I apologize if I'm asking you to repeat yourself. We need to do that sometimes."

"I just find it hard to talk about it," said Papadoupolous.

"How long did you know Amelia?"

"Just three years. Since I came to the school."

"Did you teach together?"

Papadoupolous straightened up a bit. "We did, sometimes. The school encourages a lot of integrative learning, which I like. She was a wonderful teacher. Her whole self was transformed in the classroom. I've never seen anyone like her."

"You admired her?"

"Yes. As a teacher she was the best I've ever seen. Maybe one or two of my former professors come close. She had the gift of being able to teach several things at once. So while she was teaching history, though the students didn't know it, she taught writing and drama and critical thinking. I don't know how to describe it. In my head I called it holistic teaching though I don't know if such a term exists."

At that moment, Papadoupolous had tears running down her cheeks. "Excuse me, Inspector," she said. "I can't help it."

"No excuses necessary. Of course you're in mourning for your friend."

"In mourning?"

"That's what it seems like Ms. Papadoupolous. I didn't mean anything by using the term."

"Do I look like I'm in mourning?"

"Yes. You must have had a very close relationship."

"Oh, no. I told your partner. We were colleagues."

"Nothing more?"

Papadoupolous simply collapsed in tears. Danny sat still, giving her time and space to get settled.

When she was composed, Papadoupolous answered. "Nothing more, Inspector."

Danny leaned forward, his body and face indicating he was doing some thinking. Papadoupolous was having a hard time keeping in control.

Finally, Danny broke the silence. "I don't believe you, Ms. Papadoupolous."

In tears still, Papadoupolous said, "Is it that obvious?"

"Yes. To me and to my partner. That's why we're having this conversation."

"How confidential is this?"

"What you tell me can be confidential as long as it doesn't have to be made public in a courtroom. I can't guarantee confidentiality. I can say that we're not in the business of embarrassing anyone or making people's lives hard."

Papadoupolous ceased crying. She blew her nose and sat up straight. "I've seen you on television, Inspector. I'm going to choose to believe you based on what I've seen."

"I have faults, Ms. Papadoupolous. Lying is not one of them."

"OK. Let's talk. You will be, as far as I can tell, the first to know. I'd like to keep what I'm telling you private."

"If I can do so, I will."

She took a deep breath. "Amelia Broadhurst and I were lovers. We had an affair. It began last summer. We met here every Thursday evening since the school year began. I loved her, Inspector. There was no other person in my life like her."

"I am, Ms. Papadoupolous, very, very sorry for your loss. It's got to be very difficult."

"It is, Inspector. Call me Nikki please. I can't even really talk about it with anyone. It's all bottled up until now. I go to the school and teach and pretend it's just a colleague. I probably don't do it very well."

"I'm not changing the subject, Nikki, but I have to ask. You know that you have no clear alibi."

"Of course not. We were here. She left at 9:15 to go home, as she did every week. As far as most of the world knew, she was doing her choir. She's my alibi, Inspector. And she's dead."

"I'm going to believe you, Nikki, but I have to pursue this further."

"Inspector, do you have someone you love?"

"Yes. Several people who matter more to me than anything."

"Well, that's what Amelia was to me. I wouldn't believe you would harm anyone you loved like that. You must believe me too."

"I accept that, Nikki. I'm going to ask. You will have thought of it. Who might have killed her? It wasn't random."

"There's a complication. Do you know about the thefts of the book tokens? Do you know how Amelia handled it?"

"I know the whole story."

"I don't think it was one of the other six people who are leaving the school. By the way, do you know now why I left the school?"

"To avoid the very difficult matter of being daily in the school with your lover. To avoid possibly revealing anything. To avoid the conflicting emotions while you were teaching together. And more."

"You got it."

"Now why isn't it any of the six others?"

"I just don't think that they're the kind of people who would do this. They were angry. And they had a right to be angry. I just know most of them and they don't have the personalities that fit being a murderess."

"Then who should we consider?"

"I don't know. I only know Amelia's life at the school, which was a very big part of her life."

"Why does the school become that big a part of one's life?"

"This kind of school is more than a school. It's a big

commitment to a community and to excellence. It demands a lot more than an ordinary school. You live it, breathe it, hang around, do all sorts of extra stuff. There are others like it, including the school I'm going to. I'll give another example. There are a couple of Catholic schools, private, that are like it."

"I'm familiar with them."

"You are?"

"Don't ask. I'm also familiar with the Hebrew Day Schools, which my son and other relatives attend."

"It's like that. And more. There are several people at all these schools for whom the school is the reason they live. I'm not one of them. I do a lot. And I'm good at what I do. But I have something of a life outside. Some don't."

"Let's get back to my question. Who might have killed your lover?"

"Have you looked at her life outside the school?"

"Yes, that's part of the ongoing investigation."

"Maybe there. I really don't know. I wish I did."

Danny again went quiet, indicating to Papadoupolous that he needed a moment to think. Then, "Can I ask you something that might seem odd?"

"Sure."

"Is your move to Havergal a step up or a step down?"

"For those who prefer traditional schools, it's a step up. But for those who know about education, it's either a parallel move or a bit of a step down."

"Why down? Havergal is one of the four leading

girls' schools. It has an international reputation."

"Because a few schools are challenging the tradition that there are only four girls' schools and a few boys' schools that are the best in Toronto. Maybe socially they're the best. But in terms of education the Castle Frank Academy, along with the Toronto French School, the University of Toronto School and a few others are seen in the field as being good as the others. Some even say they're better because they don't have the burden of the social stuff. They're far more egalitarian in terms of who goes there."

"This is interesting. Thanks."

"So, Inspector." She smiled. "I guess you're not going to arrest me."

"No, Nikki. I'll be honest and tell you that because you don't have an alibi — several others don't as well — you're still on the list. Very low on it, may I say."

"I understand."

"Thanks for your candour. It really helps the investigation."

"I'm glad to get it out of my very closed inner life. Maybe now I can mourn properly."

"I hope so. I'll be in touch. Call me if you think of anything else."

"What do you do now?"

"Keep going. We've just moved another step or two ahead. Just keep going."

XXXIII

It's over. That's what everyone says to me. It's over.

It's not over. It happened and it will be in my head and my dreams—and my nightmares—for a long time. Maybe forever.

Last night I took Debra and Nadiri out to dinner. We went to a place in Leslieville, not far from Nadiri's condo. It was a quiet bistro with really good food. And we wound up having two bottles of wine. What a crazy universe. A few days ago I was a captive in a basement, abused and raped. Today I eat in a high end restaurant and drink good wine. Bizarre.

We talked a lot. Debra and Nadiri, lovers, sometimes couldn't keep their hands away from one another, which was nice because I didn't think they did that with many people.

I asked them if they wanted to know how Depford knew me.

"Only if you want to tell us," said Debra. "Maybe you want to just move on."

"I do want to tell you" I said. "But I don't think I

want to tell you now. Another time." They nodded.

We talked about ourselves. I'm still amazed of what I learned about Debra's history. She's the ultimate survivor.

Then we talked about the Gelernters and the mystery surrounding their paintings. I thought I'd like to get involved in that. To see the paintings back on the walls of that family.

Nadiri told me about Sergeant Bellucci and how she looked after my dilemma both as a cop and as a woman. I had a lot of tough women on my side.

I'm home now, alone for the first time since I walked into Christine's museum. I spoke with Tom and tomorrow I'm going back to work.

I remember that sometime back I said that if I survived I'd like to think I would be a better person. That's what I'm going to concentrate on now.

Before this, I stayed away from all intimate relationships. I even think that being an escort was part of that. That it went much deeper than just a job. I didn't have to make any commitments to the men I saw. It was business.

And I had some friends, Doris and Fay among them. But I didn't have what Anne of Green Gables called a bosom friend. I never spoke about my real self with anyone. I was careful, sometimes consciously, sometimes just because that was who I was.

No good anymore. I learned a lot from those four women—Christine, Hayley, Debra and Nadiri. I learned that you can't just be passive and think you're doing something smart. You have to act, sometimes you have to commit. When I asked Christine why she helped me, this ragged person who she had never seen before and who wandered into her life, she said she did it as much for herself as for me. She did it because that's what a good woman does. Period.

When I left the blackmail gang and when I took down the escort site—when I was turning thirty—I said to myself that it was time to start a new life, to grow up.

Well, I didn't know then what growing up was about. It's not about having a condo and a job and stability. It's about trying to be a decent person. Debra knows how to do this. So does Nadiri. It's time I learned.

I'm making a pact with myself. I will try to be a real friend to Doris, a real cousin to Fay, and to make certain I look after my new friends. I will be vulnerable with people who I care for and who care for me.

I will try to do a good deed every so often. Even if it means just giving someone begging a loony or two, instead of ignoring them. Maybe I'll volunteer somewhere. In a school where they can use an extra adult one morning a week. Or in a hostel for women.

More. I will stop seeing men who are needy and who like having sex with me and seeing me. I need relationships, not business. I will respect my body. And maybe, just maybe, there's a nice guy who isn't gay out there and he and I can have a real relationship. I want to make love. I don't think I've ever really made love.

OK, Anna. You're no longer going to be alone in the world. You'll get hurt sometimes. You'll also do what Christine told you to do, "Pass it on." You're no long a lonely atom wandering aimlessly. You're a link in a big human chain.

XXXIV

The next morning Danny called Catherine Dunn at the Castle Frank Academy and made an appointment to see her at noon. Then he spoke with Nadiri.

"Well, sir, what did you find out from Nikki Papadoupolous? Was I out to lunch?"

"Not at all, Nadiri. Your instinct was dead on. It turns out she and Amelia Broadhurst were having an affair. She was indeed in mourning."

Danny then related the whole of his interview with Papadoupolous.

"What do we do now, sir? We're still not very far if Papadoupolous didn't do it and doesn't have any ideas. Like me, she doesn't think it was any of the Broadhurst seven, as I've been calling them."

"I think there may be a way to go. What would you do?"

Nadiri smiled. She knew what Danny was doing and didn't mind it at all. It was part of his mentoring. She said, "I'd go to Inspector Miller and ask him what he would do."

"Seriously. Wit won't get you out of answering the question."

"Damn. Give me a minute." She thought. "I'd go further into her personal life. There's got to be something there."

"No more looking elsewhere?"

"What's to look for?"

"I think there's something more we can do at the school. We're meeting with the principal, Catherine Dunn, at noon."

"I'm not getting it, sir. I'm not sure where you're going."

"Let's wait until we have the meeting with Dunn. By the way, can we at least theorize that the thefts are related to the stress and maybe even the guilt of the affair? That's what my psychiatrist friend, Dr. Donnerstein, thinks. I just spoke to him earlier."

"Fair enough. Yes. But how does that get us to the school?"

"You'll see. It's another one of my leaps. Some are right and some have been wild goose chases. Still, it's worth the chase. See you later."

A little before twelve Nadiri drove the two of them to the school. There was traffic as they drove around Queen's Park and onto Bloor Street, heading east into the edge of Rosedale. When Nadiri turned left on Sherbourne and they moved into Rosedale, she remarked, "It's like entering a park. Curving streets, lots of trees, no traffic lights, and big houses. An enclave for the rich in the middle of the city."

"I won't defend it," said Danny. "But there are some apartments and condos, and people like Gabriella can live here too. I do know what you mean, though. Still, it's better to have these people living in the city and committed to it instead of moving to similar enclaves in the suburbs."

"That's one good thing," replied Nadiri. "We need a city with room for everyone."

"We do. We can price ourselves out of what makes the city human. We mustn't do that."

They arrived at the school, parked on the local street and went to see Dunn.

After Danny introduced Nadiri and they got settled in Dunn's office with tea and cookies, Dunn asked, "Have you made any progress? I saw Constable Rahimi interviewing some of our staff and I'm guessing, Inspector, you poked around in the world outside the school."

"You guess correctly, Dr. Dunn. We've made a bit of progress, not enough for my liking. Still, we're closer than we were a few days ago."

"Before we go further into the murder, I'm wondering if you have any further information about the thefts."

"Frankly, yes. Some good information. Most of it is confidential. However, in confidence again, I'll tell you that it's my opinion that you don't need to investigate further."

"Amelia did it?"

"That's not what I said. I'm trying to save you both time and stress."

"Fair enough. I appreciate you doing so. I'll ask nothing further. However, when all this is over, I wouldn't mind getting a fuller story."

"If I can do so, you'll have it. I can't do it now."

"You're a careful person, Inspector."

"That's part of my job, Dr. Dunn. I would guess that it's also part of your job, which is why you understand my reticence."

She smiled. "That's so. Now how can I help you?"

"I could use some information about some of the people in the school. I also have to ask you a question that I've asked others, though it may offend you."

"Ask away."

"Where were you between nine and ten o'clock on the night Amelia Broadhurst was murdered?"

Again, she smiled. "I'm not offended at all. At this point in the investigation, with no clear suspect, I would have been surprised had you not asked it. I will tell you, though, that this is a first. As a principal, I've been asked about lots of matters, but never about whether I might be a suspect in a murder. The answer, Inspector, is clear. I was at an alumni dinner with a number of young women from our first four graduating classes. We are beginning to cultivate our alumnae, not merely for donations, which will come if we do this right, but because we want to have them keep the connection to the school and act as mentors and role models. As you've gathered, this school is not just a place to go to for a few years. We're a tight community and I want the alumnae to feel part of it forever."

"You will kindly give us some names to call to verify your alibi. Not that I doubt you, but I need verification."

"Of course. I'd expect nothing else."

"Good," said Danny. "That's out of the way. Now, I'd like to follow up on your remarks about being a community. That's why we're here."

Nadiri had been listening carefully, but she was still puzzled about where this conversation was going. She worked hard not to show it.

"My guess," continued Danny, "in fact it's not a guess, I know something about private schools that foster excellence because my spouse teaches at one and my son has gone to two of them...."

Dunn interrupted. "Which schools?"

"St. Michaels' Choir School for my wife and now my son is a student at Maimonides Hebrew Academy."

"Both very good schools. I have a lot of respect for what they do."

"So, I'm asking the following, your school demands a commitment from its staff that's far deeper than that asked of most public schools and many other private schools. You say you're a community. That means you give a great deal of yourself to the institution and its members. For example, on your door you are designated as Founder and Principal. That takes the kind of commitment made by professionals. There are people in my profession like that as well. If your teachers and some of my staff were members of the clergy we would say they had a calling. You don't have a job, Dr. Dunn, you have a profession and a calling."

"I've often thought of it that way."

"Now, some of your teachers, maybe some of your staff, also behave that way. Even those teachers who have families and outside responsibilities are asked to give more than teachers in most other schools. It's assumed when they take the position. But, I would think that for some of the staff, the school and its development have been at the center of their lives. It's how they define themselves."

Nadiri got it. 'Why didn't I think of this?' she thought. 'How clever of him.'

"I'm going to digress for a moment," Danny said. "I want to ask if the reputation of the school would have been hurt if the thefts—let's assume they were done by a staff member—had been made public?"

"Yes, of course," answered Dunn. "We're a new girl on the block. Our reputation has grown very quickly. But that reputation is fragile because of our newness. If that had occurred at, say Branksome Hall, it wouldn't have made a dent in their reputation. It would be forgotten in six months. Not here. We're not yet established in that manner. We may never be in my tenure. That we are now being talked about in the same sentence as the established excellent schools is, may I say, a real accomplishment. And we are about to be given accreditation by the national association of independent schools, faster than any other. Still, we're on a bit of a tightrope in the public eye."

"Thank you. Now back to my main topic. I want to know which of your staff you would put in the category of people of for whom the school is the central part of their lives. People who have worked hard to earn that reputation."

Dunn opened a drawer and pulled out a piece of note paper. "There are three, Inspector, perhaps four. If Amelia was still alive, she'd be on the list. She was not only a star teacher, original and creative, she helped build this place."

Who are they?"

"Our French teacher who is also the head of the upper division, our grades 5-8, Alice Rutherford." She wrote the name down on the paper.

"Then there's our Grade 3 teacher who heads the lower division, grades 1-4, Amy Chiu.

"And I'd include Martha Grayson, who teaches drama and coaches all of our sports teams. She's also someone who can fill in virtually anywhere.

"On the margin of all this is our Grade 1 teacher, much respected, Sofia Mardonska. However, five years ago she married and now has two children. She's wonderful, but she also now has another focus."

She handed Danny the piece of paper with the names

followed by their jobs.

"I must tell you, Inspector, I think I know where you're going. I hope with all my being that you're unsuccessful."

"I may be that, Dr. Dunn. Still, I must go there."

"Of course. Let's hope that something else arises which gets you to a solution."

They didn't end the meeting abruptly. Dunn asked Nadiri about her training and background and then wanted to discuss schools with Danny. Then they left.

"She's quite a person, sir." said Nadiri on the ride back. "Now I know what answer I would have gotten if Inspector Miller had answered my question. How did you get there?"

"It was something Nikki Papadoupolous said when we talked. It opened another door. Now, Nadiri, let's walk in and see what happens."

XXXV

They organized interviews with the four women as quickly as possible. Mardonska and Chiu had alibis, both home with husbands and children, and they had little to add.

Grayson lived alone in a condominium on Bay and St. Mary's Street. While she had no alibi, both Danny and Nadiri didn't find her a clear suspect. She was tall, fit and energetic and she clearly liked Broadhurst. "She was really good at what she did, Inspector," she said. "She didn't take herself very seriously, and was very cooperative when students had sports events. A good person for the school."

Rutherford provided another perspective. "Frankly, I found her a bit of a pain. She was full of herself and ate up all the praise she got as the great teacher. She and I had arguments about curriculum and integrative learning because she insisted on getting her way. She was a tough person to supervise. When she got directions she didn't like, she simply ignored them. I've gone more than once to our principal about this."

There was anger in Rutherford's voice and she had no alibi because she too lived alone. Still, neither Danny nor Nadiri felt that she was to be propelled to the top of the empty list of major suspects. As Danny put it, "Could she have done it? Yes. But let's not confuse school politics and personality conflicts with a motivation to murder someone."

Afterwards, Nadiri said, "Well, sir, it looks as if it didn't do what we hoped. Too bad."

"You're right. So far there no one we can look to. Sure, we can keep those who don't have an alibi on the list, but there's nothing there yet."

"What do we do? Do we start over?"

Danny sat quietly for a while. Then, he said, "I'm going to do one more thing before we say we're stumped and we start all over again. We need to have another meeting with Dr. Dunn."

That was arranged quickly and an hour later the three met again in Dunn's office.

"That's fast," said Dunn. "How can I help? Do you have a lead suspect and do you need information?"

"We have some people without alibis, Dr. Dunn," said Danny. "But we don't have anyone at the top of the list. We've interviewed the four women whose lives are closely aligned with the school. At the moment we're not ready to go further with them."

Dunn nodded and a slight smile appeared at the edges of her mouth. "I'm glad. Did Alice tell you that she and Amelia had their regular differences?"

"Actually," said Nadiri, "she did. I guess there's such a thing as school politics."

"It was two very strong personalities who occasionally banged heads," said Dunn. "Sometimes something good even came out of it. Good schools are not without a certain tension."

"Interesting," said Danny. "That fits with what my wife tells me occurs at St. Mike's. Now, I have another request, Dr. Dunn."

"Of course."

"Tell me about the supporters of the school who are lay people. There must be some people, probably parents of students, who have committed to the school in the manner we talked about. Whose lives are closely tied to the school community and its success?"

"There are several, Inspector. In this kind of school parents are very involved. And some of them have become officers and benefactors. In fact, we raise more outside funds every year and that has enabled us to enhance our building and to provide certain things— hardware and software, for example—that wouldn't ordinarily be around."

"So, like many of these kinds of schools, Dr. Dunn," said Danny, "your tuition pays for the program, for the operating expenses, and you need to raise money for capital costs."

"You know a lot about this, Inspector."

"My spouse and my son's principal are good teachers."

"Be careful, I may ask you to sit on our Board."

"I'm flattered," retorted Danny. "However, I'm much better at catching villains. Even if we haven't yet gotten very far on this one."

"I'm certain that's the case. Your reputation precedes your coming here. Now, what can I do? Why are you here now?"

"I'd like a list of those lay people for whom the school is important to their lives. Not someone who donates every so often. Rather, those who work to make the school excellent and who are committed to it."

Dunn, for a second time, opened her top drawer and took out a piece of notepaper.

"There are the Tellpores. Janine, whom you've met, and Adrian. Their two daughters went here and they became involved from the second year of our being in existence. They sat on committees, drew friends here, helped with enrolment in the early years, and, not insignificantly, have donated a lot of money to our betterment. The success of the school is something that they rightly regard as something of an achievement that they helped to make.

"Then, there is Victoria Parny. The Parnys live not far from here and they, too, have two daughters. One has graduated and the other's in Grade 7. Her husband, Ethan, is happy to write a cheque but doesn't do much. Victoria heads a small successful human resources consulting firm. She's involved deeply with governance

and advancement.

"There's a third family. The Kumars, Gajan and Rajiv. They found the atmosphere of our school, its inclusiveness, very welcoming. They've been instrumental in our reaching out to Toronto's ethnic diversity and attracting what I believe is the broadest group of students in any of the traditional girls' schools. We look more like Toronto than any of the others and I'm proud of that. And it makes us a better school. The Kumars are terrific ambassadors. They also contribute generously. They, too, see the school as central to their lives."

Dunn handed the paper to Danny. "You can get their addresses, phone numbers, and anything else you need from my assistant."

"No others?" asked Danny.

"There are others. We attract a lot of good people who like to be involved. Those three families are central."

"Thank you, Dr. Dunn. We'll be on our way."

"I'll say it again," said Dunn. "I deeply hope you are unsuccessful with that piece of paper."

"I understand," said Danny. "I'll get back to you soon."

They left, got the information they needed from Dunn's assistant, and drove back to the station.

XXXVI

Nadiri arranged meetings in the next two days with the three couples in the late afternoon or in the evening at their homes.

"Where do we go, sir, if nothing comes of this," she asked.

"We go back. I don't like saying it, but maybe we missed something. Whatever it might be. I don't like doing it, but we start all over again. We plug away."

At four-thirty the next afternoon they got into the car to drive to the home of the Kumars in the Lawrence Park area. They drove up Mt. Pleasant and turned into a leafy street bordering on a ravine. The house was charming on the outside, quiet and nearly fully private.

They were welcomed by Rajiv Kumar, an elegant man of about forty, a few years younger than Danny, with a face that Danny thought was aristocratic in shape. After the introductions he took them to the rear of the house, to a family room looking onto the ravine, where Gajiv was waiting. She was no less elegant than her husband. Nadiri said to herself, 'What a beautiful woman. I envy the color of her skin and her gorgeous cheekbones.'

"It's a very lovely home, Ms. Kumar," said Danny.

"We're happy here, Inspector. We were lucky to find it. Rajiv is an architect and we thought we might build a home from scratch. But when this came along we jumped."

She offered coffee and tea and when the coffee arrived, along with some Indian sweets, they settled to talk.

"We're here because of the murder of Amelia Broadhurst." Danny opened. "We're looking in a lot of places and one of them, of course, is the school itself. You're very active there and we thought you might help."

"If you're asking who might have done the killing, Inspector," said Rajiv, "we can't give you an answer. We did think about it, especially after you asked to meet us. But we're simply at a loss. Amelia taught our children. She was a remarkable person. A stunning teacher."

"Do you know about the thefts in the school?" asked Nadiri.

"Yes. We learned about them only recently," answered Gajiv, "when the matter went public. When Amelia started telling some parents about what was happening to her. Until then, the matter was confined to Catherine Dunn, the Chair, Janine Tellpore, and the Vice-Chair, Eva Hadling. Rightly, I think. I'm on the

Board also but I agree that the thing to have done was to try to help whoever did it."

"Do you think Ms. Broadhurst was the thief?" asked Nadiri.

"I don't think about it anymore. Amelia is gone. It doesn't matter now."

"Did you think about how it might have affected the perception of the school?"

"We did," said Rajiv. "But in the end I think the school would have weathered a theft. There are now a lot of people, ourselves included, who would remain very loyal."

"I need to ask you a question we ask everyone we see about the murder. I've even asked Dr. Dunn. Can you tell me where you were on the evening of the murder?"

Rajiv gave Danny a slight smile. "This is a first, Inspector. Though we know you need to ask. We were here on that Thursday evening. With our two children and with Gajiv's parents who joined us for dinner and stayed until the children went to bed a little after nine."

"Thank you. As a formality, I'll need the names and contacts for Gajiv's parents. I don't doubt you at all. Still, we need to check."

"We understand," said Gajiv. "You might get a harsh reaction from my mother, who would defend our honour to the devil."

"Good for her," said Danny. "My mother, gone now, would have done the same for me or my sister."

They talked for another fifteen minutes, mainly about the issue of minorities and schools in Toronto, and then Danny said. "You have two children to feed. We'll leave you now. Thank you again for your co-operation."

Driving back, Nadiri said, "They seem a lovely couple."

"This is what Toronto is turning into, Nadiri, and I'm very happy it's doing so. People like the Kumars and your sister's family are the future of the city. Now, we have the Tellpores at eight. Do you want to stop somewhere for a bite?"

"Good idea."

"They live in the heart of Rosedale, on Roxborough. Anything nearby?"

"Not that I know of, sir." She laughed. "The likes of me don't hang out in that area."

"Then let's go to the Rosedale Diner, near Summerhill. You can get anything from an omelette to a burger to a full meal. A middle eastern bent on the menu. You'll be at home."

"Sounds good."

XXXVII

After dinner, they drove to Mt. Pleasant to get to Rox-borough. It was a curved street with large, quiet homes, and they had no trouble parking.

Janine Tellpore greeted Danny and Nadiri graciously at the door. She took them into a comfortable large living room where her husband was waiting.

Adrian Tellpore looked like a middle-aged model in an ad for Brooks Brothers. Dark hair was greying at the temples. He had a rugged, handsome face, the kind of features that people find comfortable to look at. He was dressed casually, though clearly, as Nadiri observed to herself, unlike her he didn't shop at Winners.

"Janine told me about your inquiry, Inspector. I'm pleased to meet you and Constable Rahimi. Can we offer you any refreshments?"

"Thanks," replied Danny. "We just finished dinner before coming here."

"You work late," said Janine. "Like Adrian sometimes does."

"It's not a nine to five job, Ms. Tellpore," said Nadiri.

She then turned to Adrian. "What do you do, sir?'

"I'm a partner in a hedge fund on Bay and Wellington. Sometimes we need to monitor markets in other time zones and it keeps us busy."

"And," said Danny to Janine, "you are a lawyer."

"I am," she replied. "I'm now the house lawyer for a firm at the science and technology centre at MaRs, near the university and hospitals."

"Is it exciting?" asked Nadiri.

Janine smiled. "It can be. I'm usually the oldest person in the room with a bunch of young geniuses in biology and chemistry. They seem very casual, but there's a lot of intensity. They're on the edge of several patents in medicine, no small matter." She paused. Then, "How can we help you?"

"We're doing what detectives do," said Danny. "We ask a lot of questions, get a lot of data, and then sift it. Often, a lot of what we get doesn't figure in the case, but we need to do so."

"Ask away," said Adrian.

"First tell me about your relationship to the school."

"Our children went there in its early days," said Janine. "We liked what Catherine Dunn was trying to do and we bet on her ability. I think we were correct. And, of course, we were active in recruitment. We told friends about the Academy and some sent their daughters."

"We also took the lead in raising funds for the capital side of the school," said Adrian. "I chaired a capital campaign that began three years ago. We raised four million dollars, not a bad sum for a small school."

"And," said Danny, "you would have made a substantial contribution as a family."

"That goes without saying," answered Adrian.

"And you, Ms. Tellpore, you chair the Board. That takes time and energy."

"It does," said Janine. "It's worth it. We're not churchgoers, Inspector. However, we feel responsible to be engaged in the community. We have other interests, but the growth of the Castle Frank Academy has been a very important part of our lives in the last eleven years."

"Frankly, Inspector," said Adrian, "next to Catherine and perhaps one or two others, we feel we have contributed in a very important way to the success of the school. We're proud of that."

"Yes," said Danny, "helping to build a worthwhile institution is an accomplishment."

"Let me move this discussion in another way," continued Danny. "Tell me how you felt about the thefts in the past year."

"We were appalled," said Janine. "I never thought anything like that might happen."

"I think Amelia Broadhurst betrayed all of us," said Adrian.

"In what way, sir?" asked Nadiri.

"She stole the cards, as far as I'm concerned. And that created havoc and distrust and poisoned the atmosphere. Moreover, it could easily have eaten into the reputation of the school. Reputation is very important in these sorts of things. If you lose your brand it will hurt for a long time to come. She jeopardized all of us."

Janine smiled and turned to Adrian. "Let's not have this difference now. You know I'm not certain she did steal the book tokens."

"You're doing your lawyer thing again, Janine." His voice rose a bit. "Drop it. Sure you don't have a smoking gun. She did it and she didn't think of the consequences. There is this putting Amelia on the throne as the great teacher. Well, the great teacher's a thief and a danger."

The tension in the room could be felt. Behind this nice home and this perfect couple and their perfect kids there was something going on. Danny at this moment remembered his response to an Edward Albee play, *Who's Afraid of Virginia Woolf*, which he had seen five years ago at the Tarragon Theatre. 'I'd better not call them George and Martha' he said to himself.

There was an awkward silence which Nadiri ended. "So, Mr. Tellpore, you were not a fan of Amelia Broadhurst."

"She was a good enough teacher. I thought she was made into a kind of goddess and that was wrong. And then she betrayed all of us. No, I'm not a fan. Besides, on top of all this she was having an affair with the math teacher. So now the role model was a lesbian committing adultery. We put years into making the school into the best of its kind in Toronto, maybe in the country. She put that into danger."

Janine looked surprised. Danny and Nadiri worked hard not to show anything in their features.

"An affair with Nikki?" asked Janine. "How do you know? Why didn't you tell me?"

"Someone told me. You would do your lawyer crap, Janine. Unless we catch them in bed, you would defend her."

"Who told you, Mr. Tellpore?" asked Danny.

"Someone. I don't remember." He hesitated. Danny and Nadiri kept silent. Then he continued, "It was while a bunch of parents were standing outside the school, waiting for their kids to come out at the end of the day. Parent gossip."

"When did you learn this?" Danny asked.

"A few weeks ago."

"Mr. and Mrs. Tellpore, tell me where your daughters go to school."

Janine answered, "Grace is in Grade Eleven and Charlotte is in Grade Nine at Bishop Strachan."

"I'm going to take a bit of a tangent, again," said Danny. "I need to ask you a question that I ask everyone. Even Catherine Dunn, who took no offense at all."

"What is it?" asked Janine.

"Where were you both on the night Amelia Broadhurst was killed?

"That's easy," said Janine. "I was here. With the children. We were in the family room until about ten. I was watching the CBC nine o'clock news, something of a habit with me, Grace was reading in the corner and Charlotte was on her i-pad, playing whatever dreadful game was popular at the time. Adrian was in his office, as happens about two evenings each week."

Danny turned to Adrian, "Is that the case?"

"Yes."

"Were other people in the office at the time?"

"No. I stayed late to deal with some Asian bonds we have and to monitor the markets there."

"So you have no one who can certify that you were in the office?"

"I'm afraid not."

There was silence. It was clear from Danny's face and body language that he was deep in thought for about twenty seconds.

He then spoke, "Mr. Adrian Tellpore, I am taking you into custody. You are suspected of having committed the murder of Amelia Broadhurst. I am obligated to advise you that anything you say can and will be used against you, and that you have the right to counsel."

Janine looked shocked.

"You're out of your mind, Inspector," said Adrian. "You'll have egg on your face. I've heard of you. You're like Amelia. You think what you do is always correct. You're about to fall. Think again."

All was quiet. Nadiri had already called for a car to come to take Tellpore. Janine asked Danny, "Can my husband and I have a private conversation?"

Danny looked around the large room. "You can go into a corner together, Ms. Tellpore. But I can't let Mr. Tellpore out of my sight at this time."

They did so. Both Danny and Nadiri made no move to hear anything.

Then Janine went to the phone and called a lawyer. The car came and Adrian Tellpore was taken to the holding place at the station, Danny and Nadiri following in their car.

"What do you think, Nadiri? Did I leap too soon?"

"That's the first time you've ever asked me that, sir. I understand. Let me say that I think you took a chance. But there are hooks to hang him on, if you'll forgive the metaphor. His having heard of the affair in a place he probably never was. His very weak alibi. And, simply, his knowledge of the affair. No one knew. How did he know?"

"And we now can get into the kitchen to examine knives, Nadiri. You're right. It's not, as he said about the thefts, a smoking gun. But it's enough to warrant further investigation. If I didn't think he did it, at least 90% likely, I wouldn't have gone this far. We'll see."

The case against Tellpore got stronger in the next few days. His alibi was easily broken. There were three members of his firm who said they were in the office that evening until at least 9:00pm and all indicated

Tellpore hadn't been there.

They asked Tellpore to identify some of the parents who had been waiting for the end of school when he claimed he heard gossip that Amelia Broadhurst and Nikki Papadoupolous were having an affair. He said he couldn't remember. When asked why he was supposedly waiting outside the school when his children were at Bishop Strachan, he refused to comment.

Danny had Nadiri and Taegen interview a number of parents, especially those of younger students who would be meeting their children at 3:40, when the school day ended.

None remembered seeing Adrian Tellpore. The common response was, "I haven't seen him since Charlie (as Charlotte was called) left the school."

Nadiri and Taegen also asked those parents if they had heard any odd gossip about Amelia Broadhurst. They all replied in the negative, praising Broadhurst and lamenting what happened.

An examination of Tellpore's diary showed that he had booked off all Thursday evenings for the last two months with a simple line on the page from 6:00pm onwards.

They did examine all of the knives in the Tellpore kitchen. One did have a remnant of human blood in the small space where the blade met the shaft. It was inconclusive. As Danny said, "We'll be told that either Janine or Adrian cut themselves recently."

It was enough for the Crown Attorney to agree to

bring Tellpore to trial.

"Do you think he'll be convicted?" asked Taegen.

"I don't know" said Danny. "Tellpore has one of the best criminal lawyers in the country on his side. He's very wealthy and can afford anyone. So, they'll try to put reasonable doubt in the minds of the judge and jury. They'll not try for innocence, just reasonable doubt. We'll see. In thinking about it, I'm guessing the Crown will try very hard to ask about how he would have known about the affair, which no one else knew about."

"What about a plea?"

"It could be. That depends on how strong the defence feels its case is. They might accept a manslaughter charge, with, say, six years in prison. It's out of our hands now."

XXXVIII

Danny felt he had one more thing to do regarding the case. He made an appointment with Catherine Dunn for the next day. "Can I take you to lunch?" he asked. "I'd like to talk outside the school."

"A good idea, Inspector," said Dunn. "I accept your kind invitation."

"I'll pick you up at noon."

Danny called Constantine and made a booking at Elena's for the next day. "I need a very quiet corner table," he said. "This is a bit of business."

"Not a problem, Inspector. See you tomorrow."

The next day Danny met Dunn at the school and he drove the short distance to the Danforth to *Elena's*. They chatted about the weather and unimportant matters in the car, both waiting until they were settled to get to the purpose of the lunch. They did transition to first names. "Please call me Catherine," she said. "Everyone calls me Danny," was the response.

Constantine, as always, knew what to do. He greeted Danny far more formally than he normally did, was introduced to Dr. Dunn, and escorted them to a table on the edge of the room. He left menus, brought water and asked if they wanted any other beverage. Both declined.

"This seems very nice," said Dunn. "Do you eat here regularly?"

"Yes. I live not far away. My spouse, Gabriella, and I are here often. This is our regular place. Constantine and Elena are friends by now. He's being very proper because I told him when I booked that it was about business."

"What should I order?"

"Anything. I'll vouch for whatever Elena cooks. Gabriella's a sensational cook but she always defers to Elena. Ask Constantine when he comes. He'll let you know."

At that moment, Constantine appeared. Dunn said, "Mr. Miller has told me to rely on you. What should I order?"

Constantine smiled. "Do you want a meal or a lunch?"

"A lunch, please."

"Well, we knew that the Inspector was coming so Elena prepared a *salade nicoise*. Kosher anchovies from Bathurst Street."

"Excellent," said Dunn. "I'll have the same," said Danny. He looked at Catherine. "Can you tolerate a glass of wine before I return you to the school?"

"One glass would be fine."

Danny turned to Constantine. "You choose the right

wine, Constantine. Send my love to Elena."

"Danny, what did Constantine mean when he said that Elena prepared the salad because she knew you were coming?"

"As you will have guessed, Catherine, I'm Jewish. So there are certain things I don't eat. And sometimes— I'm not as observant as I should be and I occasionally fall—I'll forego meat entirely outside the home. They're very kind and look after me."

"Interesting. It tells me more about you. Now, let's get to why we're here."

"This conversation is confidential, Catherine. I have no doubt you're good at other people's secrets."

"Both of us learn a lot about others in our professions, Danny."

"I wanted to tell you that I am virtually certain that the book tokens were indeed taken by Amelia Broadhurst. We left that matter earlier in the investigation and I wanted to sort it out."

"How do you know?"

"There's a history. One that I think only her sister now knows about. Not even Norman Lin knows."

Danny then told Catherine about the shoplifting incident when Amelia was a student at Queens, by now a long time ago. "The diagnosis was that it was a way of asking for help at a time of great stress. And it seems to have been the correct diagnosis. I believe that the same thing was happening when she took the book tokens. She was under great stress, a stress she couldn't talk about to anyone. She had a lover, she was in the middle of an affair, and she didn't know where to turn."

"She had a lover? Amelia?"

"Yes. I said this is confidential. If the Tellpore case goes to trial it may become public. If not, it should remain a secret forever, except for a few people."

"Who was the lover?"

"Nikki Papadoupolous."

Catherine looked a little startled. "They certainly hid it well. So this is why Nikki decided to leave."

"Yes. It stressed them both to have to hide it every day, to be together professionally."

"And Amelia stole to ask for help. But we offered help. Not knowing, of course, what the problem happened to be."

"I don't want to go too far into psychologising a person I've never met. Once she stole, there was, yes, a call for help. But there was also shame. It gets very dense, I think."

"So poor Amelia, without knowing it, was setting up her own downfall."

"Yes, but in a strange way. The thefts caused people in the community to feel betrayed. At least some people. Adrian Tellpore in particular. She was now, if you'll forgive the use of the term, a heretic, a danger to the collective body of the community. How to negate it? Kill her. Then, the thefts would not matter. People would feel badly for the school and it would pass."

"Except, Danny, that a Detective Inspector figured

it out."

"You're giving me too much credit. Any good cop would have soon reached the same place. It took not only brains. It took tenacity. Keep going. Many cops have that quality and, though some in the public don't believe it, a good majority of them have brains. For example, I think my partner would have gotten there, or Ron Murphy, who is the second in command at Homicide. I do think my experience mattered. I just decided not to leave anything out."

"I very much appreciate your confidence in telling me all this. It helps. Thank you."

"I thought it would help you to move the school out of this crisis. Its job is to educate kids, not to be a cauldron of suspicion."

They had by now finished their salads and were lingering over the rest of the wine.

"By the way, this is the best *salade nicoise* I've ever had. Better than one I had in Cimiez, in a restaurant called *Chez Theo*, in the hills of Nice, which until now occupied first place. I'm coming back here."

"Tell Constantine. There's nothing that gives him more pleasure than praise for his wife or kids."

"Now, Danny, you've helped me. Is there anything I can help you with?"

"Yes. It's an odd matter, but it's been in my head ever since I went to see the Tellpores at their home. I found their relationship one which had a lot of tension in the background. They looked and talked like the perfect couple at first. Then, as the evening wore on, I sensed I was witnessing a lot of repressed anger and even just plain confusion. He mocked her a bit. She became very taut. He challenged her perceptions. She was acting."

"You're correct. The marriage is held together by the children and some other things, all very fragile. They are a classic Rosedale couple and want to appear to be so. They have a lot of money and use it to hide some differences. But there isn't a lot of affection between them anymore."

"Frankly, Catherine, as I was sitting there watching them go through what I'm going to call their dance, I thought I was part of an audience watching *Who's Afraid of Virginia Woolf*."

Catherine laughed aloud. "Well said. A fine insight. You're famous, Danny, for your literary allusions at press conferences. Is this what you're going to say at the next one?"

"I don't think so. I don't want to single out Janine. In fact, I doubt that this will require a full press conference. The Broadhurst murder hasn't gripped the city like several other cases in the last few years. The triple serial murders by someone abused in his youth; the honour killing of a terrific young woman; or the murder of a famous psychiatrist. Several reporters will call. But that will be it until the trial. If there's a trial."

"Why not?"

"There may be a deal. The case is strong but not totally solid. We'll see. That's out of my hands."

"I do hope," said Catherine, "that for Norman Lin's sake there's no trial and he doesn't have to learn about Nikki."

She changed the subject as Constantine brought the check. First, she reached for the check, but Danny stopped her hand. "I invited you. My treat."

"Thank you, Danny. Now, do you have any daughters or nieces who need to be educated?"

"No daughters, Catherine. Just my son Avi. Fifteen and going through the Hebrew Day School system. And, may I add, getting a fine education. I do have a niece, my sister's daughter, Deborah. A wonderful young woman. Now in law school. Do you have any children?"

"No, Danny. I was married fairly young and it didn't work out. So I founded a school."

"A good one. You make a difference. And you've influenced other educators. Apart from parents and close family, nothing's more influential than school in the long run. Some people would put peer influence second, but I'm much more traditional and know how important a good school can be."

"I'd like to think so."

They left. As Danny drove her back, Catherine said, "You know, I think the first thing I'm going to do is to call Nikki Papadoupolous and ask her to lunch. I don't know if it can happen for next year, she's committed, but I'd like to invite her back to the school."

XXXIX

It was the afternoon of the third Wednesday in June. In the last several days, Deborah had gone to meet with several tenants in two buildings owned by the Altonis in Scarborough and now she was reporting to Celia.

"We definitely have some possibilities," she said. "I didn't know that such things still existed in Toronto. Mice, vermin, electrical outlets that don't work, hot water shut off at 7:00 in the evening. It's hardly third world or a favella, but they are really neglected."

"Tell me about the people," said Celia.

"One couple are refugees from Syria. They have two children, who seem very polite and nice. He was an engineer and she is clearly educated. They had tried to follow the law and applied to the Provincial Landlord and Tenant Board, but nothing happened. When I told them you would take the case pro bono, they said they would think about it. She said, 'Canada welcomed us. We don't want to be rude or ungrateful'. I told her that the building was not what Canada is. We had a long talk. I think they'll respond."

"What are their names?"

"Raghda and Ibrahim Maghout."

"Anyone else?"

"Yes. I think the most interesting other one is a single mother with two children. Her name is Patricia Burke. Canadian born. Her husband walked out on them four years ago because, she said, he didn't want the responsibility for the children. He drank a lot, she said, and he now lives with another woman. The kids are now seven and five. Burke works full-time as a clerk at a local Loblaws. She got someone to help her and she also appealed to the Landlord and Tenant Board. Her mother, who also has no money, comes in to help with the kids. She's ambitious for the two boys. She wants them to escape the cycle. She seems really good-hearted."

"Well, two are enough to bring a case. Any others?"

"Yes. Two more families. These two seem the most interesting and articulate."

"Call them and set up appointments. I'd like them to come here if they can. Tell them we'll pay for the child-care needed in order for them to meet with us."

"Will do."

"Good." Celia looked at her watch. "Now I need the next hour to get some stuff done on another case. No hanging around this evening."

"I know where you're going tonight, Celia. I thought I'd let you know that I'll see you there rather than have you be surprised."

"You're going to the Bloor Street Chamber Group annual concert? How so?"

Deborah smiled widely. "My uncle's in the violin section and my aunt's the conductor."

Celia was incredulous. "Your uncle is Daniel Miller?"

Deborah nodded.

"How come you or he never mentioned it to me?"

"We thought that I should get the job here on my own. Uncle Danny was firm on that."

"He would be. Well, I'm glad you did get it on your own. Do you see him often?"

"Every Friday at Shabbat dinner. Sometimes other times also. We're a close family. My mother and he are sister and brother."

"And what have you said about the job?"

"Simply that he was right that I'd be happier here than in an ordinary firm. He had a lot of nice things to say about you and Clark."

"How did you know that I was going to the concert?"

"Gabriella mentioned it. We know Joshua Black and he called her to ask if it was OK to bring you as well as his grandson."

"Small world, indeed. All right. See you later. I'm looking forward to it. Let's get back to work for the next hour so we can go with clearer desks."

The church on Bloor just west of Spadina was packed. Three years ago not even the lower auditorium was full. Now both balcony and auditorium had no empty seats. There were even a few people standing in the rear. The concert was free and the smart people came early to get good seats.

All this was the result of the Bloor Street Chamber group gaining reputation over the time that Gabriella became its conductor. The world of classical music in the city was small enough that word of its excellence could spread orally. And *Toronto Life's* music critic said in the last two years that they were the best group of amateur musicians in the city. On top of that, Gabriella was written up in a cover story in *The Whole Note*, the Toronto classical music magazine. Four new recruits, taking the place of retired members, proved to be high quality performers, including a new first violinist, Gregori Lapuchenkov.

This year, Gabriella wanted to highlight a number of individual members and she chose pieces that were concertos or had parts where a trio could perform.

They opened with Telemann's Violin Concerto in G Major, with Gregori as the soloist. He was seen by the members of the group to be their finest musician next to Gabriella, and that night he was at his best, which meant that he was at the level of a member of the Toronto Symphony and got a rousing ovation. Then they performed Bach's Orchestral Suite in D Major and a short Valentini piece. To close the first half, they went back to Telemann in an unusual bit of programming. They did his short six minute Flute Concerto, with Gabriella as both conductor and soloist. She got big-time applause and '*bravas*' when it finished.

For the second half they began with Boccherini's Cello concerto in D Major, featuring the new cellist, Ida Chen, as the soloist. They then did a Corelli Concerto Grosso. And they closed with Mozart's Symphony #25, his 'Paris' symphony, which, Danny reminded himself, looking at his son in the audience, Mozart composed when he was seventeen, only two years older than Avi. The first movement of the Mozart was known by all because it was the opening music for the film *Amadeus*. For the third movement, in which there was a trio, Gabriella changed the orchestration slightly to accommodate the fact that the group had fewer winds than Mozart intended. Still, it gave their oboe, bassoon and horn players a chance to shine.

At the end they got a hearty and lengthy standing ovation, with Gabriella singling out all those who performed individually. While the applause was going on Joshua Black turned to Celia and said, "I wish I was good enough to play with them." "Me, too," answered Celia. "They're the best amateur group I've ever heard." "Gabriella's smart," said Black. "That's a big part of their strength. They're fine musicians and they just play for the joy of it. You feel it."

When the audience settled down, Gabriella led the group in an encore, the familiar first movement of Bach's first Brandenburg Concerto.

Afterwards, there was a reception in the church hall

below, a custom of many years.

Gabriella and the soloists were mobbed at first. Danny found himself in a corner with Ruth, Irwin, Deborah and Avi.

Several of his friends from the Y came over to congratulate him, most telling him with a smile that his violin playing was a lot better than his squash game.

Joshua, his grandson Aaron, and Celia found them as well. "I'll get to Gabriella later," said Joshua to the group. "No wonder she's in demand. She gets a great sound from the group."

Danny introduced Celia to Ruth, Irwin and Avi, saying, "There's no need to introduce Deborah. She's my mole in your office."

"She's doing fine, Danny," she replied. "We're glad to have her. Now, I never heard you play before. Amazing. Gabriella's terrific. I'm back at my cello but this is a standard above my abilities."

"Danny's violin has been part of his being for a long time, Celia," said Ruth. "It's seen him through both good and hard times."

Celia looked around and saw that Deborah was occupied with some other people. She leaned closer to Ruth. "Your daughter's terrific, Ruth. A fine person."

Ruth squeezed her hand in thanks. "She likes being there. She likes what you do. Danny says very nice things about you and your partners."

Then Nadiri appeared with Debra and Anna. She and Celia, close friends since high school, hugged one another and introductions were made.

Danny walked up to Anna and shook her hand. "I am so glad you're safe. Are you sound? How are you?"

Anna smiled. "I'm getting there Inspector. Nadiri and Debra have been taking care of me. I really enjoyed this evening. I know a lot about art, not much about music. I felt a lot of joy in the music and in how it was played. Your spouse is amazing."

"Sounds good."

Danny turned to Debra. "We meet at last."

They shook hands. "Thanks, Inspector, for tonight," she said. "It was very beautiful, like reading a great novel."

"That's a great compliment. I never thought about music in that way. But you're right. Beauty is beauty, wherever it's found."

"I know you read a lot because Nadiri tells me about your literary references."

"Maybe I should think about musical references for cases. It never occurred to me. Thanks for coming. I hope we meet more often."

"Me, too, Inspector. Could I ask a question?"

"Of course."

"Were you close to your mother? I'll bet you were."

"An unusual question. Yes, we were very close. She was my rock. After she died it's now my older sister, who I'll introduce you to, who keeps me grounded. Why did you ask?"

"Because one of the rules I learned growing up was

to never get close to a man who wasn't close to his mother. It's a feminine thing."

"A good rule, Debra. Not only a feminine thing. A human matter."

At the end of the evening, about eleven o'clock, Danny and Gabriella got their instruments and walked to the car.

"You did it, my love," said Danny. "It was only six minutes but I don't think I ever heard you play so sweetly."

"We're still doing the magic, Danny. It's all of us. That's because we're only interested in the magic, nothing else. Let's make that continue."

"Will you be able to sleep tonight?"

"Doubtful. But that goes with what we do. I'll sleep tomorrow night."

Part III

XL

The summer went by quickly. Danny and Gabriella took a two-week holiday, disappearing into the lush fields of Burgundy in a gite rented in the town of Meursault. They shopped locally, went no further than Beaune to the south and Nuit St. Georges to the north, and simply enjoyed taking walks, tasting the wine, and visiting local galleries.

In late July Danny flew to Nova Scotia to visit Avi at Camp Shalom. He found his son tanned and energized, strong and looking forward. They found places outside of camp to eat and took along Avi's girlfriend Molly, who Danny liked a lot. It was, he thought on Labour Day, his most peaceful and restful summer in years.

Anna Crowe did some healing. She also put into play her new resolve to live a different life. She took up Debra's invitation to join the women's book club and looked forward to the first meeting in September. And she enrolled in a program for training as a curator sponsored by the Art Gallery of Ontario and York University. She didn't yet find the man who might turn into a partner, but she decided she might not be ready for something like that emotionally. She laughed when Nadiri said to her, "It's easier for gays like Debra and me. There are a lot more nice middle-aged single gay women out there than there are decent single heterosexual men. Be patient."

Debra and Nadiri talked about living together and then negated it. "To use your term," said Debra, "we're solitaries. It won't work. I'm happy the way we are." Nadiri agreed and they now let the relationship float in its own kind of intimacy and trust.

The Gelernters, their lawyer, Helen Oakhurst, Tom Pendleton and Debra made some progress in tracing down the three images.

They found that in 1949 the German authorities, given the task of dealing with thousands of works of art stolen by the Nazis, sold those three images and two others owned by the Gelernter's relatives to Kurt Woolfstadt, who had been a senior civil servant in the Home Office of the German state from the mid-1920's to the fall of the Nazis. Woolfstadt was one the millions of people suspected of being sympathetic to the Nazis who were permitted to get on with their lives after the war. He continued as a civil servant until his retirement in 1955.

Then, Woolfstadt and his wife moved to a country home and they sold their art, making a considerable profit. The buyer was Ludwig Dahlberg, the scion of an Anglo-German family, a descendant of the nobility of both Britain and Bavaria. He shipped the works to his estate outside Oxford. When he died in 1988, many of Dahlberg's works of art, some far more valuable than the three images identified by the Gelernters, were sold at auction by his heirs to help pay the death duties on the estate.

Hence, the family of Sir Martin Harrow wound up with the images until they sold their rare books and some works of art after Sir Martin died, again to help pay the taxes. The paintings were thus part of a lot composed of books and art bought by the Altonis. By the end of the summer the Gelernters had enough information to think about proceeding.

Celia Rogdanovivi and Deborah Feldberg had a busy summer. "No rest for those who work pro bono," joked Celia on one of the evenings that the two stayed late to work on the Altoni case.

"When do you get a holiday?" asked Deborah.

"After this is over I'm taking a month," countered Celia. "I'm going to find an apartment in Paris and sleep and walk and drink good wine and eat good food and go to concerts and museums. It's been a dream. Then, I'll make it real."

The time and work put into the case was paying off. They had a thick file of violations and statements from tenants. Most importantly, the refugee family, Raghda and Ibrahim Maghout, and the single mother, Patricia Burke, agreed to become the plaintiffs.

The Maghouts were reluctant. "We have been welcomed by Canada," said Raghda. "Our children are being educated. This is not a good way to live, but it was far worse before we came here. We do not want to seem ungrateful."

Celia spent a lot of time discussing this with them, even taking them to housing for other people of little means which was run properly to show them the difference. Finally, they assented when Celia convinced them that they would be helping their neighbors, not only themselves.

Patricia Burke was the opposite. Her fist was in the air from the beginning and both Celia and Deborah realized she would need coaching to tamp down her anger when she testified. Still, as Celia said, "She's correct. And she's very bright. She'll be fine in the long run."

By the end of the first week in September, when Deborah was leaving the job to return to school, Celia had enough confidence in the possibility of success to file against the Altonis for negligence and for violation of the lease contract.

XLI

On September 10th, Danny's associate, Ron Murphy, appeared at his office door in the morning.

"What's up?" Danny asked.

"We have a murder between the Rosedale and Summerhill subway stations. A body was found an hour ago. Who do we send?"

"Me. I haven't been on a case since before the summer."

Ron laughed. "That's what I thought. I nearly sent Quincy, but you've been looking a little antsy."

"Time to get back on the street, Ron. You know the deal. It makes me a better head."

"That it does, Danny. Have at it."

Danny called Nadiri and they drove up Spadina. They made a right on Dupont to Avenue Road, a right on Macpherson to Yonge, and a left to the scene.

The location of the body was indicated by the yellow tape cordoning off the west side of Yonge under the railway bridge between Birch Avenue and Marlborough.

Danny knew the area in a general way because he sometimes ate at The Rosedale Diner, just south of the tape. He stopped for a minute or two to survey the streets.

Across the road from the body was a flagship store of the Liquor Control Board of Ontario, housed in a renovated Italianate railway station no longer in use. Across from the LCBO were several old buildings, now renovated, housing what some called "The Five Thieves," pricey, high-end shops that catered to people from Rosedale. They included a greengrocer, a bakery, a butcher and a fishmonger, as well as a second bakery and a restaurant.

The LCBO on the east side was in Scrivener Square, which in the last fifteen years had become the site of some elegant condominiums. On the west side, in addition to The Rosedale Diner, there was yet another high end bakery, a fine restaurant and some small antique shops. All this wealth was anchored on both sides by two of the country's major banks.

Nonetheless, Danny remarked to himself, it still had the look of a neighbourhood rather than a place only defined by its wealth.

He went to the body, which was guarded by two patrolmen. The one he encountered said, "I found the body, sir. About an hour ago." He directed his gaze to the middle of the bridge, where the body was lying on a mat on the ground, with a blanket that covered the whole of it.

Danny looked at his name tag. "Officer Ames, what did you do?"

"I was doing a walk through the area, sir, as I do most days. It was nine o'clock or so and I saw what I thought was a street person sleeping under the bridge. There've been some complaints lately from the people here and the shopkeepers, so I tried to wake him up. He didn't move. I pulled down the blanket and saw that someone had bashed in his head. I looked for a pulse, found nothing, and called it in."

"Has forensics been notified?"

"They're on their way."

"Do you know who he might be?"

"I know his first name. Duncan. He's a regular in this area. Has been for years. He hangs around the corner of Birch and he sometimes panhandles around the LCBO or on the corner where the stores across the street are located."

At that moment, Hugh O'Brien appeared. He greeted Danny and Nadiri and said, "What do we have?"

"I'm not certain, Hugh," said Danny. "Officer Ames tells us he's a street person who hangs around this area and is known. First name Duncan. He has head wounds." Danny looked at Ames, who nodded and said, "That's right, sir."

"Officer Ames found him at about nine. He had no response or pulse. All yours for the moment."

O'Brien turned to Ames. "Did you or anyone touch anything?"

"Only me. I thought he was sleeping. I saw his head wounds and checked his pulse. That's it."

"OK," replied O'Brien. "Let's see what we can see. My team will examine the area. Then it's all yours, Danny."

To make some use of the time needed for O'Brien and his team to do their work, Danny and Nadiri went across the street to the shops to talk with some of the owners and workers.

In 'Cornucopia', the fruit and vegetable shop, they identified themselves and got hold of the manager, who identified himself as Mauro Costellino.

"Do you know a street person who is called Duncan?" asked Danny.

"Sure, Inspector. A nice guy." Costellino then did a double-take. "Is that who it is?"

"Yes."

"Will he be all right?"

"It looks like he's dead, Mr. Costellino."

Several others in the store had gathered on the edge of the conversation to listen in. A woman spontaneously spoke, "Not Duncan. I've known him since I came here four years ago." Others joined in, lamenting the news they received.

"Can any of you tell us about Duncan?" asked Nadiri. "Do any of you know his last name?"

One of the clerks, dressed in a 'Cornucopia' T-shirt and an apron, entered the conversation. "I've been here for nine years. Duncan started hanging around soon after I came. That corner by Birch isn't developed and he sometimes slept there at night, near the train rails, but hidden from pedestrians. Everybody knew him. He made conversation. But he didn't annoy anyone. He was polite and always thanked people who put a loony into his cup. Sometimes, if we had fruit or vegetables which were still OK but that we couldn't put out on the counter because of the way they looked, we gave him a package. He was always nice. He usually said he'd bring it to his tent city to share."

"Any last name?" again asked Nadiri.

The woman who spoke earlier answered. "I don't know. He was Duncan to everyone. But he has a health card. Last year he broke a leg while trying to climb a fence. He wound up at Mt. Sinai and they fixed him up."

Danny and Nadiri heard more information like this. Then Danny asked, "Do we know where he lived or did he just sleep anywhere? Someone mentioned a tent city."

"Yeah," answered the male clerk. "He moved around, like a lot of homeless people. But lately he told me that he was mainly living with a small group that pitched its tents behind the Castle Frank subway station, in the ravine."

When they left the store, Danny and Nadiri were summoned across the road by O'Brien. "There's not much yet to say," he told them. "He's dead. Probably from the blows on the head, but I'll learn a lot more during the autopsy. He had some change on him and his health card. He's Duncan MacNeil. Fifty-five years old. My people tell me that there's probably not much to be found on the ground, but they'll still be very thorough. Do you want to look at the body before we take it to the morgue?"

"Of course." Danny and Nadiri went to the body. Duncan MacNeil wore ragged jeans and a cloth shirt. His shoes were very worn but serviceable. His head was a mess. What Danny had initially thought was a mat were pieces of broken cardboard boxes on which lay the body. The blanket covering him was thin and had several tears.

Danny looked at the Ontario Health Card which was in a plastic bag given to him by O'Brien. He saw a weary face and some unruly hair, and fixed the face in his mind. He didn't want the battered face which he had just seen to be the one he was going to talk about with lots of people.

The rest of the morning was spent going in and out of shops, learning about Duncan MacNeil and the neighbourhood.

Most of the people working in the shops echoed what the clerks in 'Cornucopia' had said. However, there were a few dissenters. In the butcher shop the manager told Danny that they weren't happy having Duncan as part of the scene. "Some of our customers were annoyed about having a bum panhandling where they shopped," he said. "They would remark that they didn't want that kind of thing here."

"What about you?" asked Danny.

"We didn't mind Duncan. He wasn't aggressive or loud or rude. But we also felt that he didn't belong here."

Danny told himself to resist making any social comments which might be interpreted as hostile. He was there to gather information.

While Danny worked the east side of the street, Nadiri went to the west side. "A good guy," said the owner of The Rosedale Diner. Not a bother at all. He was just part of the neighbourhood." The owner of one of the antique shops dissented. "I'd rather that he not have been here. It's a toney place. He didn't fit."

The LCBO manager was more positive. "He had a right to be on the street. He really didn't bother anyone. A lot of people stopped to talk with him. He occasionally bought a bottle of cheap rum or gin here. I'm sorry someone hurt him."

Danny left Nadiri to continue working the area to determine whether anyone saw anything.

It was one o'clock when he took the subway to the Castle Frank Station. When he exited he turned left and then, after walking about thirty meters, turned left again on a path leading down into the ravine and to Rosedale Valley Road. Before getting to the road he spotted the tents of the small group of homeless people. They were close to a fence marking the property of a large co-op which had entrances on McKenzie Avenue and Dale Avenue.

He made his way to the temporary shelter wondering who he would find at this time in the afternoon.

As he drew closer, Danny counted six shelters, mostly small tents, though one was put together from cardboard boxes and pieces of wood. He noted that several people were sitting on some logs that had broken off in one storm or another and were being used as benches. Some of the five people seated had cups in their hands; some were smoking what his nose told him was either tobacco or marijuana.

He walked slowly to the seated area and took out his identification. One of the two women and one of the three men looked up as he approached. The others continued to look on the ground or into the ravine.

"Hello," he said. "I'm Inspector Daniel Miller. I'm from the homicide squad and I have some bad news."

"What do you mean?" said one of the men. "Do we have to move? Are you cops jerking us around again?"

"No. Nothing like that. I'm here to tell you that one of your group, Duncan MacNeil, died yesterday."

They all then looked at Danny. "How do you know?" asked the same man. He was unshaven but not dirty. Danny noticed that he wore a jacket that was fraying at the cuffs but was also clean, if rumpled.

"Who are you, sir?" asked Danny. "It's nice to know who I'm talking to."

"Joe. Joe Grace." Grace turned to three others on his left and said, "This is Penny, Doris and Pete." He turned right. "And this is Quincy, sometimes known as Quint."

"Thanks. I'm pleased to meet you, though the circumstance is not a good one."

"What happened?" asked Doris as a tear ran down her cheek. "He wasn't too healthy, you know."

"I'm afraid he was murdered, folks. I wanted to let you know. He lived here, didn't he?"

"He lived with us, Inspector," said Grace. "Some people come and go. Duncan was a regular here. He was a good guy. He brought us food when he got some at the corner where he worked."

"He lived with me," said Penny as she pointed to one of the tents. "Over there. I wondered when he didn't come back yesterday. But sometimes he slept on the street or in a hallway."

"Thanks, Inspector," said Grace, seeming to dismiss Danny.

"Sorry," said Danny. "I need to ask some more questions. Mind if I sit down?"

"Help yourself to a piece of wood," said Penny.

Danny looked around, spotted a log and went to retrieve it. He placed it on the ground facing the five people and sat.

"Do any of you have any idea who might have wanted to hurt Duncan?"

"He was a good guy," said Doris.

"So I understand. I've talked to some people at Summerhill about him. He was liked."

"There's people who don't like most people, Duncan included," said Quint.

"Why not?"

"Inspector," said Grace. "We're not normal. Some of us are a little crazy. Sometimes we see things that are strange. So some people have a beef against the world and they take it out on others."

"That I do understand, Mr. Grace. That happens regularly in my world. We, too, have people who aren't what you call normal."

"Well," said Grace, "a cop who actually admits that the straight world isn't always straight. What will we hear next?"

Danny was already intrigued by Grace's comments, but this wasn't the time to explore them. He asked again about people who might want to harm Duncan.

Grace again took the lead. "There are people among us who might want to harm others, However, I don't know of anyone who might want to harm Duncan in particular."

"There's Jimmy," said Penny.

"Jimmy who?"

"Jimmy the Mechanic," answered Penny. "He fixed things good. He lived with me for a while. I threw him out. He would go crazy sometimes. He didn't like that Duncan moved in."

"Where can I find Jimmy?"

"I don't know," Penny answered. "He doesn't come around much. Only sometimes when he's drunk. I don't know where he sleeps."

"Anyone else?"

There was silence.

"Are there other communities like this?" continued Danny.

"Many," answered Grace. "More than all the straight people would care to admit to, Inspector. They move around. Sometimes you guys kick us out of a place. That's what we thought you were doing. So we find another place. The ravines are good places to go to. Then people like you don't have to be bothered. Your precious consciences are clear if we're not in sight."

"Mr. Grace, this isn't the moment for us to have a philosophical discussion. I'm interested in Duncan MacNeil."

"What's going to happen?" asked Doris.

"What do you mean?"

"Does Duncan get buried? What's going to happen?"

"If you want one," said Danny. "We're doing an autopsy and we then release the remains to the family or the closest relative."

"We're not in the relative business," said Grace. "We're his relatives."

"Did he live with you, Penny?"

"Yeah."

"I think that in the absence of any relatives, you're his closest relative."

"Can we have a service and a funeral?"

"I know that the City of Toronto's Employment and

Social Services Department provides financial assistance on behalf of dead Toronto residents who don't have money to cover the cost of a basic funeral and burial. There's an arrangement with Toronto funeral directors. If Duncan or you don't have the funds, the city will cover it."

"Really?" asked Grace.

"Really, Mr. Grace. Penny, you'll get your service."

Penny was now in tears. "How do we do this?" asked Grace.

"You stay here. I'll get someone with Social Services to come and help make the arrangements. Let me add that I think there are some people in the Summerhill area who probably would want to attend. There was affection for Duncan. Maybe one of the shopkeepers could be notified."

"What do we do if nobody from social services shows up?" asked Grace.

"You get in touch with me," said Danny. He handed Grace his card.

"I'm sorry for the bad news" said Danny as he rose to leave. "I'd like to be at the service too."

There were no goodbyes or handshakes. The five of them simply went back to the posture they had been in before Danny arrived.

The next day Danny got a call from Hugh O'Brien. "He was beaten up, Danny, as we know. However, the cause of death wasn't the beating. His heart, which was weak, gave out under the trauma and the strain.

The beating was done with something like a broomstick rather than something like a baseball bat."

"Time of death?"

"Between six and eight yesterday morning. One more thing. I can't be certain but I think he may have been beaten elsewhere and carried to the bridge. We should look for blood elsewhere in the area."

"Thanks, Hugh. I'll get on it."

Blood was later in the day found in the back of the parking area of the LCBO. It matched.

Danny and Nadiri learned little else in the next few days.

Duncan's death—and the way it happened—became news. Both the *The Star* and *The Sun* made it a lead story, for there was a lot of interest in his person and in the event. Danny met with reporters from the two papers, but had little to tell them.

The service was held two days later at a funeral home on Bayview Avenue north of Moore. There was no visitation. A small chapel was reserved and an Anglican priest presided.

Danny and Nadiri attended. Near the front of the chapel they saw several people from 'Cornucopia', clearly a place where Duncan was liked and was part of daily life, and some from several of the other shops on the east and west side of Yonge. Officer Leonard Ames was among those in front, in uniform, along with his partner. There were about a dozen others, who Danny later learned were residents of Birch and Alcorn

Avenues, and the buildings on Scrivener Square. In addition, Danny recognized three reporters from Toronto newspapers.

At the rear there were another fifteen attendees, all street people, including the five Danny had met when he went to the Tent City in the Rosedale ravine.

The priest invited people to say a few words. Mauro Costellino said some warm words, as did the female clerk in 'Cornucopia' and the manager of the LCBO. One of the residents of Birch Avenue told some anecdotes about the many conversations she had had with Duncan over the years.

Then there was a rustle at the back. Joe Grace stood up. "Can one of us speak from here?" he asked.

"Wherever you're comfortable," answered the priest. "All are welcome."

Joe turned to Penny who was sitting next to him and whispered something.

Penny stood up, tears on her cheeks, a tissue in her right hand. It was clearly an effort, and she was silent for a time and then spoke. "He was a good person, father." Several seconds went by. "He treated everyone nicely. He shared his food and whatever he had. We had some good times together. He should rest in peace."

Nadiri said, in a voice that could be heard by everyone, "Amen." And the entire group, together, repeated, "Amen."

"Thank you, ma'am," said the priest. "You gave him the right send-off. May he rest in peace and may God rest his soul."

Again from the whole group, "Amen"

When Danny and Nadiri left the funeral home there was a truck outside from CTV. Their reporter, Linda Moorhouse, put her microphone in Danny's face. "Inspector, do we have any progress on the case? Do we know who murdered Duncan?"

"We're making progress," answered Danny. "We'll find Mr. McNeil's killer and bring that person to justice."

"Are you putting a lot of resources into this case?"

Danny disliked the question, though he knew he had to answer it.

"Yes, we're giving this case all the energy we have, as we do in every instance. Mr. McNeil was a good citizen and, as I said, we'll find the killer."

"You don't seem to be getting far."

"We're moving as quickly as we can. We want to be thorough and professional. When we arrest someone we want to make certain the case holds up."

Before Moorhouse could speak again, Danny said, "Thanks for your time, Linda. We need to get back to work." He turned away and joined Nadiri to get their car.

The next day Danny was in his office when he received a call from the reception desk at the station.

"Sorry to bother you, sir," said the sergeant at the desk. "There's a person here who insists on talking with you. He seems more like a street person than anything else."

"What's his name?"

"Joe Grace, he says."

"Send him right up."

Three minutes later Grace appeared at Danny's door. "Come in, Mr. Grace," Danny said. "Can I get you a coffee?"

Grace gave a slight smile. "Best offer I've ever had from any cop. I'd like a cup."

"I'll join you," said Danny. "I'll be back in two minutes."

Grace didn't sit. He stood near the entryway and surveyed the office while Danny was out.

"Sit down, please," said Danny when he returned. "What brings you here? By the way, I thought it was a good ceremony yesterday."

Grace nodded in agreement. Then he said, "What brings me here, Inspector, is that I'd like to help you catch the murderer."

"Is there something new that you have to tell me?"

"No. You don't understand. I want to help."

"Mr. Grace, we have a lot of very able police on the case."

"I'm sure you do. And I kind of like you, Inspector. You're different than most of your fellow cops. You may even be smarter." He smiled. "If not smarter, than wiser. So listen to me."

"I'm listening."

"I'm a bum. I'm a homeless person. I can go places

and talk to people who you and your people would never meet. I know where they sleep. I know what they eat. I know who has which corner as his turf. I'm one of them."

"And if I asked you to tell me where they sleep and who I should talk to what would you do?"

"I'd tell you some things. I'd also tell you you'll get nowhere. We're experts at being stupid. Sometimes we're stoned and sometimes we pretend to be stoned. As they say when a cop appears, 'nobody knows nothin.' You're the people who move us on, you're the people who sometimes push us or use their nightstick...."

"You should report that. No one should get away with that."

"Bullshit, Inspector. What are you? A child? Naïve? Cops get away with murder, much less pushing people nobody wants to have near their neighbourhood. Get real. There's a whole world of the homeless out there and your people have no way of getting any information out of it or about it. Besides, most people treat us as if we were invisible. What are you going to do? Put Penny in jail because she won't talk to you? You're being fucking ridiculous. Excuse the language."

Danny sat quietly for a time. Then, he said, "You may be correct, Mr. Grace. I'm willing to consider it. First, I'm going to ask why you're doing this."

"Because Duncan was my friend. Because Penny and Quint and the others are decent people. Different from what your kind call decent, But decent. And yes, some homeless people are not decent. And yes, unless you've failed to recognize it, in which case I'm here foolishly, some of your so-called decent people are not decent. They cheat, they lie, they hurt others. Not all. But enough."

"I'll buy that, Mr. Grace. Now tell me how you think you might help."

"I'll be your mole in the underground, Inspector. I'll dig up things about Duncan and about others you couldn't find out.

"And what if Duncan was killed by someone in my world, Mr. Grace?"

"That's your job, Inspector. Although you'll be surprised. Sometimes your kind of people talk in the presence of a homeless person about things that they think are secret. Because we're invisible. And, of course, we're also strange and stupid."

Danny thought some more. "This would be irregular. How do I know you'll follow up? How do I know you can keep all this confidential?"

"You'll have to trust me. I'm trusting you. If word got out that I'm helping you, that puts me in danger with some people."

"I have a few more questions."

"Sure."

"Is your name Joe Grace?"

"That's my name now. And for the last three years. I had another name but as far as I'm concerned that person is dead."

"How do I get in touch with you? You don't have a phone, I assume."

"Actually I do. But you can't use it. I'm willing to report to you in any way and at any time you think is good."

"What did you do, Mr. Grace, before three years ago?"

"None of your business, Inspector. I'll just say I was an ordinary person in your world. Something happened."

"Am I reading it wrong or does the name Joe Grace have some larger meaning?"

"Good for you. Nobody really gets it. Think about Joe, just an ordinary Joe. And think about Grace. I want people who see me, people like yourself, Inspector, to know one big thing."

"What's that?"

"Inspector, but for the grace of god, you could be sitting in this chair and living on the street. We street people are you, but you won't recognize that."

"I do, Mr. Grace. Things in life are fragile. There but for the grace of god go I. I agree."

"I thought so. That's why I tried to talk to you. Am I hired?"

"Yes. It's very irregular, but I'll take the chance and the opportunity. Before we go further, I'm going to call my partner in. I'm not always around. You can trust her the way you would trust me."

Nadiri was summoned, introduced to Grace and she

listened to what was happening. "No one else is to know, Officer Rahimi," said Danny.

"Yes, sir," she replied, and she gave Grace her card.

The three of them then discussed Grace's first tasks and arranged for him to report.

After Grace left, Nadiri said, "This is very odd, sir. Does it make sense?"

"It makes great sense. He's right. He can do things we couldn't even think about. I'm taking a chance. The one thing I hope is that nothing happens to him."

"I'd like to know his story," said Nadiri. "It's almost as if he wants to be a street person."

"Not almost. He's choosing it. Maybe along the way we'll find out his reasons."

XLII

When Celia filed the papers accusing James and Jeanette Altoni of negligence and violation of the lease contract, the Altoni's lawyers at the Bay Street firm of Hardings LLP immediately went into action. They filed a brief stating that the court had no jurisdiction in the matter. Rather, they claimed the plaintiffs, in order to seek redress, needed to file again with the Landlord and Tenant Board.

Celia expected this, for the first act of defence is often to challenge the filing itself. She submitted a brief outlining what had happened in the past. In it she argued that a lease was a contract and that both the landlord and the tenant have the right to go to court if there is no other legal remedy available to address the problem. In short, having exhausted all other legal avenues, the last resort was the courts.

The judge in charge of this matter ruled in favour of the Maghouts and Patricia Burke. They could go to court. The lawyers at Hardings made it clear that they would appeal this ruling if the court found the Altonis guilty.

Celia received an email from Philip Kelsall at Hardings, asking for a meeting to discuss the matter. She had experience in this sort of thing, both from the days she worked at Wilson, Campbell on Bay Street and from the recent time she led the team on the Echoiman case at her new small firm, Clark LLP. 'The dance has started', she told herself.

Celia invited Kelsall to the offices of Clark, on the top floor of a renovated house on Huron Street, just north of Bloor. Kelsall had a junior associate, Faith Wilson, accompany him. Celia asked her partner Ken Trussman to join her.

After coffee was poured and introductions were made, Celia began the meeting. "You requested this meeting, Mr. Kelsall. Tell us what you'd like to discuss."

"As you know, we disagree with the ruling that the court has any jurisdiction in this matter. And we'll appeal if we have to. In the meanwhile the case is going forward. We prefer to ask how we can take care of the matter now. There seems no real reason to go to court when some simple remedies are available."

"What remedies are you suggesting?"

"We can make certain that the Maghout's and Ms. Burke's apartments are looked after. The complaints about the building can be taken care of. We acknowledge that our clients may have been remiss in getting to the problems in a timely manner. We're even prepared to give the Maghouts and Ms. Burke some compensation for their past troubles. I can assure you it won't happen again."

"That seems generous," said Celia in a serious voice, trying to mask her sarcasm. "Can I ask why we had to do all this to get your clients to act? Do all those who have complaints against the Altonis have to do the same thing?"

"I understand your concern. We're interested in solving the matter before us. That's all I can deal with at the moment."

"Well, as you know, I'm obliged to take your request to my clients. I'll do so and get you an answer in a week or so."

"What will you recommend?"

"I need to think about it."

"Is there anything you'd like to ask us?"

"I don't think so. The papers make clear what we're asking. We'll see what happens."

"A short meeting, Celia. Can I talk a bit off the record?"

"Of course, Philip."

"We are naturally aware of the work your firm did on the Echoiman case. I congratulate you on the result. My guess is that the Altonis are your next David and Goliath endeavour. We'd like to settle this soon without going to court. Please think about how this might be done."

Celia pursed her lips, did some thinking, and replied.

"Philip, we believe our clients have been treated badly and illegally by the defendants. They tried to get a solution to problems which could be solved by a reasonable landlord. They are living in squalid conditions. So I'll think about what you say. But there are no guarantees from our end."

"I understand," replied Kelsall. "You know you can't win them all."

"No one wins them all, Philip. All we can do is our best."

"Fair enough. I look forward to hearing from you in a week or so. Let's save everyone time, effort and aggravation."

"Thank you for coming. I'll talk with you soon."

After Kelsall and Wilson left, Ken said, "They again don't want the publicity, Celia."

"Of course. That's part of the strength of what we're doing. I didn't tell him that getting it to court, whatever happens, is a kind of win because the Altonis don't mind treating people badly, they just don't want it in the media or in front of a judge. At least they didn't do what Echoiman's lawyers first did and tell us how stupid we were."

"They're scared. That's a good thing."

"It is. Let's remember that we represent our clients, not us. Let's see how they react."

Coincidentally, James Altoni faced another matter of jurisdiction with respect to the three images he possessed which had been taken by German authorities in 1939.

Minnie and Michael Gelernter's lawyer, Helen Oakhurst, had a hard decision to make. The law regarding works of art that had been owned by people in several countries was unclear, even fluid.

The big question was, which court must the Gelernters go to in order to request that the images be returned? They had been in the possession of the United States authorities after the war. Then, they were turned over to a German commission along with thousands of other works for distribution. That commission sold them to a German citizen who then sold them to a citizen of both Germany and the United Kingdom. That person took them to the United Kingdom and after he died his heirs sold them to a UK citizen. Then, a year ago the Altonis bought a lot which included a number of rare books and other images as well and brought them to Canada, where they were offered for sale. Now, James Altoni claimed ownership.

There were a bundle of precedents, which was the problem. One principle which was sometimes applied in a case within the field of Conflicts of Laws was called the *lex loci delicti commissi* rule. This would mean that the jurisdiction which would rule was Germany, for that was where the initial sale of the images took place.

Oakhurst didn't want to start there. When she discussed the problem at a meeting with the Gelernters, Tom Pendleton and Debra Castle, she suggested that they first try closer to home. "I think our best chance," she said, "would be to get a ruling in Canada."

"But," said Debra, "the images only came to Canada a year ago. Isn't that ignoring what happened before?"

"It is. I'm going to argue that the just decision can be made here since all of the players are now Canadians. There are fewer cases in which this has occurred than the *lex loci* rule, but there are some. There's no international agreement on what is appropriate, and each country has its own laws. I'll argue that this makes a ruling in Canada the right one."

They agreed that this is where they would begin rather than start by going through German or British courts. "In fact," said Oakhurst, "one can even make a case we should go to the US because they had possession of the stolen images initially. The whole world of law surrounding the many thousands of works of art stolen not only by the Nazis, but by others—even in the Iraq war recently—is very fuzzy."

So they filed for restitution of the images in the court of the province of Ontario.

And they won this part of the effort. The judge used a precedent from the United States in which he applied something called interest analysis, seen by some to be a variation of the rule of *lex loci*. He ruled that the case should be heard in the jurisdiction with the greater interest in the outcome of the dispute rather than the jurisdiction where the transaction originally occurred. He said that *lex loci* would mean that two Canadian citizens would have to go to Germany to settle the dispute when the images had left the country many years earlier. The lawyer from Hardings was outraged, as they were now faced with a situation which could not be handled by infinitely delaying it in the argument over jurisdiction.

After his ruling, the judge in his chambers suggested to the two lawyers that the parties might go into mediation to reach a settlement rather than continue the process through the courts. In doing so, he remarked that the Altonis might—"I emphasize the 'might'," he said— have a case against Sotheby's.

XLIII

That Miller guy is better than most. He still doesn't fully get it. He's a little too sure of himself.

But he did something that no other cop would probably do. He took me on. He saw I could help. He trusted one of us invisible people.

We agreed that I'd look for Jimmy the Mechanic first and keep my ears open.

I went from the station to my studio apartment on Balliol near Yonge. I needed to get some money and I keep my card there. Then I went to the ATM at the bank and drew out some cash. I returned to the apartment and took a nap on the bed. I felt guilty doing it, though it's an indulgence that helps. I got some ragged clothes from the drawers and closet and returned to the ravine.

No one of our group knew where Jimmy stayed or slept. I decided to go to the Tent City in the Don Valley ravine, not far from ours. I changed into torn clothes, got them a little dirty with earth and mud, and set out.

When I got to the Don Valley site, there were eight

tents and two cardboard places. Six people were milling around. I went to a corner where there was a piece of wood to sit on and I took out my cigarettes and smoked. I didn't look at anybody or talk to anyone. I just sat for about an hour and smoked a couple of cigarettes.

A woman came up to me. "Got an extra butt?" she asked. I looked up and saw a person of about fifty, her face worn and tired. She had on clothes which matched mine.

I reached into my pocket, took out my crumpled pack of cigarettes and offered her one.

She took it and the matches I held out to her and lit the cigarette. Then she sat on the other side of the log. Neither of us said anything.

She finished her cigarette and just continued to sit. I waited about fifteen minutes and took out the pack again. "Here's one for later," I said.

She took it and put it in the pocket of her sweater. "I've seen you around," she said.

"Yeah. I've seen you too."

"What are you doin' here?"

"I'm looking for Jimmy the Mechanic. Somebody told me he might be here."

"What do you want him for?"

"I have a message for him from someone who knows him."

She was quiet for a while. She took out the cigarette from her pocket and I again passed her the matchbook. She lit up and said, "He's not been around here for a while. I think he's moved near the Gerrard Street bridge. There's a setup there."

"Thanks. My name's Joe"

"I'm Louise. You got any more cigarettes?"

I stood up and gave her the rest of the pack. Then I walked away.

I went to the place near the bridge. He was there along with five others.

Again, I took a seat on the edge, waited my time, and smoked. This time, Jimmy came up to me. I took out the new pack. He took a cigarette and he sat down, an almost empty half bottle of rum in one hand.

"You got any dope? he said.

"No. Just cigarettes."

He offered me the bottle and I shook my head.

He lit up and we sat together smoking until he was finished and stamped out the butt.

Then he said, "Too bad about Duncan. Penny must be in bad shape."

"Penny'll be OK. She needs a little time."

"Maybe now she'll let me back in."

"Don't count on it, Jimmy. You beat her once too often."

"It's the booze, Joe. When I'm into the booze I don't know what happens to me."

"Bullshit, Jimmy. And you know it. Don't blame the bottle. Blame yourself."

"Fuck you, Joe. There was a time women understood they got beaten sometimes."

"Fuck you back, Jimmy. That time is over. How'd you feel if someone said they had the right to beat you sometimes? Cut the shit."

"You here for a reason? You want to move here?"

"No. I'm here to talk to you."

"There's nothin' to talk about."

"There's Duncan to talk about."

"Why? I got no time for Duncan. Alive or dead."

"I hear, Jimmy, that the cops think you might have done it. Everybody knows you and Duncan had words. Everybody knows your temper."

"So what if I did?"

"If you did it you should get away now. Because they'll come after you."

"There's nothin' to get away from. I could'a done it. I didn't do it."

"How do I know? What will you say when Mr. Homicide Cop comes to talk to you?"

Jimmy got up and said, "Come with me."

We walked over to a tent where there were two people sitting outside. I knew them as Pete and Mary.

"How did we learn about Duncan?" Jimmy asked them.

Mary answered, "We learned from Mario. The bricklayer. He wandered here that night. He wanted some supper if we had extra food. He told us."

"Where was I that day?" Jimmy added.

"You was here. We had some fixing of the tent to do. We went to the Salvation Army to see if we could get *some blankets. And we panhandled in Chinatown. We got enough for some rum and some beer."*

Jimmy looked at me. I wondered whether he had made it up and rehearsed Mary and Pete. I decided it was probably true.

"So fuck you," said Jimmy to me. "Maybe I should'a done it. Maybe I'm sorry I didn't do it. Go find someone else.'

"Why are you so interested?" Pete asked.

"Duncan was my buddy, you know that. I want to know who did it."

"Why?"

"I don't know. I just want to know."

"You should stay out of things, Joe," Pete said. "Someone might get word of your interest. You know what I mean."

"Yeah. Maybe you're right. You guys got any idea?"

"I keep myself to myself," said Mary. Pete nodded. I passed the cigarette pack around and each of the three took two cigarettes. Then I walked away.

Maybe I'm dumb. I thought it would be simple. I find Jimmy, he gets drunk, he brags, I report it. Now I'm left with nothing.

I decided to walk to the station and see Mr. Big Homicide Detective. Maybe he did better than I did today.

I got to the station and he was out. I asked for his partner. They called upstairs and she told them to send me up.

She was different for a cop. They're usually white guys, some with bellies. Now, in the new Toronto, they could be anybody. She was dark, slim, studs in one ear. And a name from the Middle East. Mr. Big Homicide Detective said I could trust her. I'll see.

"Welcome, Mr. Grace," she said. "Coffee?"

"Coffee would be good."

She went to get it and I looked around her office. Not much to see. The usual computer stuff and lots of paper. Whoever said that the computer would end the paper in an office should come to a cop station. Another false prediction.

She had pictures on the edge of her desk. Two older people, her parents probably, and a family. The woman looked like she could be her sister. She left her purse on her desk, a good sign.

She brought coffee for both of us and asked me to sit.

"I forgot to ask if you took milk and sugar, Mr. Grace. I just put in a little milk."

"That's fine, Officer. I drink it anyway I get it."

"Well, you came here. To report, I assume. So tell me what you found."

"I'd rather tell the boss."

"We're partners. You tell me, you tell him. You tell him, you tell me. That's how it works."

"I found nothing. I learned a long time ago that nothing can be something, so I'm reporting.

"You're right. What nothing did you find?"

"I saw Jimmy the Mechanic, as we discussed. I checked with him and I don't think he did it. I'm not a hundred percent certain, just ninety per cent. He also has an alibi. Two people who live in the same place as him, a bunch of tents near the bottom of the Gerrard Street Bridge.

I reviewed my conversation with Jimmy at her request.

"It sounds as if you're correct, Mr. Grace. You know we'll have to meet with Jimmy ourselves. Just to make certain."

"I figured so. You're not going to trust a bum."

"We don't trust any citizen, including the Mayor. You've been a big help. We have to make certain you're correct."

"What do I do now?"

"What do you think you might do?"

"Did you learn that from Mr. Big Homicide Detective or did you figure it out for yourself? Answering a question with a question."

She laughed. "I learned it from him. But I'm serious. How do you think you could help now?"

"I'll put it back to you, Ms. Partner. How do you think I could help?"

"You could continue to probe among the homeless community. Find out what the gossip is. Find out what people are thinking. You said it yourself. You can find things that we so-called normal people couldn't. Add to our knowledge."

"What good does that do?"

"You'd be surprised. This isn't a science like biology. In a case like this, a small fact can lead to big things. Most of what we will know won't matter. But now we accumulate data. Then we piece things together."

"Can I ask if you and Mr. Big have gotten anywhere?"

"I'd rather not go there now. Let's say we're doing what you're doing. There's progress, but it's slow. Too slow for my taste."

"Well, I guess I have my assignment. When do I report?"

"If you find something you think is important, report right away. In any case, report no later than two days from now."

She hesitated. Then she said, "Mr. Grace, could I ask what might be a personal question?

"No," I said, very quickly. Then I got up and left.

XLIV

After the funeral, Danny decided he needed a broader perspective to help understand matters. He called his friend Howard Mandlebaum, who was a regular consultant for the police department in addition to being a sociology professor at the University of Toronto.

While Nadiri was talking with Joe Grace, Danny was in Mandlebaum's office near Spadina and Bloor.

When Danny entered the office, Mandlebaum said, "I take it, Danny, that this isn't just one of our regular get-togethers over a cup of coffee."

"No, Howard. This is a formal consultation with my resident sociologist."

They exchanged news about their families and then got down to business.

"I'm here about the 'Duncan case', as it's being called in the papers and the rest of the media," said Danny. "We're not getting very far and I'd like to learn about that community."

"I thought that was why you called. Do you mind if I invite one of my colleagues, Joan Tabor, to join us.

She's a specialist in what we sometimes call parallel communities. I signalled her to be available. She's very smart and totally trustworthy."

"Sure. You're ahead of me."

Mandlebaum summoned Tabor, who joined them in five minutes. Danny noted that she was probably a touch younger than Nadiri, about thirty-five. She wore jeans which somehow looked elegant and a gypsy blouse. Her hair was dyed blonde, she had on earrings a bit too large for her face, and no make-up. She was handsome rather than beautiful, with lively green eyes and a firm chin.

"A pleasure to meet you, Inspector," she said. "I've seen you on TV and Howard has talked about you. Please call me Joan."

"I'm Danny. As Howard may have mentioned, there's a lot I don't know, so I come to people like you for information."

"A cop and a male who admits he doesn't know much," she replied. "I have a feeling that can be dangerous if I actually believed it."

"Well, I'm here for help."

"Tell us what you need, Danny," said Howard.

"Joan, Howard will have told you that this exchange is confidential." She nodded.

"It has to do with the murder of Duncan MacNeil. I want to know about the community he belonged to. That doesn't mean we think that the murderer is part of that community. That could be so. But I need to understand the life he led, so I can get into his skin and maybe that of the killer."

Howard looked at Joan and said, "You start."

"Do you want the two hour lecture, Danny, or the short version?"

"Of course, the latter. I don't need a course, Joan, just some insight."

"Good. This is different from an academic matter. I needed to be reminded. Thanks. Now. There are lots of what we can call parallel communities, especially in large urban areas. There are sub-communities, like ethnic groups, religious collectivities and the like. And there are others. Toronto has a very big hockey sub-community. People whose lives revolve around the game, ranging from kids to adults who coach, referee, etc.

"But there are communities on the edge of the law, maybe even off the edge at times. The most obvious one, which everyone knows, is the biker community, especially the organized clubs."

Danny interrupted. "I'm very familiar with them. In fact they were central to a case I dealt with not long ago. I had a good deal of interaction with the Hell's Angels."

"Then you know that they don't really see themselves as part of normal civic life. Not like someone who goes to church, or who hangs around with fellow ethnics or plays hockey. In fact, they resent intrusions by the so-called 'normal' people. They have their own rules, their own laws, their own acceptable ways of behaviour, and their own justice.

"The homeless have something like that. They are apart. They believe, with good reason, that ordinary people look down on them. It's not like they don't belong. Many can't belong. They're marginal. But a person like Howard, who is also very Jewish, is marginal looking in. Their people are so marginal, they're looking out. In fact, it wouldn't be wrong to call them outsiders."

"Then why would a homeless person hurt another homeless person?" asked Danny.

"First," Joan answered, "for the same reasons so-called normal people hurt other normal people. Greed. Revenge. Anger. Jealousy. You know about this better that do I."

"And second?"

"There's still a relationship to the 'normal' world. A lot of the homeless people are so because they're eccentric. Some have delusions, others can't get along without drugs or alcohol, and others see someone taking their space or what few goods they have. A blanket, for example. Not much different than the rest of humanity. Except that they have their own customs and rules. For example, you don't go to a shelter in a ravine and say good morning. You sit around on the edge until someone recognizes you. If they do."

"I get it," said Danny. "Now, maybe an odd question. Why would someone choose to be homeless?"

"Do you know that there are prisoners who choose to be in prison? When released they immediately commit a crime so they can again be incarcerated."

"So some, maybe many, become comfortable because that's the world they understand. And maybe that world understands them?"

"Yes," answered Howard. "There comes a moment when many people are only comfortable in certain environments. Like Orthodox Jews. Or some Catholics. They need to be there."

"OK. This helps. I have to stop thinking about the homeless as different from other human beings."

Joan brightened. "You got it, Danny. They're like us."

"That's what one of them told me. He was correct. Now, one more question. I've encountered something which causes me to ask it. Why would a 'normal' person suddenly choose to live in the streets when they don't have to do so?"

"I think you're in the wrong office for that question, Danny," said Howard. "You need a psychologist."

"Try it, anyway," Danny countered.

"I'll try it," said Joan. "I could be wrong. But in some cases in could be a trauma that occurred in the normal world that seems to make it impossible to live there anymore. For whatever reason, the person had to abandon their former identity."

Danny sat and thought for a time. "You may well be right, Joan. I'll think hard about that."

They then moved on to other topics. Howard inquired about Nadiri, his former student. Joan asked about how the police used consultants. Danny talked about how he had recommended to the chief that more sociology be part of the training of new cops.

Joan returned to her office and Danny and Howard lingered for a while, catching up on personal matters. Danny left feeling satisfied that he had learned some useful things.

XLV

I decided to keep going. Back to the homes of the home-less.

First, the next morning I had my weekly appointment with my shrink, Dr. Patricia Morrison.

The meetings are a pain sometimes and sometimes, most times, they're useless. For some reason I keep going. Maybe I just like Patricia and she serves decent coffee, from Starbuck's.

We sit across from one another, she in a desk chair, me on a leather easy chair. She always waits for me to talk. Sometimes I don't start. Including today.

I know what she will say and I wait for it. "What would you like to talk about?"

"What do you think we should talk about?"

"Don't go there Peter," she said.

"I'm Joe."

"Don't go there Joe."

"I had a strange thing happen this week."

"Yes?"

"Did you hear about the killing of Duncan?"

"The one around Summerhill?"

"Yes.

"What about it?"

"I knew Duncan. I knew him well. He lived in the tent city with me and the others." I went on to describe what happened and how I got in touch with Mr. Big Homicide Detective. It took a bit of time but who cares.

"Did you get anywhere with your inquiries?"

"No. I got to Jimmy the Mechanic. I'm convinced it wasn't him. So I reported that yesterday to Mr. Big's partner.

"So why is all this strange?"

"Cut it out, Patricia. Don't do the innocent naïve shrink routine with me. You know why it's strange."

"I do. I want to hear why you think it's strange."

"I'm bothered. I don't like it. This is the first time in three years that I did something like this."

"Why did you do it?"

"I just did it. Duncan was my friend and I wanted to help. I think I should stop."

"Why?"

"Because I don't want to feel anything. I don't want to take responsibility for anything. I don't like having this feeling that I should do something for someone, for Duncan."

"But you felt it."

"Maybe I just let my guard down. I just want to be Joe Grace and not feel much."

She was silent. She wrote down some things on the

pad she always has on her lap.

"Fuck it, Patricia," I said. "You know what I think. I'm a coward. I'm a coward who doesn't have the courage to kill himself. So I kill all my feelings. I don't want to feel. I just want to disappear."

"Maybe somewhere inside you're waking up."

"I don't want to wake up. After the crash, after Vicky and Jeremy and Michelle died, after I came out of the hospital, after the ridiculous trial and the short sentence the bastard got, I don't want to wake up. The only reason I might wake up is to kill the bastard when they let him out."

I was getting really loud. Patricia didn't move.

I took a tissue and wiped my eyes. Now I know why the tissues are there.

We were both quiet for what must have been three minutes, a very long time of silence in a place where people talk.

Finally, Patricia said, "What are you going to do about Duncan?"

"I'm going to find his killer." It was almost time. I stood up and left.

I spent the next two days wandering around to different homeless places.

I went to the Humber, to the Cedervale ravine in several places, and further up the Don Valley. There was little information to be had. Some knew of Duncan's death, others were so wrapped in their own heads that they learned it from me, if they were paying a little at-

tention to what I was saying, which I sometimes doubted.

Then I went to the Salvation Army and to the largest men's shelter on College Street. Still nothing.

I decided to end my investigation—I was certain that Mr. Big would have done better than I did—by seeing Molly.

Molly was Molly Muldoon and she was the administrator of Tessa's House, the major women's shelter. She was also known to all of the street people as the most prominent and successful advocate for us with the city, the province and the cops. If anyone knew anything it was Molly, because she had spent many years building up trust. To us, she was a kind of saint.

I got to her in the late afternoon. She was busy— when isn't she busy?—but we had met before and she told me to hang around. I was good at shutting off my head and an hour passed very fast.

She came out and asked me into her space. "How're you doing, Joe?" she asked.

"I'm still here, Molly."

"That's good. Too bad abut Duncan. I hear you've been asking around about him."

"How do you know?"

"I hear things. Isn't that why you're here?"

"No one can keep anything from you, Molly. Yeah, that's why I'm here. Duncan was my friend. I want to find out who killed him, so I've been asking around."

"And what have you found?"

"Nothing. I thought I knew. Jimmy. Jimmy the Mechanic. But it wasn't him. No one knows anything."

"Did it occur to you, Joe, that maybe there's nothing to know."

"What do you mean?"

"Everyone says—at least the papers and the TV do, and probably the cops—that it was a street person that did it."

"That's what seems logical."

"Shame on you, Joe. You, of all people, know that life and logic don't usually go together."

"I'll buy that."

"So here's what I have to tell you about whether a street person did it." She paused. "Nothing. I have nothing to tell you."

"You have nothing to tell me or you don't know anything about it?"

"Reasonable distinction, Joe. I've been listening. And I have no information about any street person who might have been involved. You're looking in the wrong places."

"Then who did it?"

"I don't know. I only know that I would bet that a street person didn't do it. Who does that leave?"

"All the normal people who think we must have done it."

"Good thinking. I don't know anything about your life, Joe. And I don't want to know. But you must have had some schooling."

"Maybe."

"So instead of looking in the ravines and the shelters, maybe you should look on the street."

"I'll have to think about that. Thanks a lot, Molly."

"Be careful out there, Joe. The cops don't like people working on their turf."

"I will."

I decided to go directly from Molly to see Mr. Big. I had bought a cheap phone at a shop, one that had a few calls and couldn't be traced. When I got back on the street I took out Mr. Big's card and the phone and gave him a call.

It took a bit of time convincing the officer I needed to talk to Mr. Big in an emergency. However, I finally got to him.

"Can I see you now, Mr. Big? I need to report and I have something important to tell you."

"Where are you?"

"In Toronto."

"How long will it take for you to get here?"

"About a half-hour."

"Come over. I'll tell the desk to let you up."

When I got to Mr. Big's office he was there with his partner.

"Coffee?" she said.

"Yeah. I had Starbuck's yesterday. You should try it."

The Partner went to get three coffees.

"How are you, Joe?" asked Mr. Big.

"Is this small talk or do you really care?"

"I don't care as much as I would care if you were in my family, but I do care."

"I'm OK. I got stuff to report. First, I have to ask. Have you gotten anywhere?"

"We usually answer that to the public by saying we're proceeding and we're making progress. Since we agreed to trust one another I'll tell you we haven't gotten very far."

The coffee came. We opened the lids and he continued.

"We've gone to all the shopkeepers and to many of the residents. Nothing significant has turned up. We'll just keep plodding along. What about you?"

"I'm certain—no, that's too strong—I'm pretty sure that it wasn't one of the street people. I've been to seven tent cities and some shelters. Nothing turns up. I've talked to the one person who knows most things that happen on the street..."

"Who's that?"

"...and that person says that nothing has turned up. I'm willing to bet that the solution is to be found in your world, not mine."

"We did talk with Jimmy and we agree that he's an unlikely candidate. We talked to some others in tent cities and didn't get much."

"Of course not."

"So I guess, Joe, that there isn't much you can help us with any longer."

"Bullshit, Mr. Big. You should be smarter than that. You're demoted. I can do something that might work."

"What's that?" asked the Partner.

"Mr. Big, Ms. Partner, here's what I can do. I can go to Summerhill and take Duncan's place. I can hang around. I can panhandle. I can talk with people. I can even be polite if I have to. And some people won't like that I'm there. Some won't mind, but I think someone didn't like it that Duncan was part of the neighbourhood. If a millionaire who made his money by robbing widows and orphans was part of the neighbourhood, that's fine. If a bum who harms no one and even helps his friends is there, that's bad. That's how your world works."

"And what would happen?"

"Maybe someone will try to hurt me. Or even try to kill me."

"I can't ask you to take that risk, Joe."

"You're not asking. I'm offering." I held up my hand. I wanted to think for a bit. Then I said, "If you don't accept my offer, I'll still do it. You can't prevent a citizen from being on the street."

Mr. Big actually smiled. "You're tough, Joe."

"I'll do what I need to do. I'm not breaking any laws."

"I need to think about it and if I go along to make a plan. Can you come back tomorrow morning and we'll sort it out."

"Do we do it?"

"I'll tell you in the morning."

XLVI

Celia arranged an evening meeting in Scarborough, at a local restaurant, with Patricia Burke and Raghda and Ibrahim Maghout. Patricia brought along her eight-year old daughter and six-year old son, explaining that she couldn't afford child-care. They sat in the rear at a quiet table and ordered soft drinks and some appetizers to nibble.

"I've met with Mr. Altoni's lawyers," explained Celia. "They want to offer a settlement...."

"Excuse me," said Raghda, "we do not know the law. What does that mean?"

"They don't want to go to court. They would like to reach an agreement soon. What they are suggesting is that they take care of the violations in your apartments and the building. They said they would consider giving the three of you some money because of the difficulties you had in the past."

"Very generous of them," said Patricia Burke, in her best sarcastic tone. "Now that we did something they'll do something. If we do nothing, they do nothing."

"Would that end it?" asked Ibrahim.

"If we agree on a settlement it means that we all don't go to court. It's over."

"Did they say anything about the many violations and complaints from other buildings owned by Mr. Altoni?"

"No. The way the law works here is that we deal with a particular case. We can raise the matter, and they can make promises, but the big issue is that they want you three to drop the case."

"Why?" asked Raghda. "Do they think they are guilty?"

"I think it's more complicated than that," answered Celia. "They know they're guilty, though they will never admit it. They rely in part on your poor financial circumstances. I won't tell you how much Mr. Altoni is paying his lawyers. I'll just say that it's more in a day than the three of you combined earn in a month."

"He can afford that?" said Patricia.

"Yes. He's very wealthy, Patricia."

"So why can't he afford to fix his buildings?"

"Because he doesn't want to. He makes more money if he doesn't do any fixing."

"We do not want to be ungrateful," said Ibrahim. "Canada has been good to us. Toronto has been good to us. Our children are getting medical and dental care. They are in school. They have a future here. But this seems to be an unfair matter. Justice should not be about who has the most money."

"Ibrahim, I totally agree with you. The system is not as fair as it should be..."

Ibrahim cut in. "But, Celia, it is much better than what we came from. We do not want to seem rude in our new home."

"It's not rude to ask that they follow the law. And when they don't do so, to go to the court. That's good and necessary. No one will criticize you, Ibrahim. A lot of people will be on your side."

"Forgive us, Celia," added Raghda. "We still find it hard to understand all of the complex things here."

"Sometimes it seems more complex than it should be," said Patricia. "What do you think we should do?"

"I'll tell you the alternatives. You have to make the final decision.

"You can accept their offer. They'll fix your apartments and they'll look after the building. Yes, that's because we did this. In addition, they've offered financial compensation as part of the settlement. You could ask for a sum or we could ask them how much they're offering. I recommend we ask them. That starts negotiations."

"Would it be a lot of money?" asked Patricia.

"To them, no. To you, yes. It would be in the thousands, maybe even five thousand if we can get it."

There was a time of silence, as the Mahouts and Patricia took this in.

"What should we do, Celia?" asked Patricia.

"You have to decide. I'm your lawyer. I'll follow

your instructions."

Patricia continued, "If we make a settlement, what happens?"

"I don't understand, Patricia," said Ibrahim. "Then they do what they do, they give us some money and it's done."

"No, Ibrahim. It's not done."

"What do you mean?"

"They'll start all over again. Also, we can try to get them to fix up other people's places, but they'll probably go back on their word. I don't have a lot of trust in Mr. Altoni. And what happens to our neighbors who have been treated badly? Do they get money too?"

"Now I see what you mean," responded Ibrahim. He turned to Celia. "Why do you think they are offering a settlement?"

"If you accept a settlement that means there's no issue of guilt. It goes away. However, to answer your question, I believe they don't want the publicity that will come with a trial. Two things come with the publicity. First, they may have to fix a lot more than your two complaints. Second, perhaps more important, the Altonis lose face. Their reputation is hurt. They value that a lot. They travel in the circle of the rich and powerful."

"We from the Middle East are experts in matters of face," said Raghda. "That we understand very well."

"So it's not about money alone," said Patricia. "Is that right?"

"That's correct," answered Celia.

"What do you recommend, Celia?" said Ibrahim. "We need advice."

"I would keep going. You can get much more done for yourselves and for your neighbors if we keep going. But there's a risk. If he's found innocent, then we will lose what we can get now."

"That's worth doing," said Patricia. "Altoni is a real bastard, a nasty guy. We should take him to court. If we settle, he wins."

Ibrahim looked at Raghda with a furrowed brow. She nodded.

"We agree," he said. He turned to Celia, "I ask again. People in Toronto will not be angry at us for this?"

"You will be applauded by most people. Mr. Altoni will have very few supporters."

Celia looked around. "Then it's settled. We keep going as we were doing."

"Great," said Patricia.

"Yes, that's what we should do," added Raghda.

"Excellent," replied Celia. "Now let me tell you what might occur."

They chatted for a bit and shook hands at the end. Celia drove home feeling very good about what had transpired.

The next day she called Philip Kelsall. "I met with my clients," she said after the usual greetings, "and they don't want to accept your proposal. We're continuing."

"Do you think we could meet about this? I believe they're moving in the wrong direction."

"Philip, I assure you that I put all the alternatives on the table. They want to continue."

"What would it take to make a settlement?"

"I don't know. All I can tell you is that we're not accepting the offer. If you have another offer to make, do so. I'm not calling to bargain. I've been instructed to continue."

While saying all this, Celia was smiling to herself, for something similar also happened in the Echoiman case, and now she was confident in how to handle it. The difference now was that Kelsall and his firm respected her and Clark LLP, and treated them as equals, whereas with Echoiman there was some condescension from his lawyers for a time.

"I'll convey this to my client, Celia," concluded Kelsall. "Thanks for taking it up so quickly. Let's see what happens."

XLVII

After Joe Grace left his office, Danny did some thinking and then called his former boss, Sydney MacIntyre, now head of the Major Crimes unit. The two had worked together for five years in Homicide, Danny succeeding Sydney as head of the unit, promoted to Inspector, as she moved over. They kept in close touch, Sydney asking Danny several times for assistance in her new job, and Danny seeking her counsel in his position.

He summarized the Duncan case and said, "I'm inclined to use Joe Grace in a way which might help solve the case. He's certainly more than willing. But it may put him in danger. What do I do?"

"It's very unusual, Danny. Beyond unusual. Not that you haven't come up with creative ways of solving hard cases in the past. You're known for that. A lot depends on how you read his character. And I would clear it with at least the Super, maybe even the Chief."

"I read him as someone who is doing this almost in spite of himself. He clearly had something really terrible happen in his life. But he's honest, and he cared for Duncan. Why he wants to do this is ultimately unknown to me because I don't know him well enough. His motives though are good ones."

"Fair enough. Check it out above. I'd do it if you have a talk with him tomorrow morning and you're satisfied he knows the danger."

"Good. Thanks, as usual. I'll be in touch."

Danny then called the Superintendant, who wasn't available. He left a message and said it was urgent.

He then shrugged and decided to call John Kingston, the Chief.

Kingston's assistant said that the Chief would call back in twenty minutes. When he did so, Kingston asked, "How are you doing, Danny? I still get asked about the Duncan case when I see the press about anything else."

"That's what this call is about, John. Something unusual has turned up and I don't want to go ahead without you or the Super agreeing. Mel wasn't available so I moved up and called you."

"Tell me about it."

Danny related as briefly as possible what had happened and the involvement of Joe Grace.

"Do we know who he is?"

"No. And he's not the mystery. I'd like to know. I'm curious about him. But that can wait. So far, he's lived up to every arrangement we've made. He's a good reporter."

"What's your judgment? Not that I don't know why you're asking."

"Let me tell you what I'd like to have him do. It'll take time. And if he doesn't live up to expectations at any time we can end his involvement."

Danny then related his thinking and a plan.

"A Danny solution. However, Danny solutions usually work. I'm fine with this as long as you give him protection. He's being a good citizen. We can't have a citizen hurt or, frankly, maimed or killed, in order to solve a case."

"Will do. Thanks. I'll speak with him tomorrow morning. If the meeting goes well, we'll move forward. If not, we'll find another way."

"Keep in touch. How's the rest of the squad?"

"Doing fine. We'll have a problem soon. Ron is retiring in about a year. I can't do without someone like him. He's really the glue holding all this together."

"Do you have anyone in mind?"

"That's part of the problem. There's no obvious person to act as my associate inside here."

"I'll give it some thought. There's a lot of talent on the force. Maybe we need to move someone over." Kingston laughed. "Of course, we could always ask the head to behave like a normal head and administer the whole department the way everyone else does."

Danny went along with the game. "Though the head doesn't like to speak about himself in the third person, I'll tell you that he'll be happier moving back down to

Sergeant."

"I'm kidding, Danny. We made an arrangement to have an experiment in order to get you to be head. And it's working very well. We'll find someone for you. You know me. I like letting the people I trust be themselves. You won this one."

"Thanks, John. I'll let you know what happens with Grace. I'm sorry to tell you that this one might take a while to get a result."

"I know that. The press is bothered, but I'm not. They need to learn that we on occasion need more time than usual to do a job. Take care."

The next morning Joe Grace appeared at ten o'clock, as they had agreed. Danny and Nadiri were waiting for him. Nadiri handed him a container of coffee with the Starbucks label on it. "I thought you'd like this," she said.

Grace actually smiled. "Thanks Ms. Partner."

He then turned to Danny. "What's the verdict, Mr. Big Homicide Detective? Do I stay or do I take my coffee and drink it outside?"

"Stay. I have a plan and I have permission for you to be part of it."

"That's good. What should I do?"

"I want you to take Duncan's place."

"Huh. What does that mean? Do I go into a coffin?"

"Cut the act a bit, Joe. Please. This is very serious and I don't need it."

"How and where?"

"I want you to be the new resident street person and panhandler at Summerhill. You are to hang around the southwest corner of Birch and Yonge. You are to go across the street and panhandle in the places Duncan panhandled. You are to occasionally sleep somewhere in the area."

"Why?"

Nadiri answered. "Because we agree with you that it's probable that Duncan was killed by someone in what you call the normal world."

Danny added, "And we think that whoever did it resented him being there as part of the scene."

Grace did some thinking. "That goes along with what my person said. And you're accepting my recommendation?"

"That's right."

"Amazing."

"Amazing or not," continued Danny, "there are some things you're going to have to do."

"What?"

"You are going to have to make conversation with folks there. You're going to have to be polite and drop the obvious cynicism and anger. You may even make a friend or two as Duncan did. We need people to like having you around. Otherwise it won't work. This is important."

"I get it. It will take an effort."

"If you can't do it, then the deal is off. This is very serious business."

"I'll do it."

"Good. Now, we'll do some rehearsal before you leave here. First I want to tell you how we're going to protect you. I want nothing bad happening to you."

"I don't mind that if it will help."

"I mind it." Danny glared at Joe. "Cut the bullshit. Got it?"

"Yes." Something happened to Joe Grace's face at that moment. It settled in a new look. Some of the ever-present tension and anger were not as evident.

"So here's what we're doing." Danny explained how the police would be helping Joe do the job and looking after him.

"Very smart, Inspector," said Joe. "A good idea."

"Do you want to take a break, Mr. Grace?" asked Nadiri. "Or can we rehearse how some encounters and conversations will go?"

"Let's keep going, Constable."

They spent an hour working through various scenarios.

"Start tomorrow, Mr. Grace," said Danny. "This morning can take a lot out of you. You report every other day unless we tell you otherwise."

"Sounds good. This may work, Inspector."

Danny stood up and said. "I want to thank you, Mr. Grace. Not a lot of people would do this." He put out his hand. Joe Grace looked at the hand for a second or two. Then he joined with Danny in a handshake.

XLVIII

James Altoni was angry that he might have to go to court as a result of his firm ignoring property violations. Also, he didn't want to be seen by the public as someone who was depriving two descendants of the Holocaust of their inheritance. He did believe that he had bought the three images and that therefore he owned them, but he realized the publicity would paint him differently.

Hence, he told his lead lawyer in the matter, Anthony Banno, the expert in copyright and related matters at Hardings LLP, to try mediation. "See what you can do," he instructed Banno, "I don't want this in the public realm."

They agreed on a mediator, the veteran Susan Velasquez, and they began meeting. As often happened, the two parties were in separate rooms and Velasquez shuttled between them.

It began with Velasquez telling Helen Oakhurst and an associate, the Gelernter's lawyers, that Altoni was willing to sell the images to the Gelernters at a reduced price.

"You know that's ridiculous, Susan," said Oakhurst. "He tried that before, when we informed him of what was happening. Our position is that we own the paintings. We want them returned."

"Anthony Banno is going to insist on some compensation for his client," replied Velasquez. "They're not ready to just turn them over."

"What compensation do you think is appropriate?"

"That's not for me to determine at this time. What would you offer?"

"Tell Anthony that we went through the lot that Altoni bought from Sotheby's and the Harrows carefully. There were over one hundred and fifty rare books, eight of them very valuable. In addition there were over forty paintings and drawings. Some far more valuable than the Cezanne, Boudin and van Gogh. The Altonis bought the whole lot for under four million. They weren't interested in the art and so they're selling it. I could argue that they got a bargain and the images we are talking about really cost him a hell of a lot less than what he asked for at the Pendleton Gallery. I could even argue that they obtained them virtually for nothing."

"Nothing won't work."

"Well, the judge gave us a hint. He in effect said that Sotheby's, or the Harrows if you like, didn't do due diligence in the matter. I would argue that Altoni didn't do due diligence either. *Caveat emptor*, Susan.

Let the buyer beware. That he bought stolen art is his problem, not ours."

"I'll see you later," said Velasquez, as she exited the room to talk with Banno.

When she returned forty-five minutes later, Velasquez said, "They're not buying it, Helen. Or at least they're not fully buying it. You did surprise them with the due diligence argument and that got them into moving back to thinking about the sellers."

"Well," said Oakhurst, "that's a little progress."

"I agree. What I'm going to do is to suspend this for now. I don't think we can make further progress until both of you discuss all this with your clients and also have the opportunity to quietly do some thinking. We'll set up a meeting for next week."

When Helen Oakhurst left, she called the Gelernters. She met them at her office and reported what had transpired.

"What do you think?" asked Michael.

"I'm certain Altoni doesn't want this to be something that the media will get hold of. I've learned that he's being sued by some of his tenants and the lawyers are the same people who won the Echoiman case. That will be bad enough for him."

"I have a suggestion," said Minnie. "I've thought about it."

"Tell us."

"I don't want the nasty Altoni, a person with no *menschlichkeit* whatever, to profit from this. I won't pay him for the paintings."

"Then, mother," said Michael, "I don't know what we can do."

"We can, Michael, suggest that we will make a donation in the names of the Gelernters and the Altonis to an appropriate charity. *Yad Vashem* in Jerusalem, for example. Or to a foundation that looks after a memorial to Holocaust victims. It could be in any of many places. Berlin or Amsterdam. Or Warsaw."

The three sat quietly for a time, reflecting on what Minnie had said. Helen broke the silence. "Minnie, you may have found a way to go. I don't know why you hire me. That's ingenious."

They talked about what would be an appropriate amount and about the strategy for the next mediation session. All three felt they were closer to a solution.

XLIX

So now I'm somebody choosing to be a bum playing at being a bum.

I hang around the corner of Birch and Yonge and nod or chat with people. A few street people come by occasionally and we have a smoke together.

I go across the street with some community news-papers and sit near the entrance of the LCBO or on the street in front of 'Cornucopia' and panhandle. I have a small box in front of me with change in it.

It's been a week now and some of the people rec-ognize me.

There's a guy who lives on Birch Avenue, retired, who takes his dog for a walk and does some shopping. His name is Bernie, he told me. He always stops and asks how I'm doing. He started talking about the weather, but now he'll talk about anything. He has this way about him which makes him a terrific listener. So we talk about all sorts of things—from global warming, which I know nothing about, to the Blue Jays, which I also know nothing about. He takes a paper and always puts a loony or a toony in my box.

A woman named Marie is trying to reform me. She tells me that she could find me a job. "It wouldn't be much," she says. "You could get a place to live and you could maybe do better." I don't like to disappoint her, so I listen instead of telling her that I don't want to do better. In fact, I've done better and it didn't do me any good. Doing worse works for me. Marie is kind, though, and she twice brought a sandwich.

The local cops don't especially like what I do. One told me, "A bum like you was killed here a few weeks ago. Maybe you should move." I told him that the bum was my friend Duncan who was a good guy and liked by a lot of people. Another cop told me to move on, or else. "Or else what?" I said. "Or else you might get hurt." "How?" "I don't know. Someone else got hurt here." "I'm allowed to do this," I answered. "I'm legal." Then he told me that people didn't want me around. "This is a nice neighbourhood. They don't want people panhandling here." "It is a nice neighbourhood," I replied. "Let them tell me they don't want me here."

On the fourth day I panhandled in front of 'Cornucopia'. At the end of the day the manager came out with a box full of fruits and vegetables. "Did Duncan have any relatives?" he asked. "He lived with a woman called Penny. She spoke at the funeral." "Could you give these to her and anyone else who needs them?" "Sure. Thanks, sir, it's really appreciated." "You take care," he answered.

There's one person who harasses me every day, also telling me that I ruin the neighbourhood. "My name's Joe" I said. "What's yours?" "None of your fucking business. Just leave." Do you say fucking a lot, sir? I thought that's a word the grand people in Rosedale never used." "Just get the fuck out of here." "Oops, you did it again. Three times and they make you leave Rosedale." "Go away. We don't want your kind here." "Sorry, sir, your kind are not nice."

Many people just say hello and are very polite. When I offer the paper, they usually say "No, thanks." Some just leave a coin and don't take the paper. Several stop regularly and we talk about their day. I think that for some people, apart from a clerk in a store, I'm the only person they speak with that day. One nice woman said jokingly that panhandlers should be licensed and that they should take courses in psychology as part of the training.

Some want to know my history. "How'd a nice guy like you wind up in the street?" I lie a lot and tell whatever comes into my head. I do tell them that street people are the same as everyone else. Some good and some nasty. Some kind and some greedy. Some crazy and some sane.

The owner of the bakery twice asked me to move. "Why?" I asked back. "Because my customers don't like having a panhandler where they shop." I answer, "Am I nasty? Do I hurt anyone?" "Well, they live in the neighbourhood and they don't like it." "I live in the neighbourhood, too. On the street. Do I get a say?" Then the veiled threat, "You're asking for trouble." "No, sir," I say. "If you think about it, you're the one asking for trouble. I'm a citizen just like everyone else."

The Inspector and the Constable come around once each day. We don't talk. They just nod and let me know they're keeping an eye on me.

What have I learned? Not a lot. I think that a few of the people I've met might have decided to hurt Duncan, but nothing stands out. The Inspector tells me that this is a long haul operation. "It won't yield quick results, Joe. First we have to get you into the neighbourhood. To be a normal part of the scene. Then something might happen."

Yesterday the three of us met in the Inspector's office.

"It's not a bad experience, Inspector," I said. "How long does it need to last?"

"As long as necessary. Do you hear any gossip?"

"No. People refer to Duncan, but I've heard nothing of any use."

The Constable spoke, "Maybe we need to go further," she said.

"What do you mean?"

"I think that once people are used to you, you should sleep in the area. That's when Duncan was killed. I have a feeling that whoever did it wanted to beat him up. His heart gave way before his head did."

"You could be right, Constable," said the Inspector. He turned to look at me. "What do you think?"

"The sooner, the better. Yeah, I'll start sleeping there. Maybe even near the place behind the LCBO where Duncan was killed."

"Start sleeping near Birch for one or two nights," said the Inspector. "Do it in a fairly public place. Then move to the back of the LCBO."

They went over all the safety stuff with me again. "I don't mind taking a blow or two if we catch the killer," I said.

"I understand," said the Inspector. "Let me put it this way. There's necessary pain and unnecessary pain. I don't think it's necessary for you to get hurt in order to get the job done. Above all, I don't want two people killed so we can catch a killer."

"You're nicer to me than I would be to myself."

"I know, Joe. You may have to face it one of these days. You're a good guy. It's OK for you to be nice to yourself."

"I don't agree with you, Mr. Big. I'll give it some thought."

L

The idea of making an appropriate charitable donation as a way of getting around payment for the images which the Gelernters were claiming opened up the negotiations again. As well, the idea of the Altonis suing Sotheby's for lack of due diligence helped the mediator to smooth matters.

The amount agreed upon was one hundred thousand dollars, which was to be donated to the Jewish Museum in Berlin.

A problem arose about how the donation was to be made. The Gelernters assumed that each party would put forward fifty thousand dollars.

However, James Altoni instructed his lawyer to request that the Gelernters put up the whole of the donation and that he receive a charitable receipt for half of the money, which he would use for tax purposes.

"He seems to be the kind of person," said Michael Gelernter to the mediator Susan Velasquez, "who never passes by an opportunity to display what a disgusting human being he happens to be."

"I won't comment on that, Mr. Gelernter," replied Velasquez, "at least until this business is over. What I need is a suggestion about how to proceed. We're close. What do you people suggest?"

Helen Oakhurst answered, "We suggest that if he donates fifty thousand dollars, that he receive a receipt. If not, we'll donate fifty thousand dollars and that's the end of it."

"That may not fly, Helen," said Velasquez.

"Then let it crash and we'll go on from there. We're tired of this guy's manipulations on his own behalf."

Minnie Gelernter put up her hand, signalling she needed to speak. "Ms. Velasquez, we could have had the paintings on our wall a while ago. If we had paid him for them. And what he offered still made Altoni a big profit. We decided to do it in a different way. In a way that meant we were the owners, not the buyers. Now, we don't want to collaborate—I use the word carefully—in a dishonest scheme."

Velasquez was silent for a few seconds, thinking. "I get you, Mrs. Gelernter," she then said. "I'll do my best."

After Velasquez left the room, Helen spoke. "She's on our side, Minnie. That's as close as she can come to telling us that. I think she's going to push."

A little over an hour passed before Velasquez returned. When she entered she seemed more relaxed than she had been earlier.

"Here's the deal," she said. "The amount will be

sixty thousand dollars. You will make the whole of the donation and you will get a receipt in full. What we need do, however, is to write a press release indicating that a donation was made by agreement of the two parties without saying that you made the whole of it."

Michael looked at this mother. She nodded. "Done," said Helen. "We have the right to veto anything in the press release. In fact, I think I should be in on the writing of it."

"That won't be a problem," answered Velasquez. "In fact, I insist on it as part of the arrangement."

Velasquez looked around. "I congratulate you, Mrs. Gelernter and Mr. Gelernter. Your painting and drawings will shortly be on your wall at home."

"*Mazel tov*," answered Michael. "I didn't think it would happen. At least not this quickly."

"Let me leave and tell the other party," said Velasquez. "Then Helen can tell you how it happened this fast."

After Velasquez left, Helen Oakhurst spoke. "We were, of course, right, Minnie and Michael. But we had a bit of luck. There's another matter that's coming before the court related to the Altoni's properties. The word on the street is that they want both legal issues — this one and that one — settled out of court because of the bad publicity they would bring to the Altonis. So I think they were willing to go further than James Altoni would have liked. The last thing he wanted was to be seen cheating a family of Holocaust survivors. Still, he didn't lose much and he may even gain something if his case against Sotheby's has legs. In fact, Sotheby's may settle as well to keep it out of the public eye."

"However, it happened, I'm glad," said Minnie. "Now I'll have some of my childhood and some of my relatives on my wall, where they belong."

The 'other matter' was far more complicated and not so easily settled. After Celia Rogdanovivi called Philip Kelsall to tell him that their clients did not want a settlement, there was a week of quiet as the wheels of the justice system slowly turned. The case was put on the case lists for two months hence.

Once that occurred, Kelsall called Celia and asked her to lunch.

"What about?" asked Celia.

"I'd like to have a conversation about the Altoni case in a more informal setting," replied Kelsall. They made a date at Canoe for the next week.

On the morning of the lunch date, Celia found a copy of *The Star* on her desk, with a note from her partner Louise, "see the GTA section."

The Star had gotten hold of the story, yet again. And this time they played the same scenario as they had for the Echoiman case. On the front page of the Greater Toronto Area section there was a story about Altoni, the many violations, and the case coming before the court. They didn't use the term 'David and Goliath' when talking about the two law firms, as they had in the Echoiman case, but they might as well have done it, given the narrative. It was about an immigrant family and a single mother against a very wealthy owner of many buildings and much land; and also about the small firm of Clark LLP going up against the resources of the giant Hardings LLP. The story noted that while they had no knowledge about what Altoni was paying Hardings, the common fee for this kind of legal case and the resources put into it was over one thousand dollars an hour.

Celia walked to the office of Louise Xavier, the partner who acted as the Managing Partner of the firm. "Do you know anything about this?" she asked.

"Nothing," answered Louise. "No one from here did it."

"How do they get hold of this?"

"They have a lot of connections, Celia, including at the court."

"Well, as long as we didn't plant it, it can't hurt."

When she met Philip Kelsall at the restaurant and they were seated, Celia immediately said, "Philip, we didn't plant the story. No one in the firm, including me, talked to *The Star*. I'll have a few calls this afternoon, however."

"I didn't think you would do this, Celia. Thanks. Now let's order and we can get down to business."

"I'm used to a sandwich, Philip. I might indulge."

"Do so. I invited you. It's on Hardings."

Celia guiltily ordered mushroom soup and a lobster clubhouse sandwich, knowing that she would need a nap afterwards, for which she had no time.

After Celia's soup and Philip's shrimp and heirloom tomatoes arrived, they got to the business of the meeting.

"I was surprised that your clients passed up the possibility of a settlement. Especially because a financial settlement was part of it. They can't have many resources."

"You may not believe this, but they asked what the settlement would mean for all the others who have, if you'll forgive the term at this informal meeting, been abused by the Altonis. I told them it all ended if they got a settlement. They decided to keep going."

"Nice people. Not everyone would ask that question."

"Yes. They knew they were turning down thousands of dollars. They're poor, Philip. But they feel pretty strongly about it."

"What did you recommend?"

"I didn't do the bargaining thing. I didn't start talking about a bigger settlement. I told them the alternatives. They chose. I do happen to agree. Frankly, the Altonis need a spanking. In public. Then, maybe, just maybe, they'll play by the rules."

"I won't go there at the moment. I'd like to get a settlement. My client is anxious. We're prepared to go far."

"How far?"

"We'll correct all the violations in the building, including the other apartments. We'll acknowledge we were remiss in not responding in a timely manner and give a settlement of a thousand dollars to each and every tenant who had a violation that was not taken care of. I don't have the authority for the next part, but I'll say it. We'll give an added monetary settlement to the Maghouts and Ms. Burke for their expenses and trouble."

"Let me think about it."

Celia spent the next few minutes enjoying her soup. Then, she asked, "What will you do about the many violations in other Altoni buildings?"

"That's not part of this case. If people want to sue, then we'll get to them as it arises. Do think about this, Celia. If we do go to court, and if you happen to win, we'll be appealing the jurisdictional matter, among other things. That will take a lot of time. Your clients won't benefit right away. And if we win the appeal they get nothing. So there are two ways you can lose. First, you can lose in court. Second, you can lose on appeal."

"You know, Philip, I'm a graduate of Osgoode and I spent a decade at Wilson, Campbell. I never heard anything in law school or at the firm about using the system to leverage a case. Yet, it's done all the time. I wonder how the profession got there."

"You're anything but naïve, Celia. This is part of what we do. Don't tell me you never do it."

"I won't. I'm just speculating on how we got from

kids who went to law school to do good to high priced lawyers who manipulate the system in any way we can on behalf of our clients, some of whom I wouldn't invite into my home. What happens between twenty and forty?"

"That's the system. It needs us. Without the law, we're lost."

"That's the mantra, Philip. But we should ask ourselves if we really uphold the law or just use it."

"I stopped doing that a long time ago, Celia. The system works. It's important to keep it going."

"One more point and I'll get off my high horse. The system works, yes. But for whom? OK. Enough. What I'll do is convey your offer to my clients."

"Good. Please tell them that we're open to discussion. It's a firm offer. However, we're prepared to modify it, if necessary."

"I will. Now, tell me Philip. Let's have a civilized discussion. I play the cello, among other things, to keep my sanity. What do you do in your own time?"

It turned out that Philip Kelsall was a sailor, involved in the racing of small boats in Ontario and the New England states. They spent the next part of the meal telling one another about their two hobbies.

LI

I did the act for four weeks. Who knew that doing police work was unbelievably boring. At least ninety percent of the time. The other ten per cent might make up for it. I'm not sure.

After the first week, it became a pattern. I slept most nights either near Birch Avenue or in the back of the LCBO. I gave myself a break every so often and slept in the ravine. And for two nights I retreated to the apartment to get a shower and to sleep in a bed. After all, I'm not St. Francis.

During the day I hung around and panhandled at the LCBO or in front of the shops. Bernie always came around to talk. He asked me about my life and how I lived and I began to ask him about his. He had been a social worker, someone who looked after kids with no parents or those in trouble and he had a lot of stories. I told the Inspector and the constable that he was one of the nicest people I've ever met. "If everyone was like him," I said, "I might actually be part of your world."

I listened to people, looking for something about Duncan. They still talked about him, but no one knew anything that might lead to his killer. All were still wondering how it happened.

There was the usual mix of human beings. Some treated me nicely, and we exchanged 'have a good day' a lot. They would put a coin into my box. The people in 'Cornucopia' were really nice, and they regularly gave me food I could share. One of the women in the bakery brought out yesterday's bread. The way she did it made it seem that she wanted to keep it a secret.

There were those people who were hostile. The guy in the butcher store, some of the people living in the neighbourhood who tried to make me feel I was the social equivalent of a polluter, and some of the cops. I was very passive now, not wanting to get into any argument that would hurt my looking for Duncan's killer.

Another group were those people who behaved as if I didn't exist. There were a lot of them: from the manager of the bank across the street, to many shoppers, to normal pedestrians. We're used to that. In a way it's comforting because most of us don't want to exist in the world called normal.

Other than Bernie, there were five people who treated me as an ordinary person. What I mean is that they seemed to treat me the same way they treated everyone else. One was a female clerk, Rosalynn, in 'Cornucopia. Another was a woman, Ann, who said she was a retired teacher. The third was Robin, about fourteen years old, who found me more interesting than the people he regularly encounters. The fourth and fifth were the Inspector, who I used to call Mr. Big Homicide Detective, and the Constable, formerly the Partner.

Then it happened.

I was sleeping on some cardboard, inside a used sleeping bag, in the back of the LCBO, near where Duncan was killed. I learned afterwards it was about two in the morning.

Someone was poking me. And then he banged me over the head with a wooden stick. I had the whistle in my left hand and I brought it to my mouth and blew very hard and very loud. Officer Smyth, who was on duty that night looking after me, ran out from behind a pillar. He tackled the guy, who then tried to hit him with what I noticed was a police nightstick. Smyth held his own, though he was bleeding, as was I, at least long enough to identify the man. The guy got away, running out of the parking area.

Smyth asked me if I was OK while taking out his phone. I said yes and told him to get the guy. Whoever was on the other end got this from Smyth, "I'm with Joe Grace. A person tried to hurt him, maybe more. I got hold of him, but he got away. He's on foot. I know who it is. It's police officer Ames, badge number 8475. He ran out to Yonge Street."

A car came and took Smyth and me to Toronto Hospital, to the emergency department. They bandaged my head and told me I would be fine. Smyth had a broken nose, which they fixed.

In the meanwhile, the search for Ames took two hours. He was captured and arrested while pretending to be a cop on duty at Yonge and Bay.

It felt strange. I wanted to leave. I was told by the cop in charge that I had to wait in order to talk with the Inspector. Why, I don't know. I did my job. Now I wanted to go back to my disappeared self.

LII

Danny was awakened at two-thirty that morning. He went to the station to await developments and to meet with Nadiri. They kept in touch with the lead officer by phone as the search for Constable Leonard Ames went on. As well, they talked regularly with the officers sent to look after Connor Smyth and Joe Grace.

Ames was arrested at four-thirty and brought to the station to be booked. In the meanwhile Joe Grace was taken to see Danny after being patched up.

"Are you OK?" Danny asked when he saw Grace.

"Sure. I've endured worse on the street."

"What happened?"

Grace described being poked and hit by Ames and Connor's intervention. "That's it, Inspector. I'm done. I did my job. I want to go back to whatever my life happens to be."

"We may need to talk with you again, Mr. Grace. And if the case goes to trial, you'll probably have to testify. How do I get in touch?"

"You look for me. I am, as you guys say, 'of no

fixed address.' You'll have to find me. Probably in one tent city or another."

"That may not be good enough."

"Tough. That's who I am. You knew that when you agreed I would be involved. You'll have to live with who I am."

"You're a smart, able person, Mr. Grace. Why not come back into what you call the normal world?"

"I'll make you a bet, Inspector. I'll bet you that Ames will get a very light sentence. Oh, he didn't mean to kill Duncan, they'll say. Oh, he's put his life on the line for the good people of the city."

"You believe that?"

"You watch. Your police force will protect him. The union will be on his side. A lot of cops will resent a trial. And, you're a very naïve man, Mr. Miller. You think there'll be some sort of justice. How much do people think Duncan's life is worth? After all, he was just a bum."

"I don't believe that."

"I know you don't believe that. If Ames had killed one of those well dressed people who told me to go away from their precious neighbourhood, maybe some-one who swindles people but has high-priced lawyers to protect him, Ames would be in deep shit. But Duncan's just a bum. His life isn't worth the same to your normal people. You'll see."

"I wish I could contradict you."

"So do I. But your justice is sometimes really shitty,

and your weakness is that you refuse to recognize that."

"I do my best to make it right, Mr. Grace. I know it's not perfect."

"It's beyond not perfect. It's flawed. It's usually wrong."

"I can't agree."

"So I'm going back to where at least people are real. There's cruelty where I'm going, but we don't hide it behind a civilized façade. The normal world is a scam. A rich crook is a philanthropist. A poor crook is in trouble."

"Do you read novels, Mr. Grace?"

"I used to read novels."

"Have you ever read a French writer named Honoré Balzac?"

"Not that I remember."

"Try him. You'll find a person who sympathizes with your views. Try the one called *Pere Goriot*. Sometimes called *Old Goriot* in English. I won't give the story away. But I can tell you the thief is the most honourable person in the book. Maybe with the exception of Goriot, who is treated very badly."

"So you won't take my bet?"

"No. I'm not a betting man."

"You'll see. Ames killed my friend. He'll get a very light punishment. Now I'll say good-bye."

Joe Grace stood up and abruptly left the office.

Connor Smyth turned up ten minutes later, his nose bandaged.

Danny and Nadiri consoled him as they listened to his recounting of the event, which coincided with that of Grace.

With the arrest of Ames, Danny ordered his staff to collect the nightstick, these days called a baton by the police, and all of Ames' uniform clothes. "Send everything to the lab. They'll check for blood and anything else they can find."

Then he and Nadiri interviewed Ames. The first attempt turned out to be very brief. Ames refused to say anything other than to identify himself until he had consulted with legal representation.

The second interview occurred in the afternoon of the same day.

Danny identified himself, had the others in the room do so as well and then began.

"Mr. Ames, you are charged with two counts of battery and one count of manslaughter. How do you respond to that?

Ames looked at his lawyer, Gordon Mulvaney, a criminal lawyer used by the police union to represent its members.

Mulvaney responded, "My client is willing to discuss his attempt to get a street person this morning to move from sleeping near the LCBO. He had nothing to do with the other incident. He found the body and reported it according to regulations. We deny the charge of manslaughter and that he was guilty of assault. You're harassing a good policeman, Inspector. This won't win you any points with your colleagues."

"The person who was hit this morning is called Joe Grace. Mr. Grace was bleeding, had head wounds and had to go to the hospital. As well, Mr. Ames, you broke the nose of Officer Smyth when he tried to stop you."

"This is silly," said Mulvaney. "How was my client to know that Officer Smyth was a colleague?"

"Officer Smyth identified himself verbally."

"Right. And I'm the Prince of Wales. Anybody could claim at 2:00 in the morning that they are a policeman. He attacked my client."

"Then why run away?"

"It was two against one. What would you do?"

"Then why not report it rather than try to disappear?"

"My client was disoriented. He had just suffered a trauma."

Nadiri did all she could not to scream at what was happening. She had to say something. And she did, "Mr. Ames, you caused the death of someone. Doesn't this bother you?"

Mulvaney put his hand on Ames' forearm, signalling him to refrain from answering.

"Nothing of the sort happened," Mulvaney countered. "He reported the death. He didn't cause it."

Danny decided to end it at this point. "Thank you, Mr. Ames, Mr. Mulvaney. I'm going to suspend this for now. We'll pick it up tomorrow."

"I request that you release my client for lack of evidence," said Mulvaney.

"I will record your request. I'm denying it. We'll hold Mr. Ames on the charges of battery and manslaughter for the full forty-eight hours."

Mulvaney did everything but threaten in order to get Danny to reverse his decision, but it didn't work.

"We'll continue this interview at noon tomorrow," said Danny, ending it for the day.

After this Danny met with Nadiri, Connor, his associate Ron Murphy, and Taegen Brown, who had also been on duty at night looking after Joe Grace.

"What do you think?" asked Danny.

"I'm about to go out of my skull," said Nadiri. "A cop who beats up street people. Who beat one so badly that his heart failed. And he sits there playing as if he's an innocent grade school kid. Shame on them."

"Shame won't get you a conviction, Nadiri," said Ron.

"What will?"

"Evidence. I think, Danny, you ended it because it can't go anywhere until we get the lab reports."

"You're right," said Danny. "It would be futile to go further until we know if we have any clear evidence. If we do, that takes us some place. If we don't we'll have to decide what to do."

"You mean," said Nadiri, "that he may get away with it. He may even remain on the force?"

"I doubt that," replied Danny. "However, I'm certain that the lawyer and the union are currently producing a press release to be made public once we tell the press we have a suspect. We will be the bad guys, hurting one of our own just to try to get a conviction."

"So," said Nadiri, looking straight at Danny, "Joe was right."

None of the other three understood the reference but the tension was so great that no one asked.

"He was not right, Nadiri. The problem is that he's also not wrong. It's a shadowy world we live in."

Danny turned to Ron. "When do we get the results?"

"They're promised for tomorrow morning. The lab people said they'd work through the night if necessary."

"We wait then until the morning. Everybody go home for the time being. You've all worked hard and long on this."

LIII

That evening, Celia met again with the Maghouts and Patricia Burke.

"I need to tell you about the latest offer," she said. "It goes beyond the last one." She explained how all the violations in the building would be fixed and how each tenant would receive a payment of one thousand dollars to make up for their discomfort. Then, "And the lawyer said that the two of you might ask for a settlement for yourselves, above the thousand dollars, in lieu of your expenses and time."

"How much?" asked Patricia.

"They didn't say. I thought about it and I think you could get in the area of five thousand dollars each."

There was silence as the three plaintiffs thought about this.

"It's very tempting, Celia," said Patricia.

"I fear it is," said Ibrahim Maghout.

"What else?" asked Raghda Maghout.

"What do you mean?" asked Celia.

"There are hundreds of violations in other buildings

in the neighbourhood," replied Raghda. "What will they do about them?"

"That's not on the table. That's not how the law works here in Canada. They are responding to this case, to the charges that you two have put on the table. If others want to sue them then they'll deal with that."

"We can only do this, Celia, because you offered to work for free. What do they call it?"

"*Pro bono*. Latin, meaning 'for the good'. It implies 'for the good of the community'.

"A good term. Are you going to work for others *pro bono*? Is someone else going to take the time to do it?"

"My firm gives twenty per cent of its time to *pro bono* work. I know of only one other firm, also small, that does that. That's as much as we can do."

"Of course, Celia," said Raghda. "And we are grateful for your work. I am only saying that if we agree then what happens. First, one building is taken care of. Second, Mr. Altoni goes free. He'll probably tell everyone how generous he was."

"And if we don't agree?" asked Patricia.

"Then," Celia answered, "we go to court. If we lose, nothing happens. If we win, Mr. Altoni will have a lot of fixing up to do. And he will pay a big fine."

"We must ask, now," said Ibrahim. "What are our chances of winning?"

Celia did some thinking. "I'll be careful. I think the chances are a little better than even that we will win something. I think they're about fifty per cent or a bit below that that we will win everything. I need to tell you that it's not as neat as the books make it out to be. A lot depends on the judge and on other matters. No good lawyer will ever tell a client that she has a hundred per cent chance of winning."

"I will ask another way," said Patricia. "What are the chances of Altoni being found guilty?"

Again Celia thought. "About even, Maybe a touch better than even."

The three looked at one another. Raghda Maghout took the lead. "We have met a few times together, Celia. I think we are of one mind on this." The other two nodded. "We will not be bought off. Mr. Altoni spends money to buy people off. He will not spend money to help them. We also believe he does not want the publicity that a trial will bring to him. Look what happened with the story in *The Star* newspaper."

Patricia continued, "So we go to trial. Without public exposure Altoni will get away with everything."

"I'm glad," said Celia. "Let me say that I admire what you're doing. You're giving up a lot if you lose."

"But I can still look in the mirror in the morning," said Patricia. "I wonder what Altoni sees when he shaves."

"Face is important, as I said before," noted Raghda. "We have what Mr. Altoni can never have. Honour."

"You're correct," said Celia. "People like Mr. Altoni try to buy honour, because they can't get it any other way. OK, people, get ready. The trial begins in less than two months."

LIV

Danny received the results of the lab the next morning. Nadiri was sitting in his office, waiting. She felt better when Danny smiled.

"We got him, sir?"

"I think so. There were remnants of blood on the baton, in the cuffs of one of his trousers and in the epaulettes on the shoulder of his jacket. The baton matches Joe Grace's blood-type. The others match the blood-type of Duncan Smith. They're testing for a DNA match, which we'll have in two days. If the DNA matches, I think we're fine. If it doesn't we'll have to decide what to do."

"I think Ames beat up Duncan," said Nadiri, "and then realized he was dead. Of course, he feared that he had killed him. There was lots of blood where Duncan slept, some of which remained when we looked. Ames got lucky, in that he could transport Duncan to the place under the bridge. Then he called in that he found Duncan dead."

"That's my scenario, too, Nadiri. Let's set up an interview for as soon as we can."

They again met with Ames and Mulvaney a little after noon.

"Mr. Ames," said Danny, "we have some further information. The lab found blood on your jacket shoulder, in your cuffs and on your baton. The blood on your jacket and your trousers matches the blood-type of Mr. Duncan McNeill. We're now testing for a DNA match. The charge of manslaughter stands. We're holding you until the lab tests for DNA arrive."

Ames was again silent.

"I think that the blood was present as a result of an altercation Mr. Ames had in an apartment with a male a year ago," said Mulvaney. "I really don't think you have a case, Inspector. We admit to the use of excessive force on Mr. Grace and we're willing to take a month's suspension for it. That's all you have."

"Sorry, Mr. Mulvaney, I've spoken with my superiors on this one. We're keeping the manslaughter charge. We'll await the lab results."

"And if they are wrong or inconclusive?"

"Then we'll re-evaluate. Our case has gotten stronger. Let's see."

"I again ask for the release of my client on insufficient evidence."

"I will again record your request. It's denied."

"We'll sue for wrongful arrest. Come on, Inspector, this is one of your own."

"Not anymore, Mr. Mulvaney. A cop who beats up

people to the point of manslaughter is not one of my own."

Danny ended the interview, noting that he would inform Ames and Mulvaney of the DNA results.

After he turned off the tape, Danny asked Mulvaney to stay. After Ames was escorted from the room, Danny turned to him. "I want to emphasize again, Mr. Mulvaney, that Ames is not one of my own. Maybe he's one of your own and I think you should reflect on that."

"Cut the bullshit, Danny," Mulvaney replied. "This is the way it works."

"Then maybe it should work differently," said Danny. "Thanks for your advice."

Two days later the DNA results confirmed that the blood on Ames' clothing matched that of Duncan. The case was turned over to the Crown Attorney for prosecution.

The Chief, John Kingston, felt that a press conference was necessary in order to report to the city about Duncan and to deal with the delicate matter of Ames having contributed to his death.

Kingston opened the conference with a long statement on the case, lamenting what happened to Duncan, apologizing for Ames and at the same time talking about everyone's equality before the law. He stressed that the force will learn a lesson or two from what happened.

He then turned the conference over to Danny, who described how Duncan's case was solved.

Then the floor was opened for questions.

There were questions about how the case was conducted and Danny simply said, "This case was the same as any other. We worked hard and put a lot of resources into solving it." He decided it would take something away from what was done if he had to justify why someone in Duncan's social position received such treatment. So he ended that part of the conference with a short sentence. "There's nothing more to say about it."

The reporter for the *National Post*, Karam Bhinder, asked the next question, "You said, Inspector, that you had the help and support of a citizen. Who was it and what did he or she do?"

"The person asked to remain anonymous and I'm going to honour that request. He enabled us to find who was hurting street people and it turned out to be Mr. Ames."

"I've done some probing, said Bhinder, "and I understand that after Duncan McNeill died, his place was taken by a homeless person named Joe Grace. Several people in the area got to know him. Is that the person who helped you?"

"I won't go into that. The person asked for anonymity. I will tell you that the person demonstrated both good citizenship and concern for justice. It's unusual to use an ordinary citizen in this kind of case, but it was called for and it worked."

"We'd like to acknowledge his contribution," said

Bhinder.

"So would I, Karam, but I can't go against the wishes of the good person who helped us."

"Well, Inspector," asked Rosalie Daniels of the CBC, "in some of your cases you give us a book or a work of art to sum it all up. Have you thought about this?"

Danny smiled. By now he knew it was coming. He had thought he might deflect it this time in order to end the custom, but then decided against that.

"It seems clear to me. *Les Misérables* comes quickly to mind. It's not a perfect match, but it does have the inversion. The street person, Duncan McNeil, was thought by all to be a solid citizen, a good guy. And the cop wasn't Javert, but he did have a distorted sense of what was right. Like the book and the musical, there are matters to learn here."

LV

I skipped a meeting with Patricia. I just didn't feel like talking so soon after finishing up with Duncan.

I did go the following week.

This time, she opened. "I'm glad you didn't call again to cancel."

I just stared at her.

"How do you feel about what happened?"

"I don't feel. You know that."

"Then why did you help, if you don't feel?'

"I made a mistake. I got involved. What's going to happen? The cop who beat up Duncan so badly that he dies will get off. If he doesn't get off, he'll get a few years. This is just like what happened. A guy is drunk, he kills three people, two of them kids, and he gets six years. With parole, he could be out soon. Maybe that's why deep down I decided to be a coward. Maybe I should kill the bastard when he gets out. Now, it's six years for three lives. Then it'll be one life for three lives.

"I don't think that's what you believe."

"Oh, you're a mind reader, Patricia. What do I believe?"

"You wanted to help Duncan. He couldn't do anything, so you wanted to do it for him."

"A lot of good it did. A cop versus a bum."

"Did you watch the press conference held by Kingston and Miller?"

"I left. I don't watch TV. I haven't watched TV in over three years. Since I got out of the hospital."

"Your Inspector referred to Les Miserables. Did you read the book or see the musical."

"I saw it with Vicky about ten years ago. She loved it."

Patricia hesitated. Maybe she was waiting for me to say more. I kept my mouth shut and stared at her.

"He said that the case had some similarities to Les Miz."

"How?"

"The cop was the bad guy. And the man in rags was the good guy."

"So?"

"Do you think that maybe, unconsciously, you were influenced by Vicky in helping Duncan? Do you think she would have done that?"

"She would have done that. She was like that guy Bernie I told you about. She cared for everyone. Everyone was treated with dignity."

"So—to use your 'so'— so maybe the good that Vicky gave to the world can still live inside you."

"It's a big stretch, Patricia. Now you're reading my unconscious."

"You agree life is not rational. I know that. Maybe your motive for helping Duncan was a way of honouring Vicky and your relationship."

"You're nasty, Patricia. You know how to go where it hurts."

"Of course, it hurts. You've said you can't move away from what happened to Vicky and Jeremy and Michelle. Why not say that who they were is still a part of you."

"Maybe. But what society is is also a part of who we are. At least how we operate. Since you referred to Mr. Big and Les Miz, have you ever read a novel called Old Goriot? Also French. By a guy with a name like those coffee shops, Balzac."

"I know the name."

"Mr. Big told me to read it when we argued about what neither of us called justice. He's smart. He knows things are not right. He's too optimistic. You can get to him that way."

"What about the book?"

"Lots of characters. The most complicated thing I've read in years. One of them is a thief called Vautrin. He's probably the most honest person in the book. He's a thief who has a code and he lives by it. The point is that he has the same kind of feelings about the normal world that I do. To quote him, when he's arrested, he mocks the law and talks about—I put my hands in the *air and made quotes — 'the colossal fraud of the social contract'. It's a fraud. This thing called society is built on lies."*

"How does the Inspector respond to your thoughts?"

"He doesn't disagree. He just doesn't agree. I wanted to bet him that Ames, the cop, would get a light sentence. He wouldn't take me up on it."

Patricia was silent. Then, "What do you think about today's session? Time's almost over."

"I think I'm going to live by my code. The code I've had these last three years. I also think that any doctoring that says we have to stop because time is up has a certain amount of bullshit attached to it."

I got up and left.

Epilogue
Five Months Later

The results of the two trials, Altoni and Ames, came within a week of one another.

The Altoni trial, conducted before a judge, did what Patricia Burke and Ibrahim and Raghda Maghout had hoped it would do. The publicity surrounding James Altoni was devastating, erasing whatever he might have gained with his arrangement with the Gelernters regarding the art that had been in their family.

The press not only covered the trial. They did investigative reporting and publicized all of the violations in the Altoni name. *The Star* did a series which lasted ten days, in which they went to a different Altoni building each day and interviewed tenants and reported on the condition of the building.

Philip Kelsall, the Altoni lawyer, tried to mitigate the information coming out in the trial and in the media by having some of the administrators and managers working for Altoni testify to their efforts to clean up the properties. But James Altoni, as was his right, did not take the stand himself.

Ibrahim Maghout and Patricia Burke did testify. Celia had them simply state the history of the violations and their attempts to get them corrected.

Kelsall first tried to get Maghout and Burke to contradict themselves, but they had been well rehearsed by Celia. In addition, Ibrahim Maghout's basic dignity could not be compromised, and Patricia Burke's statements about trying to raise two children as a single mother in a building falling apart drew only sympathy.

Then, Kelsall attempted to prove that neither the Maghouts nor Burke had done enough to get relief from existing agencies, thereby making the trial, at least for now, unnecessary. The facts came out and the matter was left in the hands of the judge.

When Kelsall moved to challenge the process rather than the condition of the apartments and the building, Celia knew that a line had been crossed and that Altoni would not win. "The question," she told her clients, "was now how far the judge would go in his decision."

The trial ended with the judge stating he would take several weeks to consider what had transpired. When he delivered his decision, it was clear. James Altoni was found liable for breach of contract and for gross negligence in placing his tenants in harm's way. He was ordered to repair all of the outstanding matters concerning the building and the two apartments. The Maghouts and Patricia Burke were each to be given twenty thousand dollars for their difficulties and costs as a result of the negligence. And finally, the court required of Altoni a bond to guarantee the obligation to complete the work.

No statement was made by Altoni regarding the verdict, nor would he talk to the media. Kelsall indicated that he would be filing an appeal on two grounds. First, he again raised the matter of the jurisdiction of the court, rather than the Landlord and Tenant Board. Then, he also appealed the verdict as being too harsh. Neither Altoni nor Kelsall got sympathy from any forum.

The trial of Officer Leonard Ames received even more publicity than that of Altoni, for putting a policeman on trial for manslaughter was a matter of profound interest to a broad public.

Ames' lawyer, Gordon Mulvaney, adopted a strategy of trying to convince the jury that Ames was just doing his job. While he didn't put Ames on the stand, he called a number of witnesses, including some from the police force, to testify that the police routinely moved street people from public places at night.

However, the testimony that made the difference was that of the forensic pathologist, Dr. Hugh O'Brien.

O'Brien was a short, round man who looked something like a leprechaun, and who had a slight Irish accent. When he spoke he was very calm and he had the knack of looking at both his questioner and the jury as he gave his opinion. Every one of the twelve on the jury, after hearing him for five minutes, felt he was speaking to them directly.

"The wounds are consistent with very strong blows to the head," he said. "There is no way any medical person would interpret them as prods simply to wake up Mr. McNeil. He was beaten. If he had lived he would have had a long recovery, if he recovered."

In his cross-examination, Mulvaney asked O'Brien to confirm the cause of death. "But he died of a heart attack," said Mulvaney.

"Yes, that he did, Mr. Mulvaney. However, the heart attack came about as a direct result of the blows given to him by Officer Ames. I am telling you that he contributed to his death through using great force, excessive force, when he encountered Mr. McNeil."

"There is no possibility that Mr. McNeil would have had the heart attack anyway?"

"He probably would have had a heart attack in the next five years, given the condition of his heart as I examined it at the autopsy."

"Then you're saying Officer Ames didn't kill him."

"I am saying that Officer Ames hastened his death, Mr. Mulvaney. We all will die. Mr. McNeil's time was not six months ago."

Mulvaney tried mightily to sway O'Brien. The latter kept his calm to the point where those on the jury felt he was being bullied. After some minutes of harassment, the judge asked Mr. Mulvaney to move on.

In instructing the jury, the judge explained that there is a concept in law called culpable homicide. "Any culpable homicide that does not meet the definition of murder," he said, "is manslaughter.

"Manslaughter is killing someone by a wrongful act, even though the act was unintentional, provided that a reasonable person could have foreseen that the wrongful act posed a risk of serious bodily harm. In practical terms, this means that manslaughter is when someone does something wrong and someone else ends up dead as a result of it. It means the offender did not intend to kill or cause significant bodily harm that he knew may result in death. This occurs," he continued, "when someone causes the death of another person by one or more of the following, which might be applicable in this case: by means of an unlawful act; by criminal negligence; or by causing a person, by threats or fear of violence, to do anything that causes his death. You need to make your judgment," he concluded, "based on this legal definition."

After deliberating for six hours, the jury found Leonard Ames guilty of manslaughter. Ames was given a four year sentence, with the possibility of parole after two years.

One week after the sentencing of Ames, Danny received a letter. The envelope was a 'used' one. The previous address and return address were crossed out. In their place, there was Danny's address at the station and a return address which read, "Joe G., Somewhere, TO".

Danny smiled as he opened the envelope. Inside, there was one letter sized piece of paper which was on one side a flyer for a clothing store. On the blank reverse side there was printed a short message.

Cop kills bum: 2 years
Cop kills rich normal person: ???
Bum kills cop: ???
I told you.

Ackowledgements

Many thanks to my constant first readers for their support and suggestions. Martin Sable's legal knowledge and other contributions were especially valuable. Mike O'Connor was very helpful and creative in designing and producing this book.

As always, my profound thanks to Jan Rehner for her encouragement, guidance and wisdom.

About the Author

Arthur Haberman is a retired professor of history and humanities. He lives in Toronto and loves the city and its people.

CPSIA information can be obtained
at www.ICGtesting.com
Printed in the USA
BVHW040045020521
606187BV00001B/1

9 781554 834822